SCANDAL

SCANDAL

KELLY AND KRISTINA
MANCARUSO

HEAD
of
ZEUS

An Aries Book

First published in the UK in 2026 by Head of Zeus,
part of Bloomsbury Publishing Plc

9 7 5 3 1 2 4 6 8

A catalogue record for this book is available from the British Library.

ISBN (PB): 9781035912599
ISBN (E): 9781035912575

Cover design: Simon Michele | Head of Zeus

Printed and bound in Great Britain by Clays Ltd, Elcograf S.p.A.

Bloomsbury Publishing Plc
50 Bedford Square, London, WC1B 3DP, UK
Bloomsbury Publishing Ireland Limited,
29 Earlsfort Terrace, Dublin 2, D02 AY28, Ireland

HEAD OF ZEUS LTD
5–8 Hardwick Street
London, EC1R 4RG

To find out more about our authors and books
visit www.headofzeus.com
For product safety related questions contact productsafety@bloomsbury.com

For Mark & Chris,
whose support made this all possible

Charlie

Nottingham, UK

Friday 28 February 2025

The pub is heaving, as it usually is when the football is on. Everyone sipping beer, laughing, caught up in the excitement of the weekend's opening FA Cup match. They're too caught up, it seems, to notice the girl who's just stumbled through the swinging staff door, covered in blood.

Perhaps, like me, they assume she's a hallucination. I haven't screamed yet, haven't dropped my pint. Although my jaw's gone slack.

I blink, trying to convince myself the girl is a figment of my imagination. But she's still there when I open my eyes. My gaze shifts to her hand, to the broken bottle. *Red wine, not blood*, I tell myself.

But the thick droplet that falls like syrup from the shard of green glass tells me otherwise.

The jovial atmosphere at Oak & Arrow starts to shift to one of confusion and panic as others notice her. Chatter dies down. Laughter is replaced by whispers and gasps of horror. Glass shatters to the floor.

I fixate on the girl, my analytical brain taking everything in more carefully this time, assessing her like one of my patients. I try to guess how old she is, but it's difficult to tell. She could be fifteen, could be thirty. The feral, wild look in her eyes makes me wonder if she's suffering some sort of psychotic break or is on a drug-induced rampage. But then I take in her cut-up feet. Her greasy hair. Her frail body. The way her hand trembles as she clutches the glass like a weapon. Defensively, not offensively.

She is a victim. This is a crime scene.

I exhale, ready to intervene. As a psychologist, I'm trained to deal with people under severe stress. But it's usually in a safe place like my office or a hospital. Not at the scene of the crime, the epicentre of the trauma. I understand how crucial this moment is. How right now, the girl's body and mind will be in overdrive, desperately trying to figure out how best to protect herself. It's not as simple as fight or flight. It's an incredibly complex system of electrical currents computing how to safeguard its host. It could be deleting files, rewiring itself, shutting down...

I approach her, slowly, hands up to let her know I'm not a threat.

"It's alright," I say softly.

The words seem to comfort her, but she's still on edge. The tangy stench of copper and urine stings my nostrils as I inch towards her.

"It's alright," I repeat.

But before I can reach her, boisterous cheers erupt from the other side of the bar. The girl recoils in fear, stumbling backwards into a table. A hot fury courses through me at the oblivious men celebrating the goal, unable to avert their attention from the match for even a moment. I try to get the girl to focus on me again.

"It's alright," I say for the third time, desperate to keep her calm.

She opens her mouth as if to scream, or to say something, but then her eyes roll back and she collapses to the floor.

"Someone call an ambulance," I shout, dropping down next to her. "Now!"

I press my cold fingers to her neck, then her wrist, both splattered with what I deduce is someone else's warm blood. My eyes flit to the door behind her, dread pooling in my stomach wondering what horror lies behind it. But my uneasiness quickly turns into something much more disconcerting as I study the girl and notice the three small butterflies tattooed on her wrist.

It's her.

NIGHTMARE IN NOTTINGHAMSHIRE: FOOTBALLERS' GIRLFRIENDS MISSING AFTER SHERWOOD FOREST ATTACK

The girlfriends of Theo Abara and Harry Turner are missing following a violent break-in at their holiday cottage; Kaleigh Creedy, friend of the victims who escaped the assault, "working closely with police"

June 2023

ENGLAND STRIKER HARRY TURNER MARRIES "NIGHTMARE IN NOTTS" SURVIVOR KALEIGH CREEDY IN LAVISH CEREMONY

The Nottingham footballer and former Miss Teen USA tied the knot in Capri one year after welcoming their son

March 2025

FIVE YEARS ON FROM THE HORRIFIC ORDEAL THAT LEFT HER TWO BEST FRIENDS DEAD, KALEIGH CREEDY-TURNER IS GIVING BACK

"I'll never take for granted how lucky I am to be here, and I hope I can make a small difference," Kaleigh says of her fashionable charity endeavour

1

Kaleigh

Wonder-WAG Kaleigh Creedy-Turner is on top of the world. While her husband, AFC Nottingham captain and England striker Harry Turner, sets his sights on World Cup glory, the former American beauty queen continues to build a name for herself in the UK – most recently with the launch of her maternity clothing line, of which ten percent of proceeds will go to a charity close to her heart. Kaleigh is the sole survivor of the "Nightmare in Notts" ordeal, which tragically...

I close the glossy magazine, not bothering to read the rest of my interview. I'm happy with it for the most part, albeit it would've been nice to have "entrepreneur" or "philanthropist" precede my name rather than "wonder-WAG", whatever that means. But I've grown used to the three-letter acronym that attaches me to my husband – I'm proud of it, as much as I'm proud of him – so I don't let the detail spoil my first cover story.

Still, I don't need to read the rest. I don't want to. I know what it'll say.

How, five years ago, my two best friends and I were attacked at our rented cabin in Sherwood Forest. How I managed to miraculously escape, while the other two vanished. How Leila's bloated body was found in the River Trent the following week, throat slit, and Emma was presumed to have suffered the same tragic fate.

Two bodies.

The words rush to my mind, like they always do when I'm reminded of that night.

I run my fingers over the smooth cover, wondering why I'm here and not them. I imagine Leila's reaction to my feature piece; she'd be envious and proud of me at the same time.

My flawless, five-carat diamond catches the light, emitting a beautiful sparkle across the white walls. I think of what Emma would say next and shudder, imagining her rolling over in her grave.

They were supposed to be celebrating Emma's birthday. But the celebrations soon turned to tragedy.

The press loved that line.

I shake my head, forcing myself back to the present. To the black marble breakfast bar in my kitchen, where I'm savouring my morning half-cup of coffee. I cradle my protruding belly, which feels more like a giant watermelon than my usually toned stomach.

As if I manifested it, my phone buzzes with a text from my publicist, Sarah, congratulating me on the "fantastic coverage". It's followed by an email alert from my maternity line's manager about "huge order numbers coming in".

I send Sarah a few party face emojis in response before Alfie's high-pitched shriek detracts my attention from my phone. It's a gleeful sound, but my heart rate spikes nonetheless. I relax when I see the source of his enthusiasm through the glass bifold doors. My husband, dressed in nothing but his boxer briefs, carries a giggling Alfie as they both pump their fists in the air in some sort of celebration.

I wish the rest of the world could see this side of Harry, instead of just the red-faced footballer on TV.

I smile as they continue across the backyard, our "garden" as Harry calls it. Bordered by ten-foot-high hedges for privacy, the one-acre plot is the perfect size.

Harry keeps trying to convince me to move somewhere bigger, with even more land, but we don't need it. Nor do I want it. Especially if we're *here*, in Nottinghamshire. The place that will forever haunt me, and the last place I'd want to live in a secluded, remote property.

It's ironic, really. How other footballers' wives complain about being transferred. They envy that Harry has been with the same club for the entirety of our relationship, while they've had to relocate to new cities or new countries, sometimes multiple times a year. But I'm the one who envies them. I'd kill for London or Liverpool, would happily move to Munich or Madrid.

But Nottingham is Harry's home. It's the club he's always dreamed of playing for, winning championships for. And as long as he keeps scoring for them, I know a transfer is highly unlikely. So, I try to focus on the positives. The other wives who have become my closest friends. The fact that Alfie has his grandparents nearby. And our secure, gated property, nestled tightly inside a beautiful, bustling village.

I don't know how some of my friends live on their isolated, grand estates, miles from their closest neighbour. Too remote for anyone to hear them scream.

"Kay, come here, watch this," Harry shouts, saving me from a downward spiral.

I carefully manoeuvre off the bar stool, ignoring my throbbing ankles, and waddle over to the French doors. I pause when I reach it, catching my breath as if I've walked a mile rather than a few feet. I'd forgotten how difficult the final month of pregnancy can be.

A chill runs through me before I even step outside and I pull my cardigan tight across my chest. It's cold, yet my heart pools with warmth as I watch Harry gently kick the football to Alfie. I laugh to myself, wondering when I started calling it a football. I think of how my son will grow up calling it that and will spell things differently, too. He'll be taught to write some words with an "s" instead of "z", which he'll pronounce "zed" like his father. He'll add a "u" to words like colour and rumoured, the latter of which he'll hopefully never become as familiar with as Harry and me, thanks to the tabloids.

I recall the stories from when we first started dating. How difficult things were. The judgement. The assumptions. As if I didn't feel bad enough about it all at the time. How I fought against the feelings I had for him. Because Harry was Emma's boyfriend.

And you can't just start dating your dead best friend's boyfriend.

I instinctively run my finger across the cluster of three small butterflies on my wrist, the matching tattoo I got with Emma and Leila after graduation. It once symbolized our friendship, but now it serves as a painful reminder that they're gone.

I swallow hard, remembering how I didn't want a tattoo. It was something that had been ingrained in me since I started on the pageant circuit as a child. Right after Gretchan McCarthy, an eleven-year-old girl with a mop of blonde hair, called my family trash. She was saying it to her friend, but looking from me to my mother, who was crouched next to me collecting our things. The bending had pulled her jeans down just enough to expose her lower back tattoo, coiling like black ivy across her milky-white skin.

I clenched my fists and took a step toward the girls, but Mama stopped me, hand clasping around my wrist, pulling me back. *"Kaleigh Anne,"* she whispered. *"Beauty queens don't fight with their hands, understand?"*

I understood. And five years later, I used my wits to beat that same girl to the crown for Miss Teen Alabama. The ultimate revenge.

"Mummy, watch!" Alfie yells. *Mummy, not Mama, not Mommy.*

"I'm watching!" I call out, my breath visible in the cold air.

"Alright, Alf, show Mummy your big, strong kick!" Harry winks at me as he crouches into a defensive stance. Alfie boots the ball as hard as he can, giggling with joy as it drifts past Harry into the goal.

"Oh, well done, baby!" I say to Alfie before smirking at my husband. "Good thing you're not a goalie."

"Good thing I'm not a *keeper*, yeah," he corrects me.

I roll my eyes playfully, just as my phone alarm goes off. Time to get ready. It's a big match day for Harry – round five of the FA Cup – so he needs to get to the stadium for warm-up while I run errands and finish prepping for my baby shower tomorrow afternoon.

Harry doesn't love that I'll be running errands in town by myself nearly eight months pregnant, but a girl has to do what she has to do. I remember my own mother working the county fair when she was nine months pregnant; it's in my blue-collar blood.

"Alright, time to come inside and get ready," I call out to my boys.

"I want to keep playing," Alfie whines.

"You can play with Granddad before Daddy's game later," I say.

He pouts and kicks at the ground. Harry places his hand on the back of Alfie's head. I can't hear what he says to him, but Alfie perks up.

"Daddy said I can have chocolate!"

"Oh, did he now?" I glare at Harry. He beams at me cheekily, knowing what he's done. But I can't be mad, especially looking the way he does, like last year's Georgio Armani ad – sweat shining off his washboard abs in the sunlight, despite the low temperature.

Get Alfie ready. Get hair and nails done. Film content before Harry's game...

I start listing all the things I have to do today to distract myself and keep my hormones at bay. *We don't have the time*, I reason as Alfie sprints toward me.

Alfie trips and I automatically lurch forward. But Harry is already there, swooping him into his arms and brushing away the tiny wisps of hair that fell into his eyes. Alfie lets out a laugh as Harry begins to tickle him and I burst with joy, like I'm watching my heart run around outside of my body. It's a love I never knew existed and one that still takes me by surprise, even three years later.

"I can't believe how much I love him," I remember Harry saying to me one night when Alfie was only a couple months old, and the relief knowing he felt the same about our son, whose conception came as a huge shock to both of us – and the rest of the world.

The internet wasn't kind to us at first, people assuming Harry and I must've gotten together when Emma was still… around. But the more I talked about our story and finding love after loss, explaining the timeline and how we were just two people grieving who found solace in each other, people started to root for us.

I think back to when it started, during the UK's second lockdown in November 2020, almost ten months after the attack. The entire year still feels like a fever dream, a traumatic nightmare I never thought I'd wake up from, wondering why God spared me that night to just endure a worldwide pandemic. Mama told me it was because He must have other plans for me. So, from my small, city apartment, I began posting on social media, opening up about my grief and my daily struggles. And people started connecting with me, telling me how my videos made them feel less alone. I continued to post, documenting everything from my allotted daily walks to hair and make-up tutorials to cooking videos. It was the one of me making my Granny's Thanksgiving stuffing that caught Harry's attention.

I'll never forget that stuffing, he messaged, referencing the few "Friendsgivings" I'd organized when I lived with Emma.

We kept in touch after that, but at a distance. It wasn't until the anniversary of the attack two months later when he asked if he could visit, sensing I didn't want to be alone.

We didn't kiss that night, despite the butterflies in my stomach willing me to. We talked and listened to country music, which I was surprised to learn was his guilty pleasure, and simply enjoyed each other's company. It'd been so long since I laughed that much.

Every day after that I fought my growing feelings for Harry, tried to keep him at arms' length. *Just a friend*, I'd tell myself. But we were never meant to be just friends. Alfie is proof of that. He was conceived the very first time Harry and I slept together a few months later. I'd taken it as a sign from God that it was okay, that we were meant to be.

I wish I could go back in time and tell my younger self that I had nothing to worry about. That the worst period of my life would be followed by the best. That Alfie would only bring us closer.

My Harry. Our son. Our perfect little family.

I close the glass doors before I head upstairs to get ready, but as I turn the lock, a lone magpie perched on the hedge catches my eye. *One for sorrow.*

"*You have to salute it, Kay.*" I recall Emma referencing the British superstition. "*Salute it and say 'ello to your brother!' or you'll be cursed. It's what my gran taught me.*"

I laughed at her, thinking she was being as nutty as a squirrel.

It is nuts, I tell myself, turning away. *A stupid superstition.*

I ignore the fact that the last time I didn't salute a lone magpie, my two best friends died.

2

Kaleigh

I take my sunglasses off as I walk into my favourite bar and restaurant, a converted nineteenth-century church in Nottingham's Lace Market. Stunning stonework arches over the imposing space to my left and right, and a mediaeval-style chandelier hangs over the bar in front of me. It's framed by stained-glass windows spanning most of the grand structure's back wall.

As I follow the hostess to the booth at the back of the venue, I catch three girls staring at me. Two blondes and a brunette, they remind me of *us* back in the day – of Emma, Leila and me – and I can't help but smile. It quickly fades though when the all too familiar gut-punch reminds me I'll never sit around a table with Emma and Leila ever again.

Realising that the girls are now trying to covertly take photos of me, I stand up straight and cradle my belly. That's the worst part about being in the public eye – always having to be on. You never know who's watching, or how they'll interpret every facial expression, every conversation. Being noticeably pregnant makes it easier though, it softens me. I give the girls a kind smile and wave, and they smile back.

I let out a sigh after I awkwardly slide into the booth, pushing the table out to fit, and take a minute to appreciate how I finally made it out of the negative spotlight. From victim to survivor. From betrayer to loving "mum" and wife. Famous enough to spark the occasional whispers and covert photos but not enough to be followed by fans or paparazzi. *A perfect level of fame.*

A ping interrupts my thoughts and I instinctively tap into the notification. It's a text from my event planner saying she's on her way. I respond with a heart emoji. As usual, Lily's right on time. I'm the one who is early. Lucky enough to have had a good morning with no nausea, heartburn or acne to complicate the filming of my "Get Ready With Me" video earlier.

I click into Instagram and review the draft Alison, my social media manager, saved based on the raw footage I sent her an hour ago after I had my hair and nails done. I look cute, glowing even, as I brush my long golden curls over my shoulder to show off the hunter green dress from my maternity line. I double check the caption and hashtags, making a few quick changes before previewing one last time.

"Perfect," I mutter under my breath, scheduling it for an hour before the game.

As I wait for Lily, I scroll down to see how yesterday's post is doing. It's a reel of Harry kissing me in front of his new sports car, set to Harlow Hayes's "Ferrari". I had my doubts, thinking it was a little cheesy when Alison pitched the idea, but to her credit it's already at forty thousand likes.

I click out of my profile and start scrolling through my feed, which features a mix of private videos from some of the other wives and girlfriends I follow, mixed with random cooking videos and fashion content. I swipe up and see a post from one of my friends, Natasha, whose husband was recently transferred to Barcelona. She's pregnant, explaining to him how her baby is the size of a large mango. But he replies that her stomach is way bigger than that. The next scene cuts to her dragging him out of the room after he's been knocked out.

I roll my eyes, although the corner of my mouth crooks into a smile. Her posts can be "so cringe" as Harry says, but I miss her, wishing I could be in Spain, too. But friends coming and going is part of the lifestyle. And staying in touch through social media is the only thing that helps. That and planning amazing trips to catch up.

Laughing out loud, I comment with a bunch of emojis. Miss you! Need to plan something soon xoxo

I continue to scroll, pausing when a thirst trap of my husband appears. It's a slo-mo of Harry taking off his shirt and flexing on his knees after scoring a goal, set to "Started from the Bottom" by Drake. My lips curl back into a smile as I share it to my story with the smirk emoji, giggling like a schoolgirl. I think about how proud my teenage self would be of me, of how far I've come. From Miss Mobile County to Miss Teen Alabama to Miss Teen USA to Mrs Harry Turner.

When I return to my homepage, I see my friend Abby has posted. Her husband also plays for AFC Nottingham, so I make a point to heart and comment since I'll be seeing her at the game later.

So beautiful, I write under the sepia-filtered photo of her daughter giving her husband a kiss on the cheek.

I swipe left for the rest of the photos, chest tightening when I realise where they are. At Center Parcs in Sherwood Forest, riding bikes through the trees. The same trees I sprinted through five years ago. My heart races as if I'm back there again, desperately searching for cover before collapsing against a large oak tree. I can suddenly feel the insects that crawled all over me as I hid, frozen in the dark.

On instinct, I scratch at my skin, now prickling like it's covered in tiny ants. I still can't believe I managed to make it out of the forest that night. It was like I had a guardian angel guiding me to safety.

I close my eyes and I'm there again, at the service station off the main road. Cradling myself under the fluorescent lights, covered in my friend's blood as the police question me.

"Did you see who it was?"

I shake my head, no. I couldn't see. I could only hear.

Two bodies.

"Kaleigh, I'm so sorry! Am I late?" Lily's frantic voice brings me back to the present. To where I'm safe. Where I'm happy. *Safe and happy. Safe and happy.*

I smile widely as I stretch out my arms. "No, no I'm early, you know me."

She bends down to hug me. "You alright?"

I've been living in the UK long enough to know that this is just a greeting, not an actual question. When it's said in that tone at least.

"You look so cute," I say, admiring her chic blue pantsuit paired with pointy stilettos.

"Aw, thanks, babe, you too," Lily responds as she takes the seat across from me. "So, are you excited?"

"Yes, very! I just hope the game goes well tonight so that everyone will be in good spirits for the shower."

It wasn't ideal, holding such a big event in the middle of the season, right after an important game. But there's never a good time to do anything mid-season, so all you can do is hope for the best.

Lily flicks her straight brown hair behind her shoulder and waves her hand dismissively. "It'll be fab, don't worry."

I nod, hoping she's right, before asking for updates on her love life. I tell her I know a couple footballers I can set her up with if she's interested.

She laughs and shakes her head. "Thanks, but no thanks. You probably have one of the only good ones."

I shrug, thankful she's right.

"Do you need another minute?" the server asks.

"No, we're ready to order," I say, before turning to tell Lily that lunch is on me.

We place our orders, both getting the three-course pre-set menu with the salmon and mash before jumping into the final planning details of my dream baby shower. One that I couldn't have with Alfie due to the awkward timing of everything. Not to mention baby showers weren't really a thing in the UK back then, but thankfully, they're gaining in popularity.

Just in time for you, little Alice.

I glance down at my bump, paying attention to the way the name sounds. It feels right. Harry prefers Chloe and Olivia, but I'm drawn to Alice more and more every day.

My preferred name for her makes me wonder if I'd picked the wrong theme. That maybe I should have gone with Wonderland rather than pretty in pink. But then I realise I can do the Wonderland theme for her first birthday. *One-derland*, I think. *Genius.*

"I've already checked with all the vendors – the florist, the musicians, the venue and the baker," Lily says. "Everyone is ready to go but I just wanted to confirm the schedule."

She passes me a piece of paper with a breakdown of the event, planned out in fifteen to thirty-minute increments.

I study the schedule, double-checking every detail.

10:30 a.m. – florist set-up

10:45 a.m. – decor and place settings

11:15 a.m. – bakery delivery

11:30 a.m. – Kaleigh and photographer arrive (get early photos of venue and Kaleigh)

11:45 a.m. – string quartet sets up, ready for guests' arrival

12:00 p.m. – guests arrive (greeted with champagne or orange juice, plus canapes)

12:30 p.m. – first course served (guests encouraged to fill out "Wishes for baby" cards and "Guess the baby" game on seat placements)

12:45 p.m. – main course served

1:15 p.m. – cake, pie and coffee, and "Guess the baby" answers

1:30 p.m. – Harry arrives with Alfie, followed by gift unwrapping and photos

I nod once I reach the end, happy with the order of events. "Let's swap these last two. I'll tell Harry to get there before dessert so they can see the cake and the pie bar before we cut into it. Otherwise, it looks perfect."

I slide the piece of paper back to Lily, who scribbles a note on the last line. She places it back in her folder before handing me another sheet.

"Okay, so, moving onto the seating chart…"

"What's happened now?" I ask, thinking we had it all sorted yesterday.

Lily takes her pen and circles an empty chair next to Abby. "Paige Santos texted and said she can no longer make it, since her son got the flu."

I fight the urge to curse Paige for cancelling, making me have to rethink the seating arrangements *again*. But then I remember the last time Alfie got a fever and I had to do the same.

"I'll have a chat with Zara and get back to you later tonight," I sigh.

Lily nods, knowing Zara Becker is the perfect person to ask. Not only is she known for throwing the poshest parties, but she's also an expert at navigating the WAG political scene. A skill of hers that I leveraged at the start of our relationship. After she finally stopped resenting me for "taking Emma's place".

Lily circles another spot on the paper. "What do you want to do about this one? Is your mum coming?"

I shift in my seat as I share my rehearsed response. "She can't make it, unfortunately. She was hoping my dad would be feeling better by now, a little more mobile after his hunting accident, but she's just not ready to leave him yet."

I pronounce leave like lay-ve, my Southern drawl betraying me like it does every time I talk about home.

"*Layve*," Lily giggles, caught off guard by the slip. Heat rushes to my cheeks, but I laugh it off. "So none of your family will be there?" she double-checks, a sad look on her face.

"No," I confirm, feigning regret.

The truth is that I never invited them, not officially at least. A wave of guilt washes over me, wondering if I should have let them know after all. But then I think of my last visit to Alabama, seven months ago, around the time I found out I was pregnant again. My dad and brother, having a belching contest in between beers, their hairy bellies popping through their dirty white tanks. My mother and sisters, cooking up sloppy joes for dinner, windows open to let the cigarette smoke out as my nieces and nephews ran like feral animals around the house.

I start to sweat just thinking about them all being here. I've spent too long curating an image, crafting my brand. It's something I've been working toward my whole life, ever since I started pageants and realised judges wanted to crown girls who exuded clean-cut Southern belle rather than fairground trash. Someone they imagined picking berries in a red-checkered sundress and baking pies in a charming farmhouse kitchen, not shovelling down macaroni and ketchup from a paper plate in the back of a motorhome.

I cringe, imagining my mother at the shower in her Walmart's best, telling stories about how I used to wrestle pigs at the county fair for pageant money, like she lovingly divulged at my wedding.

Needless to say, that's not the aesthetic I'm going for.

I shake my head and reconfirm my decision not to extend the invitation. No, it's best they stay put for now and I will visit them after the birth.

After we finish our meals and decide on the final details, Lily and I exit the restaurant together.

"You ever been to the caves?" Lily asks as we cross the street. She points in the direction of the City of Caves, one of Nottingham's most popular tourist attractions. "Thinking about taking my boys one day, not sure if they're old enough though."

I picture the network of caves running beneath our feet, an underground world where people once lived and worked. Harry took me there on one of our first dates and I freaked out, feeling claustrophobic and out of sorts. "I've been once. It was really... eerie."

"Yeah, that's what I figured," Lily sighs. "Oh, but speaking of eerie, there was a huge police cordon outside Stoney Street when I drove up. Blocked off with blue and white tape, loads of police."

I frown, wondering what happened.

"Probably some drunkards from last night," Lily guesses.

Ding. Ding. Ding. A tram pulls up in front of us, slowing down as it nears the Lace Market stop.

"Oh dear, they're out early." Lily gestures to the boisterous football fans in AFC Nottingham green jerseys, tumbling off the tram into the city streets.

Some are drunkenly "singing" unrecognizable songs, while others are busy starting fights with supporters wearing Sheffield red.

Heat rushes to my face as I picture Davey Allen, the Sheffield supporter who stalked us to the cabin that night and killed Leila and Emma. All because he was angry at Harry for scoring against his team. So stupid. So senseless. So... violent.

My eyes flit to the red-faced fans already fighting with each other. I feel woozy, off balance, as they swarm across the street toward us.

Thankfully, Lily keeps me upright, and together we hurry along the cobblestones, away from the horde.

3

Kaleigh

I take in the grandeur of the stadium as I reach the top of the stairs to the family section, looking out across a sea of fifty-thousand people. About three quarters of the stadium wears green and white, the other quarter red.

The colours aren't blended though, something I was surprised by when I first attended a game here. I'd assumed it would be like American sports, all the fans sitting and mingling together. But no, in European football – and football across most of the world – fans have to be separated. Or else it'd be a bloodbath.

I search the pitch for Harry to distract myself and feel an instant sense of comfort when I see him in the left corner, sprinting toward the ball.

"Let's go, Turner!" a group of fans yell to my left. I instinctively glance in their direction, my face flushing as they notice me. They holler in excitement, elbowing each other until they're all leering at me, hands pumping in the air. I smile and nod, before turning my attention back to the stairs.

I tense when I see a man running toward me, but then I crumple in relief when I realise it's Simon, Harry's brother. He quickly links his arm into mine, helping me balance.

"Thank you!" I yell, hoping he hears me over the crowd, who now chant in unison. It's a deep, booming war cry that causes the metal railing to vibrate beneath my grip.

"We'll have to roll you down soon," he jokes.

"Tell me about it," I laugh. "I can't believe I still have another month of this, I don't think my ankles will make it."

I eye Simon's suit. He's dressed more for a horse race than a football match.

"You look nice," I say, an air of intrigue in my voice.

"Cheers," he replies, fingering his collar. "Came straight from a business meeting, figured I'd try and look important."

"Very important indeed." I nod approvingly. "Have I missed much?" I tightly grip the railing as we make our way down. I try to watch my step, but all I see is the very tip of my Chanel sneakers jutting out beneath my huge belly.

"Just Harry's goal," he says.

"No, really?" My heart sinks. "The game only started like two minutes ago."

"I'm jokin' with ya, Kay," he laughs. "You've missed fuck all."

"Mummy!" I hear Alfie squeal as we make it to our row. Robbie, Harry's dad, holds Alfie as he reaches out for me.

"Hey, baby," I say, trying to catch my breath. I give my son a long kiss on the head. "How are you? Have you had a lovely day with Nana and Granddad?"

"Yep, we pwayed football aw day," he says proudly.

"Did you now?" I glance at Robbie. "I bet Granddad is exhausted."

"He is," Robbie confirms.

"Thank you," I reply, giving my father-in-law a kiss on the cheek.

"Ay up duckie." Harry's mom, Lorraine, leans across Robbie to greet me with my favourite Midlands saying.

Like Robbie, she's sporting an AFC Nottingham jersey with Turner on the back, while Alfie dons his special "Daddy" shirt.

"Thank you so much again for watching him today," I say.

"Oh, it's our pleasure. You know we love having him. How was—" Lorraine's question is drowned out by the crowd's screams. I whip my head toward the field where one of Harry's teammates is rolling on the pitch, clutching his ankle. It's Jake, my friend Lucy's husband.

The ref then whips out a yellow card to the opposition, and the crowd booms in approval.

"Alright, ref, alright!" Robbie claps.

While the medical team attends to Jake, I search the crowd for Lucy, frowning when I don't see her. Instead, I catch Victoria's attention. She smiles, her white teeth bright against her dark skin as she cradles Henri, her four-month-old baby. He's wearing a green onesie and black leather headphones. I glance at her long, thin waist peeking from under her cropped jersey and feel a pang of jealousy.

At the risk of staring, I look in the other direction and spot Abby taking photos of the crowd with her camera, which she rarely goes anywhere without. It's currently pointed at a group of men covered in green paint from the waist up, all wearing little green hats with feathers sticking out. I smile at the jovial fans, but then my face contorts into disgust as one hurls a giant loogie onto the steps next to him, before whistling with two pudgy fingers. Abby makes a similar facial expression and laughs as she catches my eye. She turns her camera to me, and I place my hands over my belly, tilt my head and smile for a photo.

I jump as someone wraps their arms around my bump.

"Hey babe," Zara says, laughing.

"Jesus, you scared me!" I jokingly swat her and then give her a double air kiss. "Love this," I say, touching the green leather blazer draped over her shoulders. She looks effortless, wearing a light layer of foundation and a thick curtain of perfectly applied lashes.

"Thanks, hon, you're looking…"

"Swollen AF," I respond, pursing my lips.

"But still beautiful as ever," she assures me.

"Hey, where's Lucy," I ask.

She rolls her eyes. "Did you not see? There's a new headline about Jake and a mystery woman."

I groan. "Not again?"

Zara presses her lips into a thin line and nods. "Again."

I suddenly don't feel so bad for him being tackled now. "Is she okay? Should we skip Oak & Arrow later? Go visit Luce instead?"

The Oak & Arrow is where we usually go after home games. The owner, Gaz, shuts the place down so the AFC Nottingham squad and their friends and family can celebrate together.

Zara leans back and opens her mouth as if she's aghast. I frown. She usually isn't bothered about going to the

Oak & Arrow, so I don't understand her reaction. My attention is diverted though as the crowd erupts in cheers.

"Let's go, Har! Let's go, son!" Robbie bellows next to me as Harry races down the pitch with the ball.

"C'mon, babe!" I cheer.

A collective sigh of disappointment sounds throughout the stadium as the ball bounces out of play.

"No one's ever fucking there for him," Robbie grumbles, prompting a swat from Lorraine.

"Watch your language in front of Alf," she says. Alfie didn't seem to hear him though, too distracted by his toy car that he's showing his Uncle Simon.

I turn my attention back to Zara and yell louder, thinking maybe she misheard my question. "I said maybe we should skip..."

Zara cuts me off with a shake of her head, the motion sending her cherry-scented Tom Ford perfume wafting in the air.

"Haven't you heard what happened?"

My stomach sinks, suddenly remembering the police cordon Lily mentioned on Stoney Street. The same street as Oak & Arrow.

4

Harry

Harry Turner, it's Harry fucking Turner!

Harry can still hear the fans chanting his name, despite being in the changing room now. It's over. They won. They're through to the next round of the FA Cup.

He takes a seat, letting out a sigh of relief that he did his job tonight. He scored and helped send the team through after a rough first half. He pictures the fans wildly cheering for him after his goal. How he skidded on his knees over to the corner and raised his hands, and they went fucking mad. Just like Harry always dreamed.

He squirts a stream of water down his throat as he leans back, reflecting how far he – a working-class kid from the Midlands – has come. The weight his name now holds.

The moment Harry steps onto the pitch and hears the thousands of fans screaming his name, he transforms. He's no longer Harry Turner the father, husband or son – a human prone to emotions like anxiety and fear. He's an unstoppable force.

He'd say he never imagined this success, never thought he'd actually make it, achieve this kind of glory and fame. But that would be a lie. It's the one thing he pictured every single day of his life. His wife would say he manifested it. But to Harry, "manifested" implies luck. Something being handed to him. Nothing was ever handed to Harry Turner. He made the sacrifices. Put in the blood, sweat and tears. Over and over again.

Again.

Again.

Again.

His dad's voice plays in his mind. He's taken back to ten years old, cold and wet in the rain, feet bleeding as Robbie pushed him to keep training until he hit the ball on target ten times in a row. Harry wriggles his toe in his boot, a phantom pain haunting him.

He closes his eyes, reliving his 85th-minute goal one more time. Him cutting through the grass, moving straight past Hughes – his opponent today, but his teammate in a few weeks' time when they'll both be playing for England. Harry pictures the sequence as it happened, the one he and the squad had been practising all week. Porter taking three calculated steps back, all at a precise left angle to get the best curve on the ball. Evans making a run down the wing, while Harry sprints straight down the middle. Then everything accelerating as Evans controls the ball and Harry finds the gap.

And then it was touch, step, score.

Touch. Step. Score.

If any pundit tries to say he didn't play well today, they can go fuck themselves.

Harry sits forward to unlace his boots. The conversation in the changing room is a bit more depraved than usual after the game, as it is when they're on a winners' high. Raucous laughter and banter, everyone feeding off each other. But nothing Harry isn't used to. Nothing that he hasn't taken part of in the past. He catches the end of Evans' conversation with Becker and Adeyemi.

"I was so pissed, mate, the only way I made it out of the club was by keeping my eyes focused on her tight little arse. It was perfect, like a ripe peach." Jake Evans mimics biting into something juicy. "You all saw the photos. Proper fit, yeah?" He smirks as he ties chin-length blonde hair into a bun atop his head.

"Wait, wait, wait," Wolfe, the team's keeper, laughs.

He turns up his phone's volume and then holds it above him, grinning in anticipation. A$AP Rocky's "Fuckin' Problems" starts to play and the room fills with boisterous laughter.

"You love bad bitches, that's your fuckin' problem," Wolfe bellows in his German accent.

Harry tries not to laugh, Kaleigh's countless pleas not to egg Jake on in the back of his mind, but he can't help it. Evans is a lost cause anyway. Plus, who is he to judge? He used to be the same when he was younger.

He thinks of his first trip to Vegas when he was just nineteen. Simon had secured fake IDs for them, since neither were twenty-one yet, both with ridiculous names, Herbert Hancock for Harry and Eddie Cranston for Simon. Not that they needed them anyway. Harry was already making a name for himself as a rising star, invited to all the big events. Fights at MGM Grand, lavish afterparties, strip clubs...

Harry was on top of the world, with nothing or no one able to bear any weight on his decisions. His impulses. He had to be shocked out of it.

Harry checks his phone and smiles when he sees a congratulatory text from his wife. It's a selfie of her and their son from the stands, smiling. So SO proud of you, babe! Love you xoxo. He can't get over how beautiful she is, her honey brown eyes sparkling through the screen, contrasting with her golden curls. His heart bursts then, imagining their daughter. Little Chloe or Olivia. Or Alice. He wasn't sure of her name yet, but he was sure she'd look like Kaleigh. Golden hair, running around and smiling with big brown eyes and tiny little freckles. Stealing his heart like Kaleigh stole his.

When they first got together, he was worried she'd be a distraction. Assumed as a former beauty queen, Kaleigh would want the spotlight and crave more attention than he could give her. But it was the opposite. Having her own interests and goals not only kept her busy and satisfied, but it motivated him to be his best, too. He's better because of her. In his previous relationship, things were different. Things were more toxic. He knows he's to blame for a lot of it though. A twinge of guilt hits him as he thinks of Emma.

He wonders what would've happened if Leila and Emma hadn't died that night. If he and Emma would've lasted if she was still here. Or if he and Kaleigh were always end-game, they just hadn't seen it yet.

"Oh shit, you guys hear about Gaz?" Becker says, looking up from his phone, pale-faced.

"Gaz?"

"Yeah, Oak & Arrow Gaz."

"Nah, what happened?"

"He's dead. Some crazy bitch stabbed him," Becker says.

"What?" Harry says in disbelief. "Why?"

Becker shrugs.

Harry's other teammate, Porter, comes to get in on the conversation. "People are sayin' he might've been holding her hostage or something like that." He raises his eyebrows, as if to chide Becker.

Headlines from years ago flash across Harry's mind.

Emma Macy abducted.

Is Emma Macy really dead?

Police presume Emma Macy suffered same tragic fate as Leila Adler. Body never found.

Harry's phone distracts him from his thoughts. He looks down at the unknown number calling and ignores it.

5

Charlie

Sunday 2 March 2025

My chest pounds as I sprint across the court, arm and racket outstretched, reaching for the fluorescent yellow ball. It whizzes past me, bouncing just inside the lines. I hunch over, accepting defeat, and curse myself for finishing off that bottle of wine last night. If I'd gone to sleep at a reasonable hour, rather than scrolling on my phone as I half-watched the latest season of a reality dating show, maybe I wouldn't be so off my game today. But I've struggled to sleep ever since Friday night.

I swallow hard, thinking of the girl covered in blood. Her tattoo. Her face. It's been more than twenty-four hours, but still no confirmation on her identity, even though I was fairly certain who it was. I scoff, still in disbelief how a trip to the pub to watch the football with friends turned into utter horror.

I stand up straight, hands on the back of my head as I walk towards centre-court. Hot liquid rises up my oesophagus, burning the back of my throat before I swallow it back down. I visualise last night's bottle of red mixing with this morning's black coffee, all of it bubbling together, creating a pool of acid and anxiety. My heart races at the thought, the havoc it must be wreaking on my gut. As a doctor, I should know better. But I specialise in the mind, not the body; although, the two are more connected than most realise.

"You alright there?" Kate says as we reach the net.

I huff out a laugh, still trying to catch my breath. "You must be training at night…" I say to my former supervisor, now one of my close friends. "You claim you're always working but you're serving like Raducanu."

"I wish." She dabs her flushed face with a towel. "I can assure you I am still spending most of my evenings at my desk rather than on the court."

I sigh, knowing it's the truth. Kate and I are both psychologists, working for the NHS as well as the private sector. Due to the demand for mental health services and the rising cost of living, we often find ourselves working six or seven days a week.

"Any plans for the rest of the afternoon?" Kate asks as we walk towards the car park.

"Just work," I say, thinking about my stacked diary as I answer. How I have to resort to scribbling miniscule text in the margins to fit in all my appointments, tasks and reminders for the week ahead. NHS hospital appointments Monday and Tuesday, prisoner assessments and therapy sessions Wednesday and Thursday, private outpatient sessions on Friday and Saturday, plus a university talk on Friday afternoon. Not to mention consulting calls, multi-disciplinary meetings, supervising sessions, and mountains of paperwork and reports in between.

"I don't know how you keep up with it all," I say, wondering how she manages such a demanding work schedule while also making time for her two young children and her partner. I guess that's one of the reasons I'm single though.

"Well, if it makes you feel any better," Kate says, "I'm about to be buried in the Norton case."

"Oh shit, is that this week?" My stomach turns at the thought of William Norton, the former football coach at the centre of an abuse scandal.

"It's this week," she confirms, raising an eyebrow. "So it'll be a lot of prep tomorrow and Tuesday, going through files and files of..." She trails off, not wanting to go into detail. "But I will push through, make sure the court knows the lasting effects on victims."

I nod, knowing full well the kind of sordid details she's been reading. Some of the more gruesome cases I've worked on still haunt me.

"Anyway, did you watch the game last night?" Kate asks, her tone more uplifting as if she could sense me getting lost in my thoughts. "Our Merry Men could actually do it this season."

"Yeah, they played well," I reply. "Second half at least."

"Turner finally earning that sixteen mil he's on," Kate says.

I roll my eyes at the obscene number. It's laughable really, how doctors like Kate and I will never make a fraction of what he makes in one season. Essential workers deserve bugger all compared to footballers, I guess.

But my envy is assuaged as I think of the news that could be coming his way if I'm right about Emma. If his ex-girlfriend really is alive.

I return home to an unkempt flat and a judgy look from my cat, Beans. Her moniker came from my brother, who found her abandoned and hungry, picking at an empty can of Heinz. She licks her big belly, no longer the thin little kitten she once was, before giving me another wide-eyed stare.

"Now, you can't blame me for all this mess, can you?" I raise an eyebrow and point at the torn-up paper on the floor.

I stare at the scratched hardwood as I pick up the pieces and make a mental note to buy a cheap rug. But by the time I've thrown the paper into the bin, I've talked myself out of it. I don't have the time to go shopping for home decor, nor do I want to. That was always Jamie's thing, not mine.

Beans meows as if to tell me to get over it. That it's been over a year since my ex left me for being "emotionally unavailable", and it's perhaps time I try to date again. I immediately cringe at the thought though, of having to come home and be forced to talk about my feelings after I spent the entire day talking about everyone else's.

I open up a can of Beans's favourite food and scrape it into her bowl, crinkling my nose at the sour scent. I then dump a can of soup into a bowl for myself, realising her food isn't much worse than mine.

After I put my soup in the microwave, I check my phone, sighing when I see the missed call and voicemail. I determine it's probably work-related based on the local number. An emergency.

I hit play on the recording.

"*Dr Singh, this is DCI Maynard with Nottingham City Police. If you could give me a call back, that'd be great.*"

I frown at the DCI's name, not recognising it. Intrigued, I call him back.

"Maynard," the man declares.

"DCI Maynard, this is Dr Charlotte Singh returning your call…"

"Hi, yes. I was given your information from the officers you met on Friday evening under… unfortunate circumstances."

I freeze, caught off guard but happy to have answered.

"Yes," I say, clearing my throat. "Has her identity been confirmed?"

I think back to the tattoo, the slight crook in her nose. It has to be her, has to be. I'm surprised by the anxiety swirling in my chest as I wait for his reply.

"As you suspected and mentioned to the DC on the scene, it's her. It's Emma Macy."

Holy. Shit.

I don't know if I should be happy or sad. It's a miracle she's been found alive, yes, but at what cost? I think of her passed out on the floor, a helpless, bloody rumple of bones, and wonder if the old Emma is even there anymore.

"Wow…" I huff out a loud breath. "Thank you for letting me know. How is she doing?"

"That's the thing, the reason I called you, actually," Maynard says. "We were wondering if you wouldn't mind taking a trip over to Queen's Med. She isn't talking, you see."

"Not at all?" I ask.

"No. We've been able to get a few head nods, blinks, but that's it."

"Have you tried explaining to her that you want to make sure there aren't any other victims out there?" I ask, my training kicking in.

"Of course, we've tried everything," Maynard replies. "First the family liaison, then the nurses, doctors, hospital counsellors, her parents... But the reports are all the same. She just stares ahead, vacant."

"Right." I deflate, knowing this is often the case. I worried when I looked into her wild, fearful eyes that her mind might shut down from the shock of whatever she went through. I close my eyes, not wanting to think what Emma was subjected to over the past five years.

"You were at the scene, so I'm wondering if she might feel a connection to you," Maynard says. "Plus, you're qualified and already have clearance at the hospital..."

I pinch the bridge of my nose tightly, knowing I really shouldn't take this on. I'm already overwhelmed with work, and today was my day to catch up on paperwork and prepare for the busy week ahead, not add to my workload.

But I also know that I can't say no, even though it will probably consume me.

6

Kaleigh

"Are you ready?" Lily asks as we stand outside an intricately carved double door.

I nod enthusiastically, trying not to squeal like a pig in mud as the doors open, revealing the baby shower of my dreams. All my planning – pinning photos, sharing ideas and meeting with Lily, the florist, the baker, and this absolutely stunning and historic estate – coming together for this. An event fit for a queen and her little princess.

My gaze flits back and forth, not knowing where to feast my eyes first, until they land on a ten-foot pink satin bow. Its tail forms the perfect curtained backdrop to a five-tiered Chantilly-frosted Lane Cake, a fancy twist on the Alabama classic that has been my favourite ever since I had it at Cassandra Gordon's eleventh birthday party.

My eyes linger on the enchanting tablescape overflowing with pink candles, peonies, roses and poppies. All so beautifully laid out. I smirk, knowing that even Cassandra,

40

the richest, most popular girl in my hometown, would be envious. Not just of this shower, but of my life turning out better than hers, despite what her social media content of motivational quotes and beige-clad babies would have you believe.

I'm overcome with emotion as I think of the future I'll be able to give my daughter. Of the parties I'll be able to throw for her. Us trying on dresses together. Getting our hair and nails done together, while Alfie plays football with his dad.

"Do you like it?" Lily asks.

I trace my fingers over my flowy chiffon dress, trying to hold back my tears so I don't ruin my make-up.

"It's perfect," I say, turning to Lily, who looks like part of the decor in a fitted, pale pink ensemble. Her dark brown hair is tied back in a low pony with a satin bow.

She beams, also pleased. "So there's just a few final details to iron out before everyone arrives…"

I nod, willing her to continue.

"I've updated the seating chart as per your message last night. I've also instructed the caterer to bring out the pies right after Harry and Alfie arrive."

"Amazing, thank you," I say, knowing Alfie will love the desserts and Harry will love the gesture. A little thank you for having to brave a party full of women, even if it's only so he can thank them for coming right at the end.

"Are you ready for your photos?" Lily motions to the photographer, a young woman dressed in black currently taking close-up shots of the table settings.

I nod eagerly and open the list on my phone to review it with the photographer, wanting to make sure I get all the right shots. Me next to the cake. Me standing at the edge of the long table smiling. Me from the side, holding my belly, hair draped down my back. It makes me giddy to think of how many likes these will get on Instagram. If I'm lucky, my publicist will be able to sell them to some of the bigger tabloids, too.

After we take my solo shots, I run through the rest of the list with the photographer. "I'll take some with my mother-in-law next..." I wave to Lorraine, who has just arrived. She's talking to Lily animatedly, no doubt telling her how beautiful the venue looks.

"And then of course, plenty of photos of me and the girls. And don't forget candids, those are my fave."

The photographer nods in understanding.

"Oh, and can't believe I almost forgot." I put my hand to my chest. "Harry will be arriving around one fifteen, and I really want some reaction shots from him, especially of him handing me the flowers, us greeting each other... that kind of thing. And then we'll take some proper ones in front of the flower arch."

I envision the photos perfectly in my head, wondering if I may be able to land an exclusive with *Cosmo* or *Elle*.

"Hello, love," Lorraine says as she clip-clops over to me, holding a large gift. "Everything is bloody beautiful, you included!"

"Thank you." I blush, leaning in for a kiss on the cheek. "And look at you," I say as we pull apart. "Gorg!"

Lorraine smiles and does a little twirl, showing off the floral knee-length dress we picked out together a few weeks ago.

"And this is for you... and my future granddaughter, of course." She holds out the gift, wrapped in baby pink paper and ribbon.

"I told you not to get anything," I say. "You already do so much for us."

"And I'm excited to do even more when this little girl arrives."

I smile, cradling my belly like a trophy as Lorraine places one hand on my back. "Sorry, your mother couldn't make it, she would've loved this."

I give her a sad smile in return, tears rushing back, this time out of guilt. I fan my hand over my face in an attempt to dry my eyes.

"Well, I'm very happy you're here," I say. And I mean it. Because as far as mothers-in-law go, I hit the jackpot. She's so loving toward Harry, an amazing grandmother to Alfie, and so supportive of me and my career. Always up for making a funny video with me, even sending content ideas my way, of things I should do or that we could do together. It's a lovely relationship I never expected, especially since she'd been so close to Emma for so long, had known her since she was a teenager.

I suddenly picture blood pooling around Emma's head before the vision shifts to Gaz, the landlord of the Oak. I couldn't believe it when Zara told me what happened last night, before Harry confirmed that Gaz had been stabbed to death.

An unsettling feeling washes over me, causing my chest to tighten. I pinch my forearm to force the images and thoughts away. *Today is my day*, I remind myself.

I exhale, breathing out the negativity, and focus on enjoying the event as I hand Lorraine's gift to Lily. After she places the gift on the table, she ushers Lorraine and me over to the wall for photos. The string quartet begins to play as we pose.

"How lush is this?" I can hear Abby before she turns the corner.

I quickly swap sides with Lorraine to finish our photos before the rest of the guests arrive.

"Holy shit, Kaleigh," Abby says, now standing under the arch, Victoria behind her. I continue to smile for the camera twice more before relaxing my shoulders and making my way to greet them. My feet throb inside my heels.

"You Americans and your showers," Vic says in her French accent, shaking her head. Her long supermodel legs on full display make me jealous.

I shrug, ready to defend the time-honoured tradition but stop myself when Lucy shows up. She smiles half-heartedly and dabs at her long lash extensions with her finger, hot pink acrylics flashing brightly against her fake tan. Her bottom lip looks more swollen than normal, and I can immediately tell she went for the one millilitre injections instead of the half syringe like I suggested. I want to tell her she doesn't need to go so over the top, but her jerk of a husband has been really playing on her insecurities lately.

I wrap her in a tight hug. "Well, don't you look as pretty as a peach," I say with an intentional twang to make her smile.

It works, even though it doesn't meet her eyes.

The next half-hour rushes by in a blur of pink, perfumed hellos followed by photo after photo. So much happens so fast that I feel dizzy at the end of all the greetings, relieved when it's time to take my seat at the table.

Zara, Abby, Vic, and Lucy – the longest-standing AFC Nottingham wives – sit closest to me, then Lorraine and her friends, and then some of the newer players' wives and girlfriends, and my other acquaintances. The only exception is Adriana Hidalgo, the wife of the new star striker from Argentina, who sits between Zara and Abby. Zara said we needed to make her feel welcome, so I sat her next to us, although part of me wondered if I shouldn't have since her husband plays the same position as Harry. Maybe I should be less worried about making her happy and more worried about her husband taking Harry's spot. But then I realised there's no need to worry at all. Harry has been and always will be Nottingham's star. And if he wasn't, well, then maybe Harry would get transferred and we could move away from here.

The menu I carefully selected seems to please every guest as well as my pregnant appetite. I pop an antacid tablet to help quell my heartburn and suddenly long for a nap. But I know that's not possible right now because I must do the rounds and speak to each of the guests.

As I make my way around the tables, catching up with some of the newer girls, I let myself imagine what it would be like to be transferred. To let Adriana take my place while I become the new girl somewhere else.

"How did you and Harry meet?" Margot, the girlfriend of another recent transfer, asks. She looks up at me doe-eyed.

The question takes me off guard, surprised she doesn't know. Or maybe, I think, what happened almost five years ago is finally old news.

"Um, through a mutual friend," I say, feeling guilty as soon as the words leave my mouth. But that's all she needs to know. And it feels nice to not have to justify how we got together after Emma's death.

As I walk away though, I can hear another girl say, "Do you seriously not know about the drama?"

I sigh and head back to my table.

"Are any of you going to the funeral?" I hear Lucy say to the others as I take my seat. "They're going to do a closed casket since his body isn't presentable..."

"Christian tells me he deserved it," Vic says cooly. "That he was holding some girl down there, so I don't think any of us should be going quite frankly."

"But he was so lovely," Lucy says, refusing to believe it.

"Oh please, Luce, none of us really knew him anyway," Zara chimes in.

The unsettling sensation hits me again, tightening around my chest.

A chorus of "awws" resounds through the room, bringing me back. The tightness dissipates as Harry walks in with Alfie, both looking as handsome as ever in matching grey trousers and white shirts. Harry holds a bouquet of pink garden roses, wrapped in a pink bow. All the women's eyes lock on him but his beautiful brown eyes are fixated on me.

I meet his gaze and push my chair back, laughing as "Pink Pony Club" plays over the speakers, the perfect song for the day.

Alfie gets to me before I can rise from my chair, and I give him a big hug and kiss before passing him to Lorraine. Harry helps me up and plants a huge kiss on my lips. His large hand caresses my belly, and I feel safe and at ease.

I smile as we pull apart, wondering why the room has gone silent after the initial cheers and applause.

My smile drops as I see the women looking from their phones to each other, whispering. Lucy covers her mouth with her hand, and Zara turns pale, despite the fresh layer of fake tan. I want to cut the chatter, demand that everyone put their phones away until the event is officially over. But I don't dare, feeling the mood take a serious shift. It jars against the upbeat music playing in the background.

Harry looks at me, his brow raised in concern and confusion.

I waddle over to Lucy and Vic, trying to get a better view of their phones.

"What is it?" I ask, annoyed. But they don't answer. Vic looks wide-eyed from me to Abby to Zara, who bursts into tears.

A pit forms in my stomach as my heart throbs, pulsating through the butterfly tattoo on my wrist.

I turn my gaze toward Abby, whose face is painted with a mixture of shock and sympathy. My heart sinks. I let out an impatient sigh and throw my hand out. "Just tell me."

But before any of them speak, I see the headline.

My heart skips before slowing to a stop. For a moment, everything is quiet. Everything is still. Then, Alice kicks inside me, harder. My heart beats faster and my temperature rises hotter and hotter, as if my body is preparing itself for the impact. For the news I prayed for, but also dreaded.

Emma is alive.

THE HOURLY

MISSING GIRLFRIEND OF FAMOUS FOOTBALLER FOUND ALIVE

According to an inside source, Harry Turner's presumed-dead girlfriend – "Nightmare in Notts" victim, Emma Macy – shocked pub-goers on Friday night when she made a heroic escape from her prison of the last five years

By Hollee S Luther   *2 March 2025*

Nottingham, UK – Friday evening, at the Oak & Arrow pub near Nottingham Castle, a woman burst into the bar area covered in blood. Witnesses claim this woman came from a door that leads to the pub's cellar, where pub landlord Gary "Gaz" Barker was found deceased from multiple stab wounds.

Police would not confirm the identity of the woman, but did confirm that she appeared to have been held captive in a hidden room behind the pub cellar, which is attached to the city's underground cave network.

An inside source tells us that this woman is in fact footballer Harry Turner's ex-girlfriend Emma Macy, who was presumed dead five years ago.

In January of 2020, right before COVID locked down the world, Emma Macy, Leila Adler and Kaleigh Creedy were celebrating Macy's twenty-fourth birthday at a cottage in Sherwood Forest. But what should've been a fun-filled girls' weekend turned into a nightmare.

Dubbed "The Nightmare in Notts", Kaleigh Creedy – who is now coincidentally married to Harry Turner – was the only one to survive the ordeal. She alleged that intruders set upon them at the cabin, after they returned from Nottingham city centre, and murdered Leila and Emma.

After a week-long investigation, Adler's body was eventually found in the River Trent, an hour away. Based on the location and injuries of Adler's body, plus other evidence such as Emma Macy's blood found at the property, police presumed Macy dead, stating they believed the England WAG suffered a similar fate to her friend, and that her body most likely had been washed out to sea.

Sheffield resident and avid football supporter David Allen, 30, was arrested on suspicion of murder after his DNA was found below Leila Adler's fingernails. However, Allen was never tried for the crimes, having committed suicide before his trial.

Our source claims that police are now wondering if Allen and Barker were working together, or if Allen was involved at all.

Nottingham local Gary "Gaz" Barker, 58, has been the landlord of the Oak & Arrow pub for the past ten years. He was formerly in the army and also worked as a mechanic. He leaves behind a brother and a sister. The connection between Barker and Macy is unclear, aside from the fact that it's a popular watering hole for AFC Nottingham fans, the same team Turner plays for.

"I just can't believe it," said Nottingham resident and Oak & Arrow patron Ross Ducker. "He was a real part of the community, a real nice bloke. Or so we all thought. Hard to believe he's capable of what they're saying, but if he did do it, then not being funny, but maybe he got what he deserved."

Nottingham City Police are said to be closely investigating the situation.

Comments

AFCNottsFan: Didn't Kaleigh say Emma was dead?

MarkyP: So poor Emma escaped hell to only face another sort of hell where her boyfriend is married to her best friend? Shit luck that is.

SianGilbert: Kaleigh Turner reading the news like 👁 👁 👁

ChrisViv: Gaz Barker aside, there are two very obvious suspects here, no?

> **TruthSeeker:** They were both cleared

Naomi Barnes: Can someone recap this for me? Idk how I missed this! Not a lot on TikTok...

> **RavenRumours:** This was pre-true crime TikTok era, you need to check the Nightmare in Notts Reddit thread. @JusticeForDaveyAllen has the most comprehensive info (obviously a little biased, but still solid)

> **BorrillsWeerdWorld:** I was just coming here to say this. Do we think that's their source? Looks like Reddit broke the news first.

OliviaBecks: How devastating for everyone involved. RIP Leila Adler and David Allen. Hope his family can get justice too if it turns out he is also innocent.

VickyVaz: I always thought more than two people were involved, especially the way K Creedy described it...

7

Harry

Harry watches on in confusion as the women at the party start to freak out. He wonders what tabloid headline they're reading on their phones, clearly something unexpected. But the way their eyes drift between him and Kaleigh begins to unnerve him.

When he looks at his wife, now pale as a ghost, he can tell it's not the usual gossip. Something is seriously wrong. He immediately puts a steadying arm around her before guiding her to a seat.

"You alright, Kay? What—"

"She's alive!" Zara shrieks, her eyes full of tears.

"*She?* Who is *she*?" Harry's mum asks as Alfie wriggles in her arms.

"Emma," Kaleigh says softly, barely loud enough to hear.

Harry reaches out for Zara's phone, one hand still wrapped around his wife.

That's impossible, he thinks. Emma died five years ago.

The room swirls around him as the memory fades in. Trudging through the forest slowly as he analysed every twig, leaf and branch for a sign of her. For a strand of white-blonde hair. For a drop of blood. He'd told himself that she must've managed to escape like Kaleigh. That he'd save her. He prayed that he'd find her around the next tree, curled up, still breathing.

He hardly slept or ate. It was the first time football wasn't the most important thing in his life. The first time football fans from all over came to help and support. But they looked everywhere, and there was no trace.

"Leila and Emma were the victims of a violent crime at the cabin, and were most likely killed on site, and then their bodies were transported and dumped in the river."

He still remembers the conversation with police. How he so vividly pictured the fragile, beautiful body of the first girl he ever loved being mutilated and then dumped in the murky waters of the Trent. The way his stomach churned. The way the nausea shot up through his stomach into his throat. The taste of vanilla protein powder as he vomited.

"It was fucking Gaz!" Zara says as she slaps her phone into Harry's hand.

Harry's shock turns to rage. "Gaz?"

He pictures Gaz's red-faced smile as he handed out pints. His boisterous laugh. Harry thought he was a friendly bloke. But what? He had Emma... all this time?

He clenches his fists as he reads the news, learning how Emma was allegedly held captive in the tunnels below Oak & Arrow.

Emma is alive, Emma is alive, Emma is alive.

The words reverberate in his mind like an alarm, forcing him to face the fact. His rage turns into an overwhelming sense of guilt. He was there, so many times. He could have saved her. He could have – should have – been the hero. But in the end, she had to save herself.

He's sick at the thought. Of her being chained up, crying out for help, while he moved on. While he did everything he could to push her out of his memory, focusing on football, getting married, falling in love. While she was *right* there.

"But they said she was dead. They told us to stop looking." He doesn't know who he's saying it to. He clears his throat, trying to ignore the burning sensation rising from his chest.

He can feel Kaleigh shaking beneath his arm now, crying.

"Oh my god, Kaleigh, I can't believe that you could've… that could've been you, too," Zara says unhelpfully as she wraps an arm around her.

"C'mon, darling." Harry's mum places a hand on his back. "Let's get you home, okay?"

Harry's dad is at the house by the time they pull in. Usually it's annoying when Robbie shows up like this, impatiently waiting to talk to Harry about something he noticed in training, but today, Harry is relieved to see him.

"Rob, did you hear the news," Lorraine says, rushing over to him.

"Fucking madness," he says. "Poor girl." Robbie shakes his head in disgust. But there's a flicker of something else there. Sadness. His eyes are red, like he's been crying.

Robbie takes a final drag of his cigarette before stomping it out on the gravel drive. Harry would usually tell him off for this, but today he doesn't care.

"You alright, love?" He kisses Kaleigh on the cheek. "Sorry, hope you don't mind me smoking."

"It's fine," Kaleigh says in a daze, walking towards the house with Alfie in hand. Lorraine follows her, declaring to no one in particular that she'll put the kettle on.

"C'mon, son, let's go round the back." Robbie wraps a tight arm around Harry and guides him to the garden gate.

Once they're alone, Harry falls to his knees, hands clasped behind his head as he finally lets himself feel the full weight of his guilt.

"It's all my fault." He holds his face in his hands, hearing nothing but blood whooshing in his ears. He thinks back to the last time he and Emma were together. *That* morning. He was worried he was going to lose her after his childish behaviour in Vegas was made public, and had been working hard to convince her it didn't mean anything. That he was going to make it up to her. They were going to look at a house, were going to go to Thailand. He was even going to propose when they were there. But he never got the chance.

His mind drifts to a dark place as he pictures Emma tied up in a dirty tunnel, praying for him to save her. *What a useless piece of shit I am*, he thinks.

Harry stands and kicks the grass as if it's a football, dirt flying on him and his dad.

"Oi," Robbie says, motioning for Harry to stop. But he doesn't. He can't. Angry at himself for kicking a ball around a field, thinking that was the most important thing while Emma was being held prisoner under his fucking feet.

Don't cry, don't bloody cry. But it's too late. He's gone.

He crouches on the ground, hands covering his face.

His dad kneels down next to him and puts a hand on his head.

"It's alright, son, it's alright." It's a surprisingly gentle gesture from a man who'd been so hard on Harry his whole life.

"This is on me…" Harry says, voice cracking. "All my fucking fault. If I tried harder to find her. If…"

"Nah, son, we did everything we could. It's not on you but those arseholes in the police for not figuring this out sooner."

Harry wipes his face with his hands before shaking his head. "No. I mean…" He lets out an exasperated groan before lowering his voice to a whisper. "That night. If I hadn't…"

"Oh no," Robbie says. "We'll be havin' none of that."

He looks around, seemingly nervous that someone is listening. But all Harry sees is Kaleigh and Lorraine talking to each other through the kitchen window. Robbie puts his arm around Harry and walks him over to the patio furniture.

"This shit with Gaz… is just more proof it was just a bloody tragic event, nothing you or anyone coulda done…" He sits Harry down next to him and trails off, frustrated. "You can't let this get in your head again."

This. As if "this" was a simple falling out with a teammate. A loss in a friendly match.

"Cause qualifiers are comin' up soon and you know how Paulo gets, he won't tolerate any kind of distraction."

The mention of England manager Paulo Santino makes Harry sweat. The same manager who cut Harry three years ago is known for his strict expectations of his players and his no drama rule. Last year, he benched a key defender from the squad after his wife and his mistress started a tabloid war.

Harry's heart sinks at the words: wife, mistress, girlfriend, ex-girlfriend. It makes him wonder how to describe what Emma is to him now. Is she still his girlfriend? Technically, they never broke up. But he's married now. To her best friend.

He hangs his head in his hands, pressing his thumbs into his eyes until it hurts. He thinks of Kaleigh, wondering what she must be feeling, and glances inside the house to see her. But she isn't in sight anymore.

"Dad, what do I do?" he asks, eyes wide like a child. "Kaleigh... Emma..."

Robbie stands and lights another cigarette. "This doesn't change anything, mate. You see Emma, let her know you're there for her as a friend, but that's it. You focus on football and your family."

Harry nods.

Robbie rubs an unusually shaky hand over his balding head as he takes a drag. "I spoke to Simon."

"Oh yeah," Harry says, thinking of his older brother.

His dad blows out a puff of smoke. "He doesn't seem as shocked as the rest of us. About Gaz. That motherfucker, if he wasn't already dead, I'd murder the bastard myself," he snarls. "But you know Simon couldn't stand the guy, ever since they got in that tussle after Gaz cut him off after the match last year."

"Not being funny, but Simon's always picking fights with someone, so that doesn't mean much." Harry thinks of the time his brother even stopped talking to him over something daft, giving him the silent treatment while continuing to use Harry's name to get into exclusive events. If it weren't for Kaleigh, Harry and Simon probably wouldn't have ever made amends.

Robbie takes another drag before putting the cigarette butt out on the metal table, away from the ash tray. Harry quickly retrieves it and brushes the burnt dust away.

He looks around the garden, wishing he could go back to yesterday. When he was outside playing with his little boy, his beautiful wife watching from the kitchen, cradling their little girl, growing strong in her stomach. When everything was perfect.

He chides himself for feeling this way. Like Emma being back is bad. He swears he's gone through every emotion possible since the news came out. Joy and relief at her being alive. Guilt and shame for not saving her. Anger and rage at Gaz. Sadness and horror at what she must've gone through. And finally: fear. Scared of what this means, how it will all play out. How Emma will feel. How it'll look.

"I think I'm gonna go for a run," Harry says, feeling like he's about to snap if he doesn't.

"Alright, mate." Robbie nods, then gestures to Harry's arm. "Just make sure you keep that watch on. With all this stress, I need to make sure you're keeping your vitals in check, yeah?"

Harry rolls his eyes, annoyed at the constant reminder. He knows. He's been wearing the smart watch ever since his dad got it for him when he was a teenager, when he became really serious about football.

"And you let me know if you get any more of those phone calls, okay?"

Harry bites the inside of his cheek as one comes through. He ignores it and looks back at his dad. "It's nothin'…"

"I don't care. You let me know, okay?"

Harry wants to be honest with his dad but he also doesn't want to deal with him being more up his arse than he already is.

"Will do," he lies, before turning to run away.

8

Kaleigh

She's alive. Emma is alive.

I repeat the news in my mind for the hundredth time, still in disbelief. Still in utter shock. For so long, I thought I wanted to hear those words. But now that it's happened, it feels like the start of a brand-new nightmare. A spinoff from the past, challenging my picture-perfect future.

Question after question explodes in my mind, the first being the scariest. Would Harry leave me for her? I immediately think no. He would never. That he loves me and Alfie, and our soon-to-be-born baby girl so, so much. That he's a different man now than when he was with Emma. That he loves *me* now. But then I mistakenly look outside and catch a glimpse of him, crouching down, head in his hands. He begins to shake and I realise he's crying.

"He'll be okay, love," Lorraine says, clutching her mug of tea.

"Should I—"

"Let Robbie settle him," she says. "I know he can be hard on the boys, but he's also good with keeping them level-headed."

I bite my lip, imagining Robbie telling Harry to get over it. But when I see him crouch down next to Harry and console him, I soften.

She lifts her arms as if she's going to pull out a barstool but to my surprise, her arms wrap around me instead.

I relax into her for a moment before I tense at a new thought. Would Emma coming back change my relationship with Lorraine? Would she prefer Emma as a daughter-in-law to me?

No, I tell myself. She already told me that she was happy Harry was with me, after I'd finally convinced him to make amends with his brother. When we'd gotten together, they weren't speaking. Something to do with money it seemed like, although he never went into detail and I didn't press. I explained that it wasn't worth it, that his relationship with his only brother was worth more, and Lorraine was so grateful I pushed them back together. One day when I opened up to her about the guilt I felt about Emma, she told me that while she loved Emma, she never thought she was quite right for Harry. That she felt they both brought out the worst in each other sometimes. "But with you, he's a different person," she said. "His best self."

See, Emma coming back doesn't change anything, I tell myself again.

As if sensing my unease, Lorraine pulls away and reaches for my hands. "Talk to me, how are you feeling?"

I glance over at Alfie to make sure he's still distracted by the TV before speaking. "I'm not sure to be honest." I shrug. "Emma... I don't know what to do. It's just... with Harry..."

I struggle to form the sentence, worried I'll sound insensitive. Like I'm more worried about my marriage than what happened to her.

But Lorraine doesn't judge. She knows how much I cared for Emma. She also knows how tough it was when Harry and I first got together. How once the press picked up on our relationship, we were tabloid fodder for weeks. But she also knows the truth of it. How I fought against the feelings I had for him, even though it'd been over a year since Emma was killed – or so we thought.

"You can't punish yourself, sweetheart. It's been five years. It's going to be difficult for her I'm sure, but the important thing is that she is alive. She's safe. And she loved the both of you."

I dab my lashes with a napkin.

"What do we do? Do we visit her? Won't it upset her?"

"I think you need to visit her," Lorraine says softly. "Both of you."

I swallow hard, imagining the awkward reunion. *She'll never forgive me.*

"Do we just... show up?" I hold my hands out, on the verge of tears. "I don't know what the protocol is for something like this."

"None of us do, darling." Lorraine places a hand on my back. "But actually, that reminds me. I really need to text Jo."

A knot forms in my stomach at the mention of Emma's mother. She hasn't talked to Harry or me since she'd found out about our relationship in the news in 2021, after which she stated her disapproval in her own interview. What little relationship we had was broken after that. I knew it was my fault. I regretted not telling her sooner. It was just such a difficult situation to navigate, one I kept putting off until it was too late.

So many things I would've done differently if I could go back in time.

"I texted her," Lorraine says. "I mentioned that you and Harry would love to see Emma when she's feeling up for it, so let's see what she thinks."

I nod, cheeks flushing like an embarrassed child. But I'm happy she's ripped the Band-Aid off.

Lorraine sighs. "I wonder if I should reach out to Mary, as well."

My heart drops as I think of Leila's mom, Mary Adler, how there's no chance her daughter will ever shock us by coming back. I heave, picturing Leila's slit throat, as if I'm back there with her at the cabin.

I close my eyes, forcing myself to swallow down the vomit. I refuse to puke in my kitchen sink in front of Lorraine.

"At least Mary has three other children and a new husband to help her through," Lorraine adds before downing the rest of her tea.

Mary is on husband number five, if my count is correct. I remember what Emma told me about Leila's mom, how she was Leila's dad's mistress before convincing him to marry her, only to divorce him, take half his money, then marry even richer. I think of Leila and how she got with Theo Abara, and wonder if the apple didn't fall too far from the tree in her case.

Lorraine's phone pings. "Ah, see." She reads out the text from Jo. "I think it'll be good if they visit her, might help."

I agree to see her tomorrow before a wave of nausea forces me to excuse myself.

I apply pressure to the P6 point on my wrist in an attempt to quell the nausea. But the sight of my tattoo makes me feel worse. I run to the toilet and let it all out, until the queasiness finally subsides.

After, I go to my side of the vanity to brush my teeth but I still don't feel better. Anxiety continues to creep up on me like the winding ivy on our home. I forcefully rub a make-up remover wipe across my skin, annoyed at the turn my perfectly planned day has taken, before splashing my face with eucalyptus-infused rose water. I step back and look at my reflection in the mirror, at my dusty pink dress now splattered with dark water stains. It reminds me of that night, when I was covered in blood.

I turn off the faucet and unzip the garment, suddenly wanting it off me, needing my whole body to be clean. I hop out of the dress, not bothering to pick it up as I step into the shower and turn the faucet as hot as it can go. I scrub vigorously as if the motion will wash away the guilt of not being completely happy that Emma is back.

I chide myself for being so selfish, thinking what she must've endured. I scrub harder as I think of Gaz Barker, imagining what must've gone through his mind every time he saw me. I picture what I once took for a warm smile transforming into a sadistic smirk. *I have your friend downstairs.* The thought makes my skin crawl, and I wince as I rub myself raw.

"Stop," I say out loud, dropping the body brush.

I inhale as I caress my belly, trying to remember that stress isn't good for the baby. I start to list all the things I need to do in an attempt to calm down. "Get changed. Eat something. Talk to Alison and Sarah about a social media pause and statement. Talk to Harry about our game plan before we see Emma. What will we say? How will we act?"

The questions cause a different type of anxiety though.

Later, I sit down on the edge of our bed. As I brush my hair, my eyes land on a photo of Harry, Alfie and me hanging on the wall. It's from our first Christmas together in Lapland. We're all wearing matching red plaid sweaters, or "tartan jumpers" as Harry calls them, smiling brightly in front of the chalet.

My eyes then move to a photo of Harry and me together in Thailand. My stomach drops.

Everything will be fine, I try to convince myself. Emma being back doesn't change anything.

But the moment of solace doesn't last long as my phone starts to buzz incessantly on my nightstand. I sigh and reach for it, intending to silence it, but find myself scrolling through all the notifications instead – multiple calls from unknown numbers, two from my mother, emails from outlets asking for comment, my publicist asking for a statement, and hundreds of social media notifications and mentions.

I feel woozy with déjà vu, like I'm reliving the moment when Leila's body was found. A vision of her appears before me as if the thought summoned her ghost. Her image quickly morphs into a long-buried memory, the last one I have of her alive. She's angry and bitter, hurling insult after insult, oblivious those would be the last words she'd ever say.

My mind starts to swirl with horrific visions as I force myself up. Leila's bloated face and body, throat slit. Emma's hair, sticky with blood.

Two bodies.

Shouts from outside cut through my spiralling thoughts. I go to the window and peek between the blinds. Three men with cameras of varying sizes argue with Robbie from behind the gate. Another wave of déjà vu crashes over me. But this time, I'm brought back to when the media first learned I was pregnant with Harry's child.

It's happening again. The wolves are at the door.

9

Charlie

By the time I arrive at the QMC, the afternoon sunshine has disappeared, the sky now fully grey. I can barely remember the drive here, absorbed in my thoughts, wondering if taking this on was the right decision. But if I'm able to help, I have to at least try.

I badge into a set of side doors, still stunned at everything that's transpired. How just forty-eight hours ago, I thought the Nightmare in Notts case was ice cold, when really, it was burning below the city all this time.

As I walk through the familiar white halls of the hospital, I think back to when the news first broke about the attack. I'd been a student at the time, studying for my Doctorate in Forensic Psychology at the University of Nottingham. Naturally, the event sent waves of terror through campus, with students advised to be extra vigilant and to travel in groups, especially at night. It also became one of the main talking points in my lessons, prompting discussions about the tribalism of sport and psychology of fans, from the positives: a sense of community, belonging and enjoyment; to the negatives: obsession, aggression, violence.

I pause outside the psychiatric unit, taking a moment to collect myself, before heading through.

"Hey, Tracy," I greet the familiar receptionist.

"Dr Singh," she says, surprised. "Here on a Sunday?"

I give her a wry smile. "Unfortunately, human suffering doesn't break for weekends, nor can I."

Tracy gives a knowing nod.

"I'm looking for—" But before I can finish my sentence, a man comes rushing towards me. He's smaller than I expected, only a few inches taller than me.

"DCI Maynard," he introduces himself. "Thank you for coming."

"Of course," I reply, smiling as I shake his hand.

"Have there been any developments I should know about?" I ask, readjusting my handbag, heavy on my shoulder with my laptop and notebooks.

"Not really." He guides me down the corridor. "The latest report suggests she's suffering from severe PTSD. Which is understandable given she was held captive by that monster for five years."

Not a monster, I think. *A man.*

Before I decided to specialise in trauma victims, I spent countless hours evaluating violent offenders. Murderers, rapists, abusers, I've seen them all. And the scariest thing about them? They're human, just like the rest of us.

"But I suppose you wouldn't say monster," Maynard says, as if he could hear my thoughts. "Psychopath maybe?"

I tilt my head to the side and shrug. "Quite possibly. Anyone who can keep a young woman as a prisoner under his pub for five years while he jokes with patrons and pours pints undoubtedly shows signs of psychopathic behaviour."

I shiver as I recall a patient from my past, a psychopath I evaluated as a trainee psychologist at one of the UK's three high-security psychiatric facilities. A CEO by day, serial killer by night. He had a popular podcast, was well respected in the business world. But in his spare time, he was raping and murdering women. I was so naïve at the time, a young doctor on a mission to change the world. But if anything, the experience changed *my* world, shifted my perception of what a psychopath is. How charming they can be. How they blend right into society, hiding in plain sight. Just like Gaz.

Most people will be relieved to know Gaz Barker is dead, but in a way it's a shame because now we won't be able to study him. We also won't be able to ask him why or if anyone else was involved.

"Any progress on a motive?" I ask. "Sexually charged, I presume...?"

Maynard raises a knowing eyebrow as a fluorescent light buzzes above us. "So we swept Barker's pub and his flat. Laptop was full of pornography, but not the kind you'd expect, not the usual graphic, violent videos I thought there'd be. They were weird... Almost tender?"

He holds his hands up as I wince. "I know, I know, but it kind of tracks with what else we found... photos and videos of Emma."

My mind puts together what he's saying and I feel more unnerved. I clench my jaw, waiting for him to continue.

"The photos date back to 2018. Barker was clearly fixated on her. He had these videos of them, forcing her to role play being a housewife..."

My face flushes as heat rises to my face. "Housewife?"

"Yeah, I guess that's why he kept her alive for so long. Usually these guys get tired of their victims after a few weeks, months, years. But it was like he made her role play WAG and footballer."

I force down the bile in my throat, imagining how Emma managed to endure this for five years. *Stockholm syndrome?* I wonder. But then I remember how unkempt she was when we found her. Not at all matching Maynard's "happy family" role play theory.

"But she was so... filthy and emaciated when we found her..."

Maynard stops outside a door, lowering his voice. "We think he eventually tired of her, moved her to the pub cellar. She'd been living off scraps for weeks."

I exhale, preparing myself for a difficult session. *Five years.* I shake my head, knowing that is a lot of trauma to process. How it's not just latent signs of PTSD we'll be working with but other possible disorders as well.

"I still can't believe the case was closed so prematurely," I say, thinking of how many years Emma was out there without anyone knowing. "I know COVID didn't help, but..."

Maynard sighs. "Regardless of COVID, the investigation would've run its course. The crime happened at the end of Jan, the first lockdown wasn't until March. I've been looking over the files and Allen was still the only lead after seven weeks. Even the Macys had given up by that point, accepted the most likely option that Emma was murdered by him, like Leila, and her body had washed out to sea."

I swallow hard as I think of Davey Allen who was blamed for the crime after his DNA was found under Leila Adler's fingernails. Before he took his own life, he claimed it was from an altercation he'd had with her earlier in the evening, but no one would listen.

"An angry football hooligan, who wanted 'Harry Turner to pay.'" That was how the papers framed it. Claiming that, after Davey recognised Emma Macy in town, he hunted her and her friends down, following them to their cabin, where he killed Leila Adler and did God knows what to Emma in retribution for Harry Turner's uncalled handball and his subsequent goal.

I remember watching the game that night. AFC Nottingham was playing in a knockout round of a major tournament. The ball hit Harry's hand in the box, but then the defender tackled him. The ref blew the whistle for a penalty, but many believed it shouldn't have been a pen – but a handball. The goal scored by Turner essentially won them the game, sending them to the next round. A fight nearly broke out on the pitch after Turner's celebration, and everyone was at each other's throats for the rest of the match, including the refs.

Turner received countless online threats, including one posted by Davey Allen.

Fucking disgrace. Turner needs to pay for that, I don't care how.

A comment the police cited as clear intent. A motive that I never bought into. Because how could, "a drunk, low IQ hooligan", as the papers claimed, also be the mastermind of a carefully covered-up crime?

Despite his less-than-noble behaviour, my heart breaks for Davey. I feel sick as I picture him swinging from his jail cell, unable to cope with the allegations.

I'm about to make a smug comment about the police's incompetence, but hold back when Maynard stops short.

"She's in here," he says.

I look through the windowpane, stomach clenching when I see Emma there, helpless and lost. *So many lives ruined that night. For what?*

Things still didn't add up.

The gravity of the situation hits me then: that in order to find out what really happened, we need Emma to tell her story.

First, help her recover, I remind myself. *Then, uncover the truth.*

JusticeForDaveyAllen

On 6 February 2020, Davey Allen was wrongfully arrested for the murder of Leila Adler. He was also accused of murdering Emma Macy (even though no body was found) and attempting to murder Kaleigh Creedy, although, once again, no real evidence of this was found, only circumstantial.

This subreddit is a community dedicated to supporting Davey, and to finish the job law enforcement is refusing to do and find out who actually is responsible for the crimes and for potentially framing and killing Davey.

Created 5 Mar 2020
Public
3.9k members   157 online   Top 17%

ADMIN POSTS

u/JusticeForDaveyAllen 1 March 2025
NIGHTMARE IN NOTTS CASE BLOWN OPEN: EMMA MACY IS ALIVE, NOTTS PUB LANDLORD RESPONSIBLE. JUSTICE FOR DAVEY ALLEN FINALLY ON HORIZON? https://clebnews. com/emma-macy-found-alive-nightmare-in-notts

u/JusticeForDaveyAllen 5 yr ago
THREAD: DNA under Leila's nails doesn't prove anything, obviously from their altercation earlier

in the night – no evidence he followed or attacked them. HE IS BEING FRAMED!

u/JusticeForDaveyAllen 5 yr ago

THREAD: The smoking gun = Not the DNA but the car leaving the cabin soon after. Who was it? Why don't the police know?

10

Kaleigh

I toss and turn, half asleep, in and out of dreams. I see myself as if I'm outside of my own body, like an observer. Or a fan.

I'm standing in a stadium, looking down at my younger self, a cropped jersey showing off my slim waist, my long blonde hair flowing beneath Harry's arm wrapped around my shoulders. I'm stung with a pang of jealousy, of longing to be that version of me with Harry on that field.

I want to laugh at myself for being jealous of a younger version of me. But when I look back, the hair is platinum-blonde, not golden-blonde. It's not me at all. It's Emma.

I shake my head, willing myself to wake up but I don't. Instead, memories seep into my dream.

It's May 2015, London. I'd moved from Alabama the semester before in 2014, spending every single bit of the scholarship money I'd won from Miss Teen USA to attend university abroad and travel around Europe.

I'm with my roommates Emma and Leila, watching Emma's boyfriend play in the championship final. He's a young, rising star, who scored a last-minute goal after being subbed on. We all squeal with joy and storm the field behind Emma, who jumps into Harry's arms.

The crowd around me chants as the players continue to take turns posing with the giant cup, adorned with green ribbons. But instead of the players, I fixate on the wives and girlfriends. I didn't know their names at the time, but I recognize them now. Zara Becker is pregnant, rubbing her husband's arm as he talks to a camera. Natasha Donahue is clapping for her fiancé as he takes a lap around the stadium. Alara Perez is posing for some photos with her now ex-husband and their newborn. And Emma Macy is standing on the tips of her white sneakers, kissing Harry.

I know I shouldn't stare but I can't avert my gaze. His large biceps glisten with sweat as he lifts her up in the air and hugs her before placing her back down. When she turns to look at me though, her face is covered in blood.

Suddenly, I'm running. Mud squelching beneath my bare feet as rocks, twigs and thorns dig into my flesh.

I stop briefly, clutching at my side in pain as I gasp for air. I look behind me, back toward the cabin. A light scans the woods. I duck, even though it's too far away to catch me. I think of everything that's happened and a sob escapes my mouth. I muffle my cries with my hand, tasting blood.

Crack. I spin around toward the noise, but it's too dark to see anything. Or anyone. *Boom, boom, boom.*

I know I should go back. Try and save them. But I know that's no longer an option. All I can hear is my heart pounding in my chest and two words.

Two bodies.

I jolt awake, startled until I register the soft feather duvet below my arms and hear Harry snoring next to me.

I wrap my arm around him, desperate to hold him, desperate not to lose him as his emotional reaction from earlier replays in my mind. Crying, crouching, even yelling at Robbie at one point about something I couldn't hear. When I eventually went outside to talk to him, he wasn't there. Robbie said he'd gone for a run, to blow off some steam. But it didn't seem to work because when Harry returned, he seemed more distant than before.

I hold Harry tighter, trying to quell my rising panic, wondering what had been going through his mind, wishing I had the guts to ask him earlier.

I hadn't had much of a chance though, since Robbie and Lorraine didn't leave until after midnight, talking in circles about the news and what to do next. I suggested that Harry and I visit separately, but Lorraine thought that wasn't necessary. She encouraged us to go together, but no touching, no holding hands. Just two people who loved Emma, letting her know we're there for her. And we agreed.

I pull his arm tighter around me, trying to fall back to sleep. But as I shut my eyes, I hear his voice.

"No. Stop." He mumbles, arm twitching. "She doesn't... know."

My eyes snap open. *What don't I know?*

"Harry." I roll his arm off me and pinch his nose, something I often do when he's snoring too loud.

I gloss my fingers over his cheek as he stirs. "Wake up. You're having a nightmare."

Harry shakes his head and groans, his eyelashes fluttering before he wakes.

"What's wrong?" he asks, trying to get his bearings.

"You were having a nightmare," I whisper. "I did too."

Harry wraps me in his arms then and I press my head against his chest, listening to the steady rhythm of his heart. He runs his fingers through my hair as I breathe in his scent. It's warm and comforting, signalling I'm safe. Home.

But there's no getting away from the awkward situation we're in. I think about Emma who was once my best friend. And the man she loved, who I now love.

I feel like for Emma's sake, I should tell Harry that it would be okay if he needed to be with her. That I would understand. But the truth is that I wouldn't understand. That it wouldn't be okay. Tears sting my eyes as I worry that the idea is going through his mind and I can't bear it if it is. So I ask the question that's been haunting me.

"Are you gonna... Would you..." I force the words out. "Will you leave me for her?"

His body tenses before he rolls over, so he's looking down on me.

"What?" he says, caressing my face. "My darling, I would never, could never."

I bite the inside of my lip, trying not to cry, feeling overwhelmed.

"When I was with Emma," Harry says, understanding that I need more reassurance, "I thought that was just how it was. You know how much we argued. We were never right for each other, but it was all we'd ever known. And I loved her, cared about her, obviously, was devastated when... I mean you know." He quickly moves on. "But when you and I met up the next year, started seeing each other, it was different. I never felt anything like that in my life. It's me and you, okay? I'm not going anywhere."

I breathe a teary sigh of relief, even though I'm still left wondering why he reacted so strongly earlier if he's so sure. But at this moment, I push the worry away and turn to kiss him. He presses his lips hard against mine, moaning as I move my hand to his thigh. I slip my tongue into his mouth, desperate to prove my love to him. Desperate for him to choose *me*.

11

Harry

Monday 3 March 2025

Harry had made his fair share of A&E visits growing up, for broken noses and fractured ankles, even a concussion from bashing his head against a rival going up for a header. And even though he knew hospitals were places where they "healed" people, there was always something about them he didn't like. He wishes he could remember the moment when he first felt this way, but there's nothing he can pinpoint exactly, just knows that he hates the fluorescent lighting and bright white floors and walls. Hates the beeping of machines and groaning of patients. The crying. The sniffling. The coughing. And most of all, he hates the smell.

He digs his face into the huge bouquet of pink flowers Kaleigh picked up from the florist that morning, needing to inhale something other than antiseptic and lingering cafeteria food.

"They smell good?" Kaleigh asks nervously as they walk down the hospital corridor.

She'd spent hours agonizing over which ones to get, researching their meanings and what each colour symbolises so she could subliminally send the right message: *I'm sorry for what happened to you but also, please don't hate me.*

Harry leans into his wife's neck, to smell her instead. The rush is instant, like a hit of cocaine.

She gently pushes him off. Her honey brown eyes meet his and it's like they have an entire conversation with one look. *Not here, not now.*

He nods, knowing she's right. He reaches his arm out instinctively to hold her, but then pulls back, remembering what they discussed. No PDA at the hospital.

A ping sounds from his smart watch then. A text from his manager wishing him the best and telling him to take the day and pick up training as usual tomorrow.

He should be grateful that the Notts manager is empathetic, but he'd much rather be able to lose himself in sport. He doesn't want to be here. Doesn't want to feel all the feelings he felt yesterday. And most of all, he doesn't want Kaleigh to see him lose his composure again, give her any more reason to think he'd ever consider leaving her.

He shakes his head, still wondering how in the world she could think that.

"That's Harry Turner!" a boy whispers to his dad as Harry and Kaleigh pass.

Harry silently curses as he catches the man following them out of the corner of his eye. He psyches himself up for the inevitable autograph and photo request.

"'Scuse me, mate," the man says.

Harry is tempted to ignore him or tell him he's in a hurry and can't stop and chat, but doesn't feel like getting hammered on social media later for being rude or "ruining" his kid's day. So he stops and faces them.

"Great game the other night, mate." The man's face is nearly as red as his hair.

"Appreciate it." Harry turns to the kid, who is holding a football. "What's your name, buddy, I'm Harry."

"I know," the kid says, giggling.

"This is Declan," the man says. "He may be your biggest supporter in the entire world." The man then stares at Harry, waiting.

Harry crouches down. "It's very nice to meet you, Declan." He holds his clasped hand out for a fist bump. Declan looks up at his dad excitedly before bopping Harry's fist with his own.

"Could we get a photo?" the man asks as Harry and Kaleigh start walking again.

"Sorry mate but it's not the best time." Harry gestures to Kaleigh, hoping the man soon remembers they are all, in fact, in a hospital, and not out for a jolly.

The man's smile drops in an instant. He lowers his voice. "Really, pal, you just gonna ruin my lad's day like that?"

Harry laughs in disbelief, but forces himself to stay calm. He should've kept walking, it was going to happen either way. He'd been famous long enough to know how these things go, ever since he played his first Premier League game when he was only eighteen, nearly eleven years ago. He learned pretty quickly when fan interactions were going to go awry, that he could never really win. He tried to take it in his stride, but it was hard to be patronised by people, swallow shit and smile.

"Declan, is it?" Kaleigh jumps in, pen in hand. Harry is grateful for her intervention. He doesn't know how she does it: reads every situation perfectly, knows how to fix it.

"How would you like it if Harry signed your ball?" She smiles up at the man and he softens. She often has that effect on people.

"That would be pretty awesome, wouldn't it," Declan's dad says.

The kid looks up at Kaleigh, giddy. He didn't want a photo, his dad did. Harry crouches down. "So you like football?" he asks as he signs the ball.

"Yes," Declan replies, fidgeting with his hands.

"You know I have a son a little younger than you. Maybe you two will play together one day."

Declan lets out a big grin as Harry hands the ball back to him.

"Cheers, mate," his dad says, not nearly as enthusiastically as earlier.

Harry turns back to Kaleigh and rolls his eyes. "Bloody—"

"Shh," she says, smirking. She glances behind them to make sure the man didn't hear.

"You just made that little boy's day, think of it like that. Isn't that how you'd want someone to treat Alfie?"

He rolls his eyes again, still annoyed at the dad – he would never be so pushy. But the thought of making the boy happy made him smile, he had to admit. He pulls Kaleigh close and gives her a long kiss on her head, inhaling her sweet cotton candy-like scent as they pass the sign for the psychiatric unit.

Harry's heart rate spikes as they turn the corner and see

Tom and Jo Macy at the end of the corridor. It feels like taking the pitch against a daunting opponent, and he fights the urge to turn on his heels and sprint away. *Man up you fucking coward*, he chides himself.

Kaleigh, who'd been adamant about following Lorraine's advice of not showing any PDA, grabs his arm. She must be feeling a similar panic. He can tell by the tremble of her hand. He hates how much stress this is putting her through. Not what she needs at eight months pregnant, for the most traumatic event of her life to be rushed back to the surface. He gives her a squeeze, letting her know he's there for her.

"Okay, so we'll go in together, but not *together*," Kaleigh reminds him. He looks at her beautiful eyes glistening with tears and hates that he can't pull her in for a hug.

Just get it over with, he tells himself. *And then you can get back to normal. Football and family.*

As they approach, Harry sees a dark-haired woman speaking to Emma's parents in hushed whispers. The woman, who has heavy bags under her eyes, does a double take when she sees Harry, who quickly averts his gaze.

"Right, I'll leave you for now," she says, gesturing to Harry and Kaleigh. "I'll be back later for my session with Emma, but you know where to find me if you have any questions in the meantime."

Harry notices her staff ID badge clipped to her faded black jumper. Dr Charlotte Singh, Psychologist. He feels exposed, like she's psychoanalysing his every move. As if in reaction, his phone vibrates in his pocket. He ignores it.

Emma's parents thank the doctor before turning to Harry and Kaleigh. Jo Macy wipes a tear from her eye as she sombrely holds her arms out to Harry for a hug.

She's thinner than Harry remembers, her black trousers and tan blouse practically drowning out her figure. Tom looks heavier, like he's been knocking back one too many ales. He makes eye contact with Harry over Kaleigh's shoulder as they embrace and gives him a half smile. Harry's heart hammers in his chest as he thinks of the last time he saw the Macys.

"Pregnant again, I see," Jo says with feigned surprise to Kaleigh.

Heat rushes to Harry's face. He'd like to assume she doesn't mean it in a snarky way but the fact that she doesn't so much as lean in for a hug or side kiss tells him Kaleigh's hunch was right.

"We should've told her," she said on the way here, gesturing to her bump. "Shouldn't have assumed she'd know from the news."

"It's our second baby, Kay," Harry replied, telling her she was overthinking it. "It's been five years, she'll be over us being together by now."

Guess he was wrong. After all, Emma always knew how to hold a grudge; she likely learned that from somewhere.

Harry awkwardly shifts from right to left, as Kaleigh replies, "Yes, a little girl."

Jo's eyes fill with tears as she looks between Kaleigh and Harry. He thinks they're filled with a mixture of envy and sadness, probably wishing it was her daughter that was standing here pregnant with Harry's child. The thought makes him feel protective of his wife.

"Thanks for coming." Tom shakes Harry's hand once Jo releases him from her grip. "Squad's looking good this year. Think you guys can take it all the way."

"Hope so," Harry replies, relieved to know he's not the only one who'd rather talk about sport than the horrible situation at hand. He wants to keep talking about football, but stops himself, knowing it's inappropriate. Thankfully, Kaleigh turns the conversation back to why we're here.

"How is she?"

Jo shrugs, tears forming in her eyes. "She's been through a lot." Her voice cracks and she covers her mouth. Tom rubs her shoulder to comfort her.

A pit forms in Harry's stomach. He knew this was going to be difficult, seeing Emma after all this time. He needs to prepare himself for the worst, because that's what she went through.

"She was transferred here from the emergency unit only yesterday," Jo continues. "They said she was malnourished and that it's necessary they replenish her with all the vitamins and minerals before she can leave." She pauses, seeming to choke on her own words. "But I don't like it, don't want her... here." She gestures to the off-white corridor. "We're hoping to bring her home tomorrow and continue her treatment there, where she'll be more comfortable."

"Tomorrow?" Kaleigh says surprised. "That's great." She tries to mask the surprise with hopefulness. "That must mean she's doing well?"

Jo's eyes fill with tears and Tom pulls her into a hug. She takes a breath before composing herself.

"Just prepare yourself," Jo says. "She obviously doesn't look well. And she's not talking at all. But we hope the more family and friends that come to see her, the more she'll open up. That's what the psychologist hopes at least."

A lump forms in Harry's throat.

Jo knocks on the door and pokes her head in. "Emma, darling, Kaleigh and Harry are here."

Harry holds the flowers in front of his face as he walks in, focusing on them and the other bouquets dotted around the room. It's as if he's trying to trick himself into thinking he's in a garden, not a hospital. But the high-pitched beeping reminds him where he is. *Whoosh, whoosh, whoosh.* His thumping heart matches the monitor.

The moment he lays eyes on the frail woman in the bed, he can't believe it's Emma. *His* Emma. The girl he used to stare at during lessons, trying to muster up the courage to ask her out. Who he smiled at from across the hall after she responded *yes* to his daft note asking *Do you like me?* The girl who he had shared so many firsts with. Their first kiss at the park behind their school. Losing their virginity to each other in Harry's teenage bed, covered in AFC Nottingham sheets. Their first flat. Their first argument.

Emma's expression is vacant though as she lies back on the medical bed, her stringy hair hanging over the IV. She barely reacts, making Harry wonder if she even recognises them. If she has some form of amnesia.

Harry sets the flowers down on the side table and stands beside Kaleigh, unable to make eye contact with Emma. Kaleigh bursts into tears and reaches out for her but Emma shies away, like she doesn't know who they are.

Emma then fixes her gaze on Harry's wedding band and Kaleigh's bulging bump, before trailing her eyes up to his face. Her all-too-familiar, ice-cold glare sends chills up Harry's spine.

And in that moment, Harry knows that she knows.

David Wells → AFC Nottingham (Public Group)

---

2 hrs ago: I just met Harry Turner at the hospital, and he nearly turned my little lad away. The cheek of these people who think they're above us just because they kick a ball for a living. His wife was a class act though. Not too bad on the eyes either!

Comments

JJ McCallister: That's a shame. Really hope this business with his ex doesn't throw him off his game, big season coming up

Ollie Miller: I mean, you approached him at the hospital, on his way most likely to visit his ex missus who's been through some pretty rough shit no doubt, what do you expect knobhead

12

Charlie

My first session with Emma Macy yesterday went as expected. Like DCI Maynard said, when I asked her anything, even something as simple as her name, she just stared vacantly ahead at nothing in particular. It was as if she couldn't hear me at all. Like I was a telly on in the background.

Even when her parents were around, she didn't show much emotion. I knew I'd have my work cut out for me, trying to bring her back.

In cases like this, I like to think of the mind as a massive cinema, full of long, dark corridors connected to various rooms, each showing a different story, a different memory. A trauma victim like Emma will be wandering the corridors, searching for a way out, but behind every door is a horror film. All ones she's seen before, ones she promised herself she'd never watch again. So she chooses to stay in the liminal space, choosing not to venture towards danger. Instead, she'll try to destroy the film or create her own stories. Or sometimes, she'll try and keep her mind empty, void of anything, because that's better than the alternative of being forced to watch the horror unfold again.

But the only way for trauma victims to truly heal is to face it head on. Discuss it, unpack it, learn coping mechanisms for how to deal with the intrusive thoughts and flashes of memories that will hit them at the most inopportune moments. On a bus. At the store. In the middle of the night. It's my job to give them the tools they need to talk themselves down, banish the thoughts, the voices. Help them realise they're safe, that it's a memory, it can't hurt them. Because if they don't have those tools, they may think the only way out is to harm themselves, or others.

I'd have to help Emma face the horror, guide her out the other side. But to do that, I'd have to earn her trust. Would have to create a safe, comforting environment. Tell her things about me, talk about places like Paris or the seaside, places her mother told me she loved. Give her coloured pencils and paper to draw, let her know she can communicate in writing or through art if she prefers.

And thankfully, my approach seemed to be working. In this morning's session, she started sketching on the paper, drawing flowers and seascapes. She even started to give non-verbal responses – a huge breakthrough that showed we were slowly knocking down the walls.

I started asking yes or no questions. "What was your favourite place as a child?" for example, gave me no response. But, "Did you enjoy holidays in Devon as a child?" prompted a flicker in her eyes, a nod of the head.

I told her then that I'd like to invite a detective to join us, that they wanted to ask her some questions. At first, Emma obliged, answering DS Banes's questions.

"Were you the only one held there?" Banes asked.

Emma nodded.

"Were you held at a house, above ground, at any time?"

A shallow, short nod. She rubbed at her wrists.

"Do you remember being moved to the pub basement?"

She twitched.

"Was this the man that did this to you?"

Emma winced at the photo of Gaz Barker, and then completely turned back in on herself, not responding.

"Emma, we need to know if there are other bad people out there. Or other victims like you. Please talk to us," Banes begged before I finally shut the interview down.

This afternoon, though, Emma seems more alive, more aware. But she has a glint in her eye I haven't seen before. Anger, perhaps.

"Just us today," I reassure her. She responds with a small smile and nod, which gives me hope our progress hasn't been totally lost.

Her mother told me she was doing a little better when I briefly spoke to her earlier, right as the Turners arrived.

I'd never been that close to a celebrity before. Kaleigh was even more beautiful in person, carrying herself like a true beauty queen, despite being heavily pregnant. Harry, on the other hand, looked pale and on edge.

I study Emma now, wondering if that's why she has a fire in her eyes. Has the betrayal set in?

She blinks rapidly, then slowly, then rapidly again. As if it's some kind of code. Possibly a coping mechanism for herself. I study her, wondering what's going on behind those eyes. The way the brain processes trauma is complicated and unpredictable, so many things can be happening right now. It's clear she's suffering from severe PTSD, and that has serious effects beyond a lifetime of anxiety and fear.

At best, Emma will wake up screaming in the night from night terrors, potentially for the rest of her life. At worst, she'll dissociate completely to cope with the trauma. The whole situation feels surreal. How this broken woman is the same Emma Macy, whose glowing smile was plastered all over the internet five years ago.

I remember scrolling through her social media profile after the attack, how strange it was viewing Emma's life through her careful selection of photos, showing off her beauty and wealth. I used to shake my head at the stark contrast of our lives, despite being the same age. Me, a poor graduate student living in a shared flat on the bad side of town, eating ramen every night since it was all I could afford. Her, getting paid to pose with a brand of protein, living in a multi-storey terrace home in the most affluent part of Nottingham. As if she needed the money with her cushy life as Harry Turner's partner. But that's how life works: the rich get richer, the poor get poorer, while the working class literally work themselves to death trying to hover in the middle somewhere.

I feel guilty again for letting my mind wander. For feeling any sort of animosity towards Emma, who can barely tolerate sunlight now. I frown as she shies away from the sliver of light cutting through the blinds next to us. She rubs at her neck and I wonder if she was strangled. Or chained.

"Emma," I say, after noting down her movements. She looks at me.

Good. She's there.

"I want to apologise for the session yesterday, with the detective. I'm sorry if that made you uncomfortable. But please know this is a safe space. You're safe. The man who hurt you is dead."

Emma snaps her head up at me, face red with anger. She then starts shaking her head "no" as her eyes well with tears.

I curse myself, knowing I shouldn't have added the last bit. All that did was remind her of him. But then Emma grabs the red pencil and scribbles on her paper.

She tries to say the words out loud as she turns it to me, her voice soft and harsh at the same time. Like cotton wool being rubbed against sandpaper.

"Not dead."

Goosebumps cover my entire body and I force myself to breathe before I speak.

"Did someone else hurt you, Emma?" I ask, moving closer but not touching her. She doesn't like to be touched. "Was someone else responsible for what happened?"

She moves her mouth, but her voice is so low I can't hear a word. Just a low grumble.

"Emma? Can you please say that again?" I can hear my pulse pounding in my ears as I wait.

Another croak escapes Emma's throat as she tries to find her voice again. When she does, the accusation comes out clear as day.

"Kaleigh… did this to me."

13

Kaleigh

I stare at the brown mulch beneath my green wellies. Brown and green, the unofficial colours of England. I picture my boots gone, bloody feet in their place.

"Higher, higher!" Alfie yells as I push him in the swing. "Mummy, higher!"

But instead I stop the swing and cradle him in my arms.

"Mummy, no," he giggles. I give him another long hug and kiss before pushing him again, trying to focus on his laughter rather than my racing thoughts.

But no matter what I do I can't stop thinking about that night. About Emma. Seeing her yesterday was even worse than I imagined. Different emotions fighting each other. My heart fighting with my head. Grief for Leila. Guilt over Emma. And guilt for not just surviving, but thriving. Living the perfect life that was supposed to be hers.

I'd been so taken aback when I saw her yesterday. She didn't look like the Emma I knew at all. Her filler had dissolved, her platinum extensions and dye job had grown out, leaving faded mousy brown strands in its place. She didn't have false lashes or acrylics. No fake tan. No megawatt smile. Only a thin frame that made her look childlike.

I remember the time we both did a social media trend that involved showing what we'd looked like in the past versus what we looked like in the present. I laughed when she showed me her photos. She was adorable but so much nerdier than I'd expected, wearing big sports goggles and oversized football jerseys. Nothing like the photos the tabloids published of her when Harry started getting famous around nineteen. By then she'd traded her goggles for contacts and her baggy clothes for skin-tight dresses. More like the version of the Emma I knew and remembered.

A faint smile tugs at my lips as I recall her reaction to my childhood pageant photos. The ones of me in a big, poofy dress with wild, curly hair that looked like I'd stolen an 80s country singer's wig, posing with my hands on my hips. She'd actually snorted with laughter, one of her cute little quirks.

My smile disappears as I picture the woman in the hospital bed yesterday. How can that be Emma? Part of me wishes she's an imposter. A changeling. But then I recall the last look she gave me, right before I walked out the door. A look that told me it was her. She knew me. And she hated me.

"You're overthinking it," Zara told me when I popped by her house yesterday afternoon. "It's going to take time, that's all."

I want to believe she's right. If I just give it time and lie low, Emma will come around and we can be friends again. But I know that's delusional. Things will never be the same.

The cawing of birds distracts me from my potential spiral, and I'm thankful for it. Because every day I feel myself being pulled further down into the depths. Where the memories live, the demons dwell. I don't want to go back there.

I think of something on my to-do list to distract myself, specifically what statement, if any, to put out on my socials. "We're relieved for Emma's return but ask for privacy at this time," I mutter the idea out loud to myself, the words sounding shallow on my tongue. I sigh, thinking maybe it's best to stay quiet for now.

I look to my left, where the cawing has grown louder, and see two magpies. I continue pushing Alfie with my left hand while I begrudgingly take out my phone with the other. I bite off my glove and look up the rhyme.

Two for joy.

Okay, that's good, I think. But just when I allow myself to feel relieved, I see another, hiding around the base of the tree. And then more. And more. I quickly count them, scrolling down to read the full rhyme.

One for sorrow, two for joy, three for a girl, four for a boy.

Five for silver, six for gold, seven for a secret never to be told.

I breathe another sigh of relief when an eighth lands, surprised at my irrational desperation for it not to be seven. But my uneasiness returns as another joins the tiding. Then another, and another. I've never seen more than six at one time before. Something tells me this isn't a good omen.

The pit in my stomach grows as I finish the rhyme.

Eight for a wish. Nine for a kiss. Ten, a surprise you should be careful not to miss. Eleven for health. Twelve for wealth...

That's good, I tell myself, thinking of my maternity line. I'd been so distracted the past couple days, I almost forgot about the launch entirely. But the distraction is fleeting.

When I look up again, I see yet another magpie has joined the flock. I glance back at my phone.

Thirteen... Beware it's the devil himself.

"Come on, Alfie, time to go, baby."

"Alabama" by Neil Young starts playing from my purse as Alfie and I walk home. I sigh, knowing that ringtone can only mean one person.

"Hey, Ma," I say, juggling my phone in one hand and holding Alfie's hand with the other.

"Kaleigh Anne, I've been callin' for days... Is it true? Is Emma..."

"Yes," I say, sounding more annoyed than I should.

"Heavens to Betsy," she proclaims. "Why in the Lord's name haven't you told me?"

Be nice, I tell myself. I look at my son, happily bumbling along the street, no idea of everything that's going on, and it soothes me momentarily. I take a calming breath before I respond, reminding myself it's not my mother's fault I don't want to talk about it.

"Sorry, I'm still processing it all."

I hear her breathing heavily on the other line. "Well, I want you to know you can talk to me. You've always been one to bottle up all your emotions inside and it's just not healthy."

I almost laugh at the irony, since she raised me and my siblings on a diet consisting mainly of fried, beige foods.

"How's Dad?" I ask, desperate to change the subject as much as I'm genuinely curious about how he's feeling after that copperhead bite last week.

She sighs. "You know him, back out there huntin' in that same ol' duck hole like he never got bit in the first place. I swear that man will be the death of me."

I want to tell her to put her foot down, to demand he stop hunting on his own like that. But I know my dad, know he'd never stop. *"So long as I can drag myself out there and pull the trigger, I'm doin' it. Ain't no slippery little creature gon' stop me."*

My mouth twitches in a smile at the thought of that stubborn man and his thick Southern accent, one I've managed to almost shake entirely.

"Well, why don't you do some research into hunting gear," I tell her. "Let me know what I can buy so he'll be more protected at least."

"Kaleigh Anne, you know he don't want your money."

"I'm not sending money, Ma, I'm sending a gift. Can just say I got it free from a brand deal or something, doesn't matter."

"You can visit and give it to him yourself then," she says passive aggressively.

I scoff. "Yeah, Mama, let me just hop on a plane, eight months pregnant."

"I mean after," she says, annoyed.

"I will," I promise, wishing I really could escape to Alabama now.

"Well, you let me know when and I'll work with Karlie Mae to fix you a little baby shower."

I open my mouth to tell her not to worry, but shut it in a tight line when I spot a black car pulling up in front of our house. I place my hand on Alfie's shoulder, stopping him. *A press van?* I wonder. *Are the paparazzi back?* But then two individuals get out of the car, dressed smartly, no cameras. They spot me and wave.

"Sweetheart, are you there?" my mother asks.

"Sorry, Ma, I'll call you back." I hang up the phone.

"Who's that, Mumma?" Alfie points at the visitors outside our electric gates.

"Not sure, baby." I give him a reassuring smile, despite my hammering heart.

"Mrs Turner," the man says once I reach them.

"Yes?" I reply, heart thumping.

"I'm DCI Maynard with the Nottingham City Police." He stretches out his hand, which I shake. "This is DS Banes." He gestures to a short woman with an ash-brown bob.

I nod in her direction, aware of my sweaty palms. *Detectives. Probably reopening the case since everything we thought we knew is out the window.*

I pull my coat around me as goosebumps prickle my arms, feeling sick all over again at the thought of Gaz being in front of us this whole time. Could that mean there's someone else too?

DCI Maynard looks down beside me, where Alfie has latched himself around my leg. I wrap my hand around his head, holding him close.

"Looks just like Harry." The detective smiles. *A fan*, I note, thinking that this expected inquisition should be easy enough.

But the woman doesn't smile. Simply raises a brow as she looks me up and down like I'm some type of criminal. White air floats in front of me as my warm breath mixes with the cold.

"How can I help you, detectives?" I ask, my accent sneaking through, like it always does after a call from home.

"We were hoping to speak to you privately," Maynard says just as Alfie screams for a snack. "Would that be possible?"

I nod and unlock the gates, making sure to hide the code from them. "My housekeeper is inside, she usually finishes up around this time, but I'll see if she can stay for another fifteen minutes?"

"That would be great, thank you," Maynard responds. His female counterpart raises an eyebrow at the mention of a housekeeper.

Once inside, I ask Nina if she can stay for a little while longer to watch Alfie. She happily agrees, but I can see the apprehension in her eyes as she glances at the two detectives.

"Okay, baby, you go with Nina," I tell Alfie. "She's going to get you a special treat."

Alfie runs toward the kitchen where Nina is waiting with open arms.

"Come on, little one," she says cheerily.

"Thank you," I mouth, before guiding the detectives to the sitting room. It's a space we rarely use, furnished with bespoke sofas and armchairs. No television, just built-in shelves filled with Harry's trophies and a handpicked selection of artwork and books I never have time to read.

They both look around the room, Maynard's eyes alight, clearly excited by the trophy display. Banes, on the other hand, looks confused and slightly amused, with her raised eyebrow and suppressed grin. It reminds me of my dad's reaction when he visited. *"So what d'ya do in here? Just stare at them trophies?"*

I want to explain to Banes that I didn't grow up like this. Harry and I worked hard for everything we have. But I contain myself and instead ask the detectives if they'd like a drink.

Maynard smiles and I can tell he's about to ask for a tea or coffee, but Banes answers first. "No, thank you. We'd like to get into some questions about the night you were attacked." She says the last word as if she's mocking me and I stare at her, confused.

Maynard gives Banes a stern look before turning to me apologetically. "Listen, we're very sorry to surprise you like this but with…"

"It's okay, I was expecting you actually." I note Banes's raised eyebrow. "I mean, not now specifically, but in general." I gesture for them to take a seat on the sofa across the table from me, where I sit in the new mohair chair Harry had delivered last month. I wasn't sure at first, but now I love it. Harry has a great eye for interior decor, another fact almost no one knows about him.

I clasp my hands on my knees and lean forward, ready to face the detectives. "I mean, everything's been thrown into question, now, so…"

Maynard nods but Banes is the first to speak. "Will your husband be home soon? We'd like to ask him a few questions as well."

"No," Maynard cuts in. "Turner will be at training, won't he?" He smiles at me, as if I should be impressed he possesses this knowledge.

I give him a smile, asking the question I already deduced the answer to. "AFC Nottingham fan?"

"Oh yes, been a Merry Man all my life." He sits up straight, wearing this fact more proudly than his badge.

"Right," Banes says. "Well, now that's out of the way, we would appreciate it if we could get your side of events again."

"Sure," I say, even though I'd rather not go back there.

A cool sweat pricks at my forehead as I recall the events. I force myself to push the nightmarish memories away and answer the same rehearsed response I'd given hundreds of times before.

"Leila, Emma and I came back to the cabin after going out in town…"

"Town, as in Nottingham city centre?" Banes asks.

"Yes. And we were back for, I don't know, a half an hour. Next thing I know I'm in the bathroom, puking my guts up, having had way too much to drink, and then I hear a scream. I go outside and…"

My voice cracks. "I'm sorry," I say, throat burning as I push through. I haven't said these words out loud in years, not since my original police interviews.

"It's okay," Maynard says. "Take your time."

"Um, yes, so I hear a scream, I go outside and… there they were."

Pools of tears have now formed in my eyes.

"Leila in the hot tub, Emma on the deck. Dead. Or so I thought."

"Did you not check?" Banes asked.

I let out something between a scoff and a laugh. "Oh, I checked," I said. "I pulled Leila out of the hot tub, thinking I could give her CPR, but—"

The horrifying image of Leila's slashed throat crosses my mind.

"It was very clear she was dead. Her throat…"

Maynard nods. "And Emma? What made you think she was dead?"

My heart pounds in my chest and I wonder if they can hear it. But I don't lie. I tell them the truth.

"She had blood pooled around her head. She was unconscious."

"And you didn't call for help?" Banes asks.

I laugh, annoyed at her tone. "We had no service out there."

"Yet you ordered an Uber earlier that night?"

"My phone, which we used earlier because I was with a different service provider, was dead. And Emma and Leila's phones had no service. Believe me, I checked."

I bubble over with frustration for being in this situation. For having to explain myself to the police *again*. For having to go back to a place I never wanted to mentally return to. For feeling guilty and horrible that Emma was still alive and I could have saved her. That maybe it was my fault she ended up as Gaz's prisoner after all. I look down at my white sneakers, imagining my bare feet underneath, my toes covered in her sticky, red blood.

I start to cry. Maynard hands me a tissue.

"I've told this all to the police before, don't you have a copy of the report?"

"Yes, but we'd like to hear it from you again. Mainly on why you thought Emma was dead, and to check the timings," Maynard says, before Banes cuts in.

"The report says that you claimed a car pulled up after you found Emma and Leila."

I nod, thinking of the headlights growing brighter as I sat frozen in fear, drenched in Leila's blood.

"So you walk out after hearing a scream," Banes says. "Your friends are seemingly dead, and *then* a car shows up? After the scream? Not before?"

I sit up straighter, feeling defensive. This was always the part of my story everyone had trouble with. And it barely made sense to me either.

"Yes," I say, holding my hands out.

Maynard scribbles something down and then shrugs to Banes, but she doesn't seem satisfied. "Do you believe the person that drove up to the house was the same person who attacked Emma and Leila?"

I stare ahead, remembering the fear I felt as the tall, shadowy figure stepped out of the car, black hood pulled over his head.

"Yes," I reply. "Or an accomplice at least."

"You think there were two people involved?" Banes asks.

"As I said in my original statement, yes."

I always thought there was another attacker out there. Especially having heard the man talking to someone on the phone.

"There's two bodies."

I shift in my seat as I recall his gruff whisper.

"Do you think Gaz was working with Davey Allen?"

Maynard and Banes exchange a look.

"We're considering various possibilities at the moment," Maynard says.

Banes smirks. "One of them being that Gaz was a professional for hire. You have to agree, it was a very impressive clean-up job. Murder weapon gone. Bodies gone…"

I look from Banes to Maynard, then back to Banes in confusion, before recalling one of the theories I heard years ago.

"Maybe," I say. "There were those who thought Leila had been attacked in retaliation for her stepdad putting that drug ring behind bars. Maybe Gaz had been involved with them?"

Banes purses her lips. "Mrs Turner, what was your relationship with Gaz Barker?"

"My relationship with…" I frown, looking between her and Maynard again. "Sorry, what are you implying?"

"It's been suggested…" Maynard clears his throat and looks down at his clasped hands. "That you may have had something to do with what happened that night." He holds his hands out, as if he also thinks it's an absurd accusation.

I inch myself up and rub my hands over my belly, feeling hot tears rush to my eyes. Of all the things I expected, this was not it.

"That is… that…" I struggle to find the words. I try to exhale but my breathing is cut short. I have completely lost my cool. I clutch my protruding belly for comfort.

"I was a victim too, you know."

I catch my breath and straighten my shoulders, knowing from pageants how important it is to appear composed. "Just because Harry and I got together an entire *year* after I thought Emma died, doesn't mean I am somehow involved.

Despite what the tabloids and internet trolls would like you to believe."

Maynard nods, holding his hands up higher now in surrender.

"Mrs Turner," he says. "As I mentioned, we're just doing our due diligence here."

I catch Banes looking at him though, like there's more to it.

"I think this should suffice for now though, don't you think?" He looks at Banes, who doesn't look satisfied but nods.

"Thank you for your time, Mrs Turner," he says.

"We'll be in touch," Banes adds.

I shake their hands and walk them awkwardly to the front door, finally glad to be waving them off.

But as they're exiting, Banes turns around and addresses me. "Oh, and Mrs Turner. This should go without saying, but you should cancel any immediate plans to travel outside of the UK."

"What?" I reply in utter confusion. But she doesn't answer, just turns on her heels and walks away.

They know you're hiding something, a voice whispers.

I silence it with the truth. That I told them everything they need to know.

NEW DEVELOPMENT: Police looking into Kaleigh Creedy-Turner, suspect she may have been involved in Emma Macy's abduction

3 March 2025 10:01pm
Buckle in, justice seekers, there's been another major update in the Emma Macy case since her reappearance. According to a source close to the investigation, Kaleigh Creedy-Turner is suspected of being involved in orchestrating Emma's abduction before fleeing the scene herself, and potentially even being involved in Leila Adler's death.

We're now one step closer to proving Davey Allen's innocence in the Nightmare in Notts case.

Do you think Kaleigh Creedy was involved? For me, the fact that she claimed both Emma and Leila were dead is a huge red flag, since Emma clearly wasn't. Let me know your thoughts in the comments.

Comments:

SandraBollocks: She's beauty, she's grace, she orchestrated the Nightmare in Notts case

HarlowsNextVictim: Can't wait to see the next "Meet the WAGS of England" article

> **Murder4Sport:** if Harry even makes the squad now with all this drama going on

MillieCrimesolver: What was her motive though?

RavenRumours: To get Emma out of the way so she could get Harry all to herself

MillieCrimesolver: Still doesn't explain Leila.

UndercoverJayne: If she hadn't said E was dead, maybe the police would've kept looking. Tragic.

14

Charlie

Tuesday 4 March 2025

"*Kaleigh did this to me.*"

I think of Emma's damning statement, how I was so sure I misheard her, implicating the person I least expected. Sure, plenty of people suspected Kaleigh's involvement in the past – survivors are usually targets of true crime theorists who are desperate for answers – but I never did.

I tried to keep Emma talking after she made the accusation, asking what she meant, but she just started crying, and then curled up in the foetal position. I didn't want to push it. So after I left her in the care of the nurses, I called Maynard.

"Kaleigh Turner?" he said, echoing my reaction. "She seems so… nice?"

"A lot of killers seem nice," I shrugged.

I try to imagine how Kaleigh could possibly be involved in this, picture her working with Gaz Barker – like notorious serial killer couples Fred and Rosemary West, or Ian Brady and Myra Hindley. But they're not a couple, don't even know each other well as far as I'm aware.

I shake my head at the depraved things humans are capable of. Nevertheless, it fascinates me.

Stones crunch beneath my tyres as I pull into the Macys' drive, ready for my first outpatient session with Emma. Despite my hesitations, she was released from the hospital this morning after her parents requested to take her home. They'd hire an in-home carer to help look after her and any doctors could treat her here. I would have preferred Emma stayed for a few more days, but I also could see the pros of moving her to the comfort of home. Hopefully it'd help her open up more.

I park my battered Toyota next to two shiny BMWs in front of the renovated brick mansion, immediately feeling like I'm devaluing the property. I forgot the Macys had this kind of money before remembering how, after the attack, Tom Macy sold his van hire business and reportedly made millions. It raised a few eyebrows at the time – never a good look to come into wealth following something like that – but the deal was already in the works before everything happened, so it was deemed above board.

I pick at a bobbly bit on my jumper as I get ready to head inside. The once deep black colour has faded to a dark grey and I realise I am wearing four shades of black. I had always pictured myself in a sophisticated trouser suit, looking demure as I sat with patients. But just as the films often wrongly portray mental illness, they also do a shit job at showing what a normal psychologist looks like. I sniff my jumper and scowl at the mildewy smell, annoyed at myself for letting my washing marinate in stale water overnight yet again.

I sigh, feeling insecure, before I reprimand myself. *Emma won't care what you're wearing or what you smell like.*

Although, she likely would've years ago.

I crumple up the Maccie's breakfast sandwich wrapper and shove it into the paper bag, which I throw on the back seat. I don't bother with an umbrella, just shield my head with my hand as I run outside into the frigid rain, foot landing deep in a puddle on my way.

"Dr Singh, please come in." Jo Macy holds the door open for me as I run inside. "Thank you so much for agreeing to do your sessions here."

"Oh, not a problem," I respond, trying not to drip all over her pristine hallway. "How is she doing? Was everything okay last night?"

As much as I understand Jo's reasons for wanting Emma home, I often find patients sleep better in hospital, with nurses and doctors constantly milling around.

I can tell by Jo's expression that it was a difficult night.

"Well, her friend Zara stopped by... you know, Zara Becker. She's married to... well, it's not important, but she was a good friend of Emma's back in the day, so it was nice to have her here. The first real friend she's seen." Her tone is tinged with disdain.

I bite my lip, wondering if she's been informed about Emma's accusation against Kaleigh Turner yet.

"Did Emma open up to Zara?" I ask, curious.

Jo shakes her head, tears welling in her eyes. "She didn't say anything, but it looked like she was listening to Zara at least, not completely vacant... like she was when..." Jo's face crumples in anguish. "I'm sorry," she says as she begins to cry.

I put a hand on her back to comfort her. "It's okay," I say in a hushed tone. "What you're going through is incredibly difficult, but you're all doing so well. Give it time."

Jo nods as she brushes away her tears. "Oh dear, how embarrassing. Anyway, Emma is in the conservatory, I'll take you to her. Can I make you a tea or coffee?"

"Coffee would be lovely, thank you," I reply, in desperate need of caffeine.

When I enter the conservatory, Emma is sitting on the settee, cradling a cup of tea in her hands. Her hair looks freshly washed, and she's wearing a large green jumper with black leggings.

For the first time, I'm starting to see the Emma I became so familiar with online all those years ago.

"Emma, hi," I say. "It must be nice to be home."

She nods. And then she shocks me by speaking. "It's very different," she whispers, looking into her mug.

"Is it?" I ask. "How so?"

"All of it, really."

My heart races as she answers me again. "Did you sleep well?"

She looks up at me, tears in her eyes as she shakes her head no. "Slept outside. Well, lay outside. In the grass..."

"Why?" I ask, although I'm fairly sure of the answer.

As she thinks of an explanation, I notice her begin to close in on herself again, so I keep talking.

"Camping can be quite nice," I say, gesturing to the large garden surrounded by woodland and fields. "Something freeing and comforting about being outside, under the stars."

Emma looks at me and nods, letting me know that's it. She'd been trapped inside for five years, now she wants to be outside. Free.

"Here you go, Dr Singh." Jo Macy swoops into the conservatory with coffee and biscuits in hand.

"Lovely, thank you very much." I smile up at her.

"Darling, can I get you another cuppa?" she says to Emma.

Emma pulls her lips into a thin line and shakes her head. After lingering for a moment, Jo takes the cue to leave. "Right, I'll leave you both to it, then."

Once she's out of sight, Emma speaks again. "Don't tell my mum please, about me sleeping outside. She'll worry."

I nod, heart leaping at the progress Emma's making, speaking unprompted. "Secret's safe with me."

"Thanks." Her voice cracks. "Sorry." She holds a hand to her throat, wincing as she caresses it.

"No need to apologise," I say. Advice I have to give far too often.

She nods. "Sorry." Then a slight smile escapes her as she meets my eye.

"Were you like this before? Did you often apologise when you didn't need to?"

She shrugs and looks at her hands, picking at a scab.

I start to feel guilty for judging her all those years ago. It was before I learned that anyone can be a victim, no matter how poor or rich, plain or beautiful. It can happen to absolutely anyone. And to see her this broken, well…

You can fix her, I tell myself. *Help her.*

I know she'll never get back to herself, not completely, but there's hope of her having a normal life, a happy life. I refocus my thoughts, checking my notes to remind myself of the aim for the session: to get her to pick up where she left off, to tell me more about Kaleigh.

But I know diving right back into that may be too jarring for her, so I approach it differently.

"So, Emma, today I'd like to start our session with you telling me about a happy memory from when you were younger." I look at my notes. "What about your twenty-third birthday? You spent it in Paris, didn't you?"

She nods, a smile forming at the corner of her lips.

"What was your favourite part of the trip? I went on a boat ride across the Seine at night when I was there, that was incredible. Did you do anything like that?"

"I did that, too," she says softly. "With Mum. It was nice." She looks up at me, eyes shining and my heart soars.

"What else did you do when you were there?"

"Went to the Moulin Rouge," she adds, looking away from me now. She picks at the scab on her lip that has yet to heal.

"Sounds fantastic. There's the musical on in the West End now, you'd love it." I'm trying to remind her that she still has her whole life ahead of her.

"Now," I say, treading carefully. "If we can jump forward a year or two, I'd love to know more about your twenty-fourth birthday. Could you tell me what you were doing that morning, starting when you woke up?"

My heart thumps as I finish the question, hoping it's worked – hoping her mind will let her venture there. Although I worry it's too close to a pain point. To my relief, Emma's expression goes from vacant to something else, as if she's recalling the memories.

15

Emma

It was a typical winter day: cold and wet. I pushed through the rain as I ran, enjoying the cool droplets on my hot skin. I huffed out an exhale as I rounded the corner through the tunnel, picking up the pace – a mini sprint before I reached the bottom of the incline. Sprinting was the only time my mind truly relaxed, so I pushed myself.

My Apple watch buzzed once I reached the bottom of the notorious Park steps, letting me know I hit the four-mile mark. *Right on time*. I allowed myself to rest before tackling the mammoth climb, proud that I'd managed a run on my birthday, slightly hungover. The bottom of my skull throbbed, like a little knife, as acid from last night's prosecco burned the back of my throat.

An old Harlow Hayes song played through my AirPods, a song Kaleigh recently introduced me to. Too slow for running, I tapped my watch to skip it, along with the next seven songs, until I landed on The Weeknd's new hit

"Blinding Lights". The skin around my tattoo stung, irritated by the sweat pooling around it under my watch. Part of me regretted the placement of three butterflies, the symbol Kaleigh, Leila and I chose to represent our friendship. Mine seemed to be the only one that still itched six months later. But when I removed the watch from my left wrist to move it to my right, and saw the fine line etching up close, I decided I didn't regret it at all. It was beautiful.

I jogged in place as I glanced at my phone, which was blowing up with notifications from friends and strangers, wishing me happy birthday. Then there were countless Insta notifications from my followers, who were commenting on the photo I'd posted of Harry and me at dinner last night. We'd celebrated my birthday early since he had a game tonight.

Heat rose in my cheeks as I thought about last night. And this morning. Him on top of me. Me on top of him. Him between my legs. Me, on my knees in front of him. I'd hoped we'd have time for one more go before he set off. One more chance for me to remind him what he has.

Not that he needed the reminder. We'd been together for ten years, ever since we met at secondary school. We had our breakups here and there, like any teenage couple, but always came back to each other.

I'm his and he is mine, I comforted myself as the awful *Daily Mail* article from the previous week resurfaced in my mind. *Air hostess claims Harry Turner romp in Vegas nightclub.*

My blood started to boil as I thought about it again – the vile rumour being spread all over the internet despite Harry's boys' trip to Vegas happening eight months ago.

So cliché. So unimaginative. I think of the blurry photo of him smiling as an ugly blonde whispered into his ear, accompanied by the caption: *Helen Baker was seen getting cosy with rising star Harry Turner.*

Helen Baker, stupid fucking slag, I thought as I pushed myself up the steps. *Who does she think she is? And waiting eight bloody months to "share her truth"? Lying bitch.*

My conscience challenged me.

Bitch, yes. But is she a liar?

I bowed over in relief once I sprinted to the top, holding onto the railing for support. I was sure my heart was trying to literally jump out of my chest based on how hard it was hammering. I grabbed one foot and then the other, stretching out my tired, aching limbs. I shook out my arms and then bent down to stretch my hamstrings.

Since it was my birthday, on my way home, I popped into the café on the corner of our street to treat myself to my favourite hazelnut latte. I was confused to see the barista in a face mask across the counter, but then I remembered the headlines from that morning, about the virus that had started in China. How fourteen people had tested positive for it in the UK.

I didn't understand why people were so worried though; it was just like any other virus or outbreak the media reported on. It would be gone soon. If anything, I felt oddly excited by the whole thing, imagining myself as a lead character in a film. Like Gwyneth in *Contagion*. Although my character would survive of course. Fight through the trials and tribulations and make it to the end – the final girl.

The door dinged again as two teenage boys entered and stood behind me in line. I quickly turned back around after making eye contact with one. "That's Harry Turner's bird," I heard him mutter to his friend.

My face flushed and I stood up straighter, hoping they wouldn't say anything else. I caught sight of myself in the mirrored drinks shelf and was thankful for my new lash extensions and brow lamination. I wondered what they were thinking. If they thought I was good enough for their hero. Some of the cruel social media comments I'd seen argued I wasn't.

She doesn't deserve him. She's so average.
Average? That's generous.
Idk what he sees in her, he can have anyone in the world.

"Americano. Black," I ordered, deciding to forgo the extra sugar.

Once outside, I forced myself to smile under the café awning as I held up my phone for a selfie, making sure to get the right angle.

My favourite part about social media was that I was in control. I got to post photos of myself the way I liked, at good angles, with the right lighting and a filter if I wanted. It was the only way I could counteract the dreadful tabloid shots. Even after all these years, they still made me insecure.

But this interest in my personal life, which exploded after Harry scored a goal in a cup match for the first time, meant I was able to turn social media into a career. By the time I hit my second year at uni, I was making enough money to afford what I wanted without having to ask Harry or my parents. So I dropped out and moved back to Nottingham with Harry after his transfer. Part of me wished I stuck it out, finished my last year with Leila and Kaleigh, got my degree. But, really, the only reason I wanted one was to *say* I had one, and that wasn't a good enough reason.

I thought through captions for my post as I walked back to my apartment. *"Birthday run: check. Birthday coffee: check."* Or maybe just a few simple emojis?

I decided on the first and posted before I scrolled through my messages. I sent a bunch of love hearts to Mary, Leila's mum, the first to wish me happy birthday this morning, then confirmed the time for lunch with my parents, and responded to comments on my latest post from more strangers wishing me a happy birthday.

Excited for tonight! Kaleigh messaged our group chat.

It'd been her idea for the forest retreat. At first, I thought she was insane for suggesting we camp out in the woods for my birthday weekend instead of our usual decadent night out, dressed to the nines. But now, I was actually looking forward to sipping champagne in a hot tub with my two best friends, surrounded by trees under a blanket of stars. I already had the perfect Instagram post in mind. Me in the hot tub in my bikini, holding a glass of fizz. I could be blowing a kiss or simply looking off in the distance. Maybe a selection of a few.

This kind of chilled weekend was exactly what I needed.

I'd expected Harry to still be in bed when I got home, but instead he was in the kitchen, waiting to surprise me.

"Made ya a birthday smoothie," he called out.

I smiled in delight as he handed it to me, nodding in approval as I took the first sip.

"Mmm, thank you," I said, letting him wrap me in his arms. I pressed my head into his chest, staring at the four gorgeous bouquets of roses on the kitchen table. The one good thing about the *Daily Mail* article dropping a week before my birthday meant that he had to step up his game this year. And he did. He surprised me with a trip to my dream destination, Thailand. We'd go later in the year, once the season ended. I imagined us on the beach, the iconic one from the Leonardo DiCaprio film, him down on one knee, proposing...

I was grateful that we seemed to be back on track again, especially after how strange and secretive Harry had been acting lately. Always on his phone. I'd almost checked it yesterday when he was in the shower, but decided against it. Told myself I shouldn't go looking for answers I don't want.

"I have one more birthday surprise for you," Harry said, smirking. "Something special since we can't spend tonight together."

"Oh yeah?" I responded, running my hands up his shaved chest.

"I thought we could look at a house next week. I found one I think you'll love."

"A house?" My heart leapt. "For us? Really?"

"For us," he beamed. He knew how much that meant to me. How much I wanted to buy our own place, move out of this rented apartment.

Excitement coursed through me as he scrolled through the photos of the gated home on his phone: a five-bedroom property in the most expensive village in Nottinghamshire. Somewhere a family would live.

"Can we afford this?" I asked.

His face flushed and he looked downcast for a second, embarrassed by the question. Because to anyone else, of course a Premier League champion could afford this. But Harry's Vegas trip had done damage to his finances as well as our relationship.

"Don't worry about that," he said dismissively, rolling his eyes. "Of course we can!"

I reached up and pressed my lips against his, parting them with my tongue. He pushed me up onto the countertop, and I ran my fingers through his hair as he kissed my neck.

If only that slag could see us now.

I thought about all the other wives and girlfriends before me who had to deal with tabloid fodder and the endless rumour mill. Even the Beckhams and Rooneys dealt with their fair share. But they withstood the storm and ended up stronger than ever.

I could get through this. It would be worth it in the end. He was mine, and would always be mine. I'd make sure of it.

16

Harry

Wednesday 5 March 2025

Harry hammers the ball with his right foot, watching it slice through the grass before going wide, missing the net. The Europa League match is tomorrow and if the best penalty taker on the squad can't even sink one during training, that's a problem.

"One more time, Turner," the manager bellows, sounding as frustrated as Harry.

Harry looks into the stands and sees his dad leaning back in one of the chairs, arms crossed, unimpressed. Harry turns away, not wanting to meet Robbie's eyes. Funny how no matter how old Harry gets, he's still just a boy wanting to impress his father.

He sets the ball down again, spinning it a few times to find the perfect placement. But everything feels off.

He cracks his neck from side to side to shake the relentless thoughts he can't escape. Of the night it all happened. After he took the penalty. He pictures the ball soaring straight to the top right corner. Perfect placement.

He breathes, hops on his left foot before taking two long strides towards the ball. But before he hits it, he pictures Emma in the hospital, frail and weak, followed by her icy stare. Micro moments continue to cloud his focus as he imagines Kaleigh with the police, being questioned, being accused. Frustration courses through him and he knows the second his foot meets the ball, he's fucked it again.

He screams this time, clenching his fists as he spins on his heel, not bothering to watch it soar over the net.

"Turner, do some laps, clear your head," Upton commands.

Harry sighs, but does as he's told. *Why can't everything go back to being simple?* he thinks. When all he had to worry about was football and family. It's a lot for him. Too much to try and process.

His only comfort is his dad's words from the other day, making him hopeful that life could go back to normal. *"See Emma. Wish her well. Then re-focus on football and family."* His dad had made it seem so easy. But what if it wasn't that simple or clean cut?

Why would the police tell Kaleigh not to leave the country if it wasn't serious? Why would they accuse her of potentially being involved? He thinks of Kaleigh then, scrunching her nose and waving off the accusations.

He doesn't know how she's able to be so positive all the time. It's one of the many things he loves about her. That she's always able to pull him out of the dark and get him to refocus on the good.

He picks up his pace, lungs burning. But what if Kaleigh and his dad were wrong. What if it wasn't a misunderstanding? What if they had enough evidence to reopen the case and analyse certain things they'd missed before? That wouldn't be good.

Harry's sprinting now, going so fast that he can barely make out any single object. Just like he can't seem to pinpoint one particular emotion. He's upset, annoyed, frustrated and scared all at the same time. All the things he shouldn't be feeling going into one of his busiest seasons yet with Premier League, Europa League, FA Cup and World Cup qualifiers…

This should be his time. His legacy. To bring the Cup home. He should be riding high, enjoying every moment of his success with his family yet he feels the opposite. Like instead of light, he's being consumed by a gaping black hole.

He lets out a groan and runs even faster, unsure he'll ever have another chance. Unsure if his body will be able to wait another four years.

It's all your fault, an internal voice mocks. He sprints so fast that his vision blurs to a mix of colours. Grey, green, black, red.

Unable to run anymore, Harry falls to his knees and struggles to catch his breath. His right hand throbs and he rubs it as he brings his arms over his head.

"You alright?" he hears Becker ask before he reaches a hand out.

Harry shakes it off, finally feeling better. Lighter.

"Yeah, fine, mate. Cheers."

Becker nods, then pushes his hair back, before squirting an electrolyte pouch into his mouth. The manager calls them in, and they walk towards the centre pitch together.

"Listen, mate, there's something I think you should know."

"What's that?" Harry says, unsettled by Becker's serious tone.

"Zara went to see Emma again yesterday. Said that Emma's been saying some things... and I... I don't know, I thought I'd give you a heads-up."

Harry stops walking and turns to him. "What did she say? I thought she wasn't talking much."

Becker shrugs. "Apparently she is now. And, well, Emma told Zara that she thinks Kaleigh was involved."

Harry scoffs. "Involved in what?"

"In everything," Becker says. "What happened to Emma and Leila..."

"That's fucking bullshit, why the hell would you say something like that?" Harry feels an irrational sense of anger and confusion, even though it all makes sense now. It's what the police were alluding to with Kaleigh. Of course, it was Emma that made it up.

But if she was going to accuse anyone, he would've expected it to be him. And he would've taken it. But this? Kaleigh? No.

"Hey, I'm just giving you a heads-up, man." Becker holds his hands up in defence. "Figured you may want to hire a lawyer or whatever. Get ahead of it."

Harry buries his face in his hands and groans. "Fuck!"

"Kay?" Harry yells out the moment he steps inside.

He kicks his shoes off, annoyed, before setting them neatly in their place.

"Ay up mi duck," Simon says as Harry walks into the kitchen, catching him off guard.

"Simon came to drop off that behemoth of a truck you ordered," Kaleigh says, cutting through a rotisserie chicken with a knife.

"Did you seriously not see it?" Simon laughs. "It's basically the size of a house."

Harry runs his hands over his eyes, frustrated. He should've been excited, coming home to the ultra-American lifted King Ranch he ordered through Simon, having a fun little spat with Kaleigh about how cool it was while she admonished him for ordering such an impractical truck. Instead, he's consumed by what Becker told him, too focused on the shit storm Emma caused to be happy about anything else. He ignores his brother and looks at Kaleigh, pausing as he takes her in. She looks so sweet, wearing her hair how he loves it, in a long braid that drapes over a red-and-white-checkered apron. Her warm honey eyes look into his and he wishes that he didn't have to ruin her day. But he can't hide this from her. He knows she'd want to know.

"The police were here because Emma is saying you had something to do with what happened to her. Becker gave me a heads-up at training..."

Kaleigh slams the knife through the chicken, making Harry flinch.

He waits for Kaleigh to say something. But it's Simon who speaks first. "Shit, man."

Harry's eyes are fixed on Kaleigh as she washes her hands and unties her apron, before grabbing her keys.

"Babe, where are you going?"

"Where do you think? To sort this out." She shoots him a look that tells him to leave her to it.

"Can I at least drive you?" Harry offers, not wanting her behind the wheel this upset. But by the time he gets the words out, she's already out the door.

17

Kaleigh

My heart races, matching the rapid speed of the windshield wipers. I'm going faster than I should in the rainy conditions, but I can't wait any longer. I need to get to Emma before this spreads any further.

Large oak trees arch over the road, forming a tunnel of grey and green, a sight that enamoured me eleven years ago when I first moved to England. Silly me, thinking I escaped to the land of fairy tales and enchanted forests. Somewhere safe and magical.

Instead, every bump in the road prompts something terrible. Screaming. Bleeding. Running. And before I know it, I'm back. I can smell the rain. Feel the cuts on my feet. See the blood pooled around Emma's head.

I want to cry, feeling helpless and angry. How could she do this to me? Does she not realise that I was a victim too? That I've also been haunted and traumatized by that night?

You are what's wrong with the world!

I hope Harry divorces you, you lying bitch.

Rot in hell.

I hope you die.

I slam my manicured hands against the wheel, imagining some of the things the internet would say if a word of this gets out. I scoff, holding back tears.

I wish the detectives had been honest with me so I could've defended myself properly. Could they not see through Emma's accusation? See that she's just upset that Harry and I are together?

The spiteful nature of it reminds me of the time Emma got an airline attendant fired after it was rumoured Harry had a fling with her. Or the time she shared the naked photos of some girl who DM'd him online. I knew how jealous and vindictive she could be. I just never expected to be on the receiving end of it. I should have seen it coming though, should've known it was a bad idea to visit with Harry. I shouldn't have listened to Lorraine or Jo. It was probably Jo's way of instigating the situation. Her snarky comment replays in my mind. *"Pregnant again, I see."*

I handled the situation as gracefully as I could, diffusing rather than igniting a fire. Jo had been through enough and I was willing to let *her* off the hook. But this accusation from Emma? There is no excuse for it.

I think of the sad, angry look in Emma's eyes. Of Zara assuring me that I was overthinking it. And of how wrong she also was. How even though Zara knew Emma longer than me, I know her better.

My heart thunders in my chest as I arrive at the Macys and old memories resurface.

The home looks completely different now: grander, more modern. Worlds apart from the first time I visited with Emma during a break from uni. Still teenagers, we spent the long weekend trying on various fashion hauls for her social media channels and talking about Harry, planning her bachelorette – or hen do as she called it – and imagining what her wedding would be like. We wondered what my future husband would be like, too, fantasising how fun it'd be to get pregnant at the same time and raise our children together.

My boiling blood cools, remembering what it was like when we'd been friends, and how devastating it must be for her to see me with Harry.

It's a misunderstanding, I tell myself. She's been through so much, and she was angry that Harry and I moved on without her. I'd be angry too. I just need her to see my side of things, explain what happened.

I pop open a giant green umbrella and glance around before getting out of the car, making sure there aren't any bystanders or paparazzi trying to get a cheap shot in. I groan as I step into a puddle, soaking my white Chanel sneakers. I think again about what would happen if word of this spread, of the countless number of outlets who would be foaming at the mouth, excited to tear me down. Emma's accusation being the exact sort of click-bait headline that would make anyone's jaw drop.

I thought you were dead. Otherwise, I would never have gotten with Harry. I press the doorbell. *Please let me be here for you.* I continue to think through what I want to say as I wait for someone to answer.

"Hello," I call out. "Is anyone there? Emma?"

Still, no one answers. "Emma, please. We need to talk," I say again.

I rock back and forth on my heels, trying to remain calm as I continue to wait in the cold, wet rain. Trying to remind myself to be the bigger person. To be as forgiving as possible to Emma and her trauma. I look around, wondering if I'd been mistaken. That maybe Emma wasn't here after all.

My phone vibrates in my pocket and I reach for it to see if it's Harry. But it's a text from my publicist, saying to call her as soon as possible.

Heat rises in my cheeks as I start to lose my patience.

"Emma!" I beg. "This is serious. We need to talk!"

I walk away from the door and scan the three-storey home, zeroing in on Emma's bedroom window, covered with curtains. I swear I see the curtain twitch, like someone's watching from behind.

I rub my belly, thinking of the stress Emma's accusation is putting my baby under. Of how much worse it will get if Emma doesn't put an end to it now. I think of how unfair it is, no matter what happened, for Emma to come back and try to ruin the life Harry and I managed to build after everything.

I storm back toward the house and hold the doorbell down, before pressing it multiple times. "Emma, I'm not leaving until you talk to me," I say, digging my heels into the front step.

"Finally," I mutter as I hear someone shuffling my way.

The door opens an inch, revealing Tom Macy behind it. His face is barely showing, only a red nose and cheeks peeking through. All signs of warmth he'd shown at the hospital are gone, replaced by a cold, harsh tone. "You need to leave."

"Mr Macy, I just need to speak with her," I plead. "She's obviously confused…"

"Kaleigh, please. Don't make me call the police."

I scoff. Call the police? On *me?* I should be calling them on Emma for causing such distress on me and my family. Yet even in my desperation, I know hurling threats is not going to make the current situation better.

"Why is she doing this? Is it money? Harry and I can match whatever the tabloids will offer. Please, we only want to help."

"Kaleigh, I'm not going to say it again. Please leave now. I don't want any trouble."

"Trouble?" I say. "You don't want any trouble? Neither do I but…" I pause, hearing a clicking noise in the distance.

I turn and confirm my worst nightmare as I stare into the barrel of a long zoom lens. I chomp on the inside of my cheek to stop from crying and cradle my belly. Or maybe I should cry? If I'm caught on camera, crying pregnant lady, surely that would get me some sympathy.

I give Mr Macy one more pleading look before deciding it's best to leave.

I take a deep breath and push my shoulders back, trying to compose myself. Not that it matters now. They probably already got the perfect shot. One that makes me look deranged and desperate.

Hot tears mix with the cold rain as I waddle toward my Range Rover. Just when I'm hanging on by a thread, the wind rips my umbrella from my hand. Frustration and rage bubble inside me as the rain lashes down, soaking me completely.

I release a guttural scream. "Why is it. Always. Fucking. Raining!" I screech, kicking the gravel with my shoe in the direction of the paparazzi.

When I finally make it inside the safety of my car, I break down, smashing my hands against the steering wheel. I pull down the mirror and wipe the mascara from under my eyes, exhaling a shaky breath. I force a smile, telling myself it's okay, but it makes me look even more deranged.

Slamming the mirror back into place, I put the key in the ignition and inhale sharply through my nose before looking up one last time in the direction of Emma's room.

I expect to see closed curtains, but instead I see her pale face, smirking.

C*Leb News ✓ @CLebNewsOfficial

WAGravated: Heavily pregnant Kaleigh Creedy-Turner confronts Emma Macy after horrifying accusation. Read more at: clebnews.com/Kaleigh-turner-emma-macy

16:03   6 Mar 2025   18.3K Views
238 Reposts 1.5K Likes

Comments:

BobTheFloppp: Omfg that photo of her

CherylsBiggestFan: Proper lost her mind, hasn't she?

ThePoshestSpice: So she orchestrated her friend's abduction, took over her life, and is… mad about it now?

QueenColeen: Idk guys I kind of feel bad for her

GeorginasRing: Don't. I saw another article with side by side photos of Emma six years ago v Kaleigh. Same friends. Same boyfriend. Same clothes. Same tattoo. Same restaurants. Kaleigh just ripped off her life. And went about it in the most diabolical way possible.

18

Emma

The sun was setting by the time we pulled off the main road and headed into the forest. Nestled between rows of tall pines, the side road was barely big enough for Leila's Mini Cooper to fit through, let alone two cars.

"This really is secluded," Kaleigh said after three full minutes of passing nothing but trees. She was sitting in the middle back seat, leaning forward between Leila and me. She glanced down at her phone, which was navigating us.

"Apparently it'll be on our left in one minute."

Leila turned onto another unpaved sideroad and the cabin came into view. Its angular wooden roof was blanketed in a golden glow.

The property as a whole wasn't as nice as the photos – which was expected, seeing as the dreary backdrop for January couldn't compare to a lush summerscape – but the cabin itself didn't disappoint. The front entrance featured a set of wooden steps that lead to a double-sided wrap-around porch, adorned in twinkly fairy lights. One of my least favourite things about a January birthday was how everything suddenly went from festive and twinkly back to bland and bleak, just in time for my celebrations. So I appreciated the extra touch.

A lone magpie landed on the railing and cawed as we exited the car. Kaleigh stopped to take a photo of it, not knowing the proper etiquette.

"You have to salute it, Kay," I called out.

"Huh?" She looked up, face scrunched in confusion.

"Salute it and say 'ello to your brother!' or you'll be cursed. It's what my gran taught me."

"Ello," she said in a bad Cockney accent as the bird flew away.

I shook my head and smiled, happy she was here with me at least. Unlike Leila.

"So we're just going to camp out here for two nights?" Leila said, unimpressed. "Weather's supposed to be shit too…"

She couldn't seem to enjoy anything anymore.

I sighed. Sure, Harry and I finally had money to jet away on fancy escapes, but we both grew up holidaying in the UK, with caravan trips to the coast and mini breaks to Center Parcs. Leila, on the other hand, had been jetting away to luxury Italian villas since her mum started marrying older men with money, so she struggled to appreciate less bougie things in life.

"But wait, just think how perfect, right…" Kaleigh cut in before I could tell Leila off for being so mardy. "Candles… rain pitter-pattering. Us having wine and cheese, gossiping… or watching a movie. There's a new romcom on Netflix…" She trailed off as she danced around the corner of the porch.

Leila looked at me and rolled her eyes in a playful way. Kaleigh was the stereotypical, annoying, bubbly American to Leila's cynical Brit – and I was somewhere in between. Although, I knew there were a lot more layers to Kaleigh than that. Despite her sweet Southern belle façade, she used to be a cutthroat beauty queen. If she weren't one of my best friends, I'd need to watch my back.

"Ah, look!" Kaleigh squealed. "The hot tub is sheltered. Perfect."

Leila perked up when she saw the huge hot tub on the back deck, relenting to Kaleigh's enthusiasm.

I pulled out a bottle of champagne from one of the M&S bags. "Well, let's get the party started, shall we?"

"So have you started packing for Thailand yet?" Kaleigh asked as the three of us settled into the hot tub.

I smiled wide. "I only found out we were going last night! So yes, of course I already have things in my ASOS basket. But wait, I didn't even tell you the best present..."

"Something better than Thailand?" Kaleigh raised her eyebrows.

"He showed me a house that he wants to look at." I smirked, waiting for their reaction.

Kaleigh's jaw dropped as she squealed in delight. But Leila just furrowed her brow.

"A house?"

"Yeah," I said, annoyed again by her extra-sour attitude, which had re-established itself after the initial excitement of seeing the hot tub.

I was about to ask her what the hell her problem was,

but then I remembered things with her and her boyfriend Theo, hadn't been great lately. Not that that was a surprise to anyone. Their relationship started on a lie, her being the other woman. It would make sense that Theo would turn around and do the same to her with someone else. I wanted to feel bad, but honestly? It's what she gets for stealing someone else's fiancé.

I cleared my throat. "How's things with Theo, Leila?"

She flushed red, confirming my instincts were right. "I don't know, I'm starting to think it's run its course."

"Oh no, why?" Kaleigh asked.

"I don't know, everything he does lately seems to annoy me."

I tilted my head, confused. Was Theo the one getting bored or was it Leila?

"No way, really?" Kaleigh pouted. "He's so fit, as you Brits say... and rich!"

Leila laughed. "Well, I too am fit and rich so he's not really bringing anything extra to the table, is he?"

"Cheers to that!" Kaleigh giggled, holding up her glass.

I wanted to ask more questions but also didn't want her drama to overshadow my night. So I just clinked my glass against theirs and drank. By eight p.m., we'd finished most of the champagne and snacks, and were sitting around, bored.

"This Wi-Fi is shit, nothing will load!" Leila whined.

I pulled down to refresh my Instagram one more time, but still got the error message. I sighed. "Same."

"Mine isn't great, but seems to be working. Barely," Kaleigh replied. "We could open up the vodka and go back in the hot tub?" She shrugged.

I could tell even her positive outlook was waning.

"Or," Leila said, smirking, "I did pack a couple of dresses, in case we changed our minds and wanted to go into town…"

I was never one to turn down a night out.

19

Kaleigh

Thursday 6 March 2025

Ping. Ping. Ping.

After parking at the stadium, I turn off the ignition and reach to silence my phone. It's been pinging non-stop ever since Emma's accusation made headlines. A photo of my angry, deranged face from my meltdown yesterday is plastered on the homepage of every online media outlet, and even worse, is going viral on social media at this very moment.

I open my phone instinctively, despite telling myself not to look. *It's not going to do you any good.* And there I am, looking like a very pregnant, very manic train wreck on Emma's driveway. My wild eyes mock me, post after post, officially a mainstream meme.

You can take the girl out of the trailer park, but not the trailer park out of the girl.
She's not trailer trash.
She is. Everyone in 'Bama knows it.

139

"Oh, it's reached America now, wonderful," I mutter. My face flushes in embarrassment as I continue to scroll through the comments.

POV: You steal your best friend's life and have to finally face the consequences.

I want to reply, tell them they have no idea what they're talking about, but then I think about the trip to Thailand, my house, my diamond ring... knowing if Emma hadn't disappeared, those things probably would've been hers.

Alfie laughs from his car seat behind me, his attention focused on a cartoon. *My son*, I think, seeing both myself and Harry in his little face. *My life, not hers.*

He giggles again and the sound momentarily distracts me from all the hate that's been directed my way. Not only from the usual suspects, but from sports fans, too. Because somehow, it will be my fault if Harry makes a mistake or if Nottingham loses the game today.

I throw my head back, fighting the tears that are pooling on my lids. I try to calm the anger I feel toward Emma as I think about what Gaz did. Try to remind myself that it's her trauma speaking, not her.

But then I think of the smirk she gave me right before the news broke. *No, she knows what she's doing.* I let out a grunt of frustration.

"Mumma?" Alfie says, concerned.

I rub my hands over my eyes, unable to hold back the tears any longer.

"Mummy..."

I try to answer but my words are choked by a sob as I think of how this scandal will affect Alfie and Alice. Will they see all these horrible things being said about me one day?

"Someone hurt you?" Alfie asks, his empathy and innocence breaking through my spiralling thoughts.

"No, baby. Mummy was just playing a silly game," I say with a tear-soaked smile, grateful he's his father's son. Sweet, kind and eager to come to my defence.

"This is classic Emma," Harry had said when I told him what happened. He thought about going to see her too, but I stopped him. Said it would only fan her flames to see him defend me. He wasn't happy about it but agreed, realising I was probably right.

"Well, it's a ridiculous accusation anyway," he relented. "No one's going to believe it. But still, maybe it's best if you don't go to the match."

I debate turning the car back and driving straight home, skipping the game like Harry said. But then I click into my unanswered texts to Zara, getting angrier and angrier that she still hasn't answered, horrified that she could actually be taking Emma's accusation seriously.

> I'm so confused. Can you try to talk some sense into her? I told you she looked upset before I left the hospital.
> Hello?
> Zara, please talk to me. Listen to my side. You have to know I would never do anything to hurt her.
> Don't you see she's just mad Harry and I ended up together?

I cringe as I scroll, realising how desperate I sound. But I am desperate. I hover over the screen, my thumbs ready to type something along the lines of how I thought our friendship meant more to her over these past five years. How she's forgetting that it's me: the other victim.

But I click out of the message, unwilling to see another text go unanswered. *No*, I think. *If she's really taken Emma's side, then she can say it to my face.*

I shove my phone in my bag and swap it for concealer and mascara. I flip the driver's side mirror down and reapply my make-up, carefully guiding the wand back and forth. When I'm done, I flutter my lashes, reminding myself that the tabloid photo was just a bad shot taken at a very bad angle. I mouth my affirmations.

You're beautiful. You're happy. You're safe.

"We're going to have a great time at Daddy's game," I say to Alfie as I pull him out of the car seat.

He wraps his little arms around my neck as I position him on my hip, and walk with purpose towards the stadium.

I hold the metal railing with one hand and Alfie with the other as I make my way down to our seats. "Excuse me, please," I say, as I come upon a woman blocking the aisle.

"Sorry, love," she says, letting me pass. But her expression contorts into one of disgust as soon as she sees me.

I squeeze by awkwardly, wondering if I'm being paranoid. That suddenly every single person in Nottingham not only recognises me, but knows about and believes Emma's accusation. But the more people I see with sour faces, and the more whispers I hear, I'm sure it's not just in my head.

To my relief, Simon meets me at the stairs again, and helps us to our seats.

"Surprised you came," Simon says as he lifts Alfie up.

"Maybe I shouldn't have," I sigh, darting my eyes around the crowd.

"Eh, fuck 'em," he says. "You're here now, let's enjoy it. It's gonna be fine."

Robbie takes Alfie from Simon and ruffles his hair before he greets me with a kiss on the cheek.

"Lorraine coming?" I ask as I squeeze past.

"Nah," he says. "Not tonight. Wasn't feelin' great."

My heart sinks, wondering if she hates me too.

I try to focus on Harry and the other players taking the field, but I'm too distracted by the tension in the air.

I look around, trying to find the other wives and girlfriends. Maybe if we can put on a united front, people will see Emma's claims are nonsense. But as I try to get their attention, I realise they're ignoring me. It's as if I'm invisible.

I see Vic and wave, hoping for a smile or any type of acknowledgement, but she quickly looks away. My stomach drops as I try to get Abby's attention next, but she won't look at me either.

"Lu Lu," I say, spotting Lucy to the right of the row in front of me. I say her name with a subtle Southern twang and the same endearing tone I used all the times I'd gone to console her when the tabloids were tearing her down. A reminder that it's now her turn to be there for me.

She turns around, cheeks flushed red, and I know she's panicking, wondering what to do. To my utter relief, she gives me a sad smile before squeezing past Jake's family to get to me.

"Kaleigh, I'm surprised you came." Her eyes dart from one side to the other, seemingly on edge.

"Why wouldn't I?" I say. "I have nothing to hide."

Lucy exhales and leans closer. "Then why would Emma say that?"

I raise my brows and open my hands. "Because she's mad about me and Harry."

Lucy's hardened expression softens, and I realise then she's looking at me in the same way I used to look at her. With pity.

I ball my right hand into a fist, letting my nails dig into my skin. Mad at Emma, again, for putting me in this ridiculous situation. *Stay composed*, I tell myself. *Losing your temper is not going to win you any favours.*

I bite my tongue and play into the pity instead. "I was a victim too, Luce. I'm not the enemy. We just need to help Emma see that…" I pause, realising that Lucy is no longer paying attention to me. Her stare is fixed elsewhere.

I cringe when I spot cross-armed Zara raising an eyebrow at Lucy. A gesture to stop talking to me. My eyes widen as I look into hers, pleading with her to talk to me. But she narrows them and turns away.

I don't mean to cry, but Zara's hateful reaction catches me off guard. I'm gutted.

"Why don't we get out of here?" a voice says behind me.

A hand touches my shoulder and I turn to see Simon. I look to Alfie and then Robbie, who mouths, "I'll bring him over later."

I nod and lean into Simon, keeping my head down to avoid the hate-filled stares as the crowd applauds my departure.

20

Harry

Harry cracks his neck from side to side, jogging in place to keep warm. A small child, not much older than his three-year-old son, beams up at him. Harry smiles down at the boy and takes his hand, copying the rest of the players and their mascots.

He should feel excited and happy to be here, despite the stakes. He pictures himself jumping in front of the crowd at the end of the game as they bellow "Sweet Caroline". That this game will prove to England's manager that Harry is ready to take them all the way.

But with all the publicity around Emma's accusation against Kaleigh, the timing couldn't be worse. And it makes him anything but excited. He hums one of his favourite country songs to try and calm down and it works momentarily. But then he thinks of Kaleigh. He wishes he tried harder to convince her not to come. He hoped no one would believe Kaleigh could do what Emma said, that

Emma was just bitter and jealous. But the chants and insults being hurled at him as he makes his way onto the pitch prove otherwise.

It takes him back to that game five years ago. The sinking feeling in his stomach the entire day. The elation when he sent the game into extra time. His team piling on top of him. His racing heart before he took the final penalty. The rival supporters chanting obscenities as he did it.

Expecting a similarly rowdy crowd tonight, Harry's manager asked to meet with him before the match.

"Remember, Turner, you're one of the guys the younger lads look up to, so tune it out, you can't lose your head like you did at training," said Si Upton, the AFC Nottingham's gaffer.

"Yes, boss," Turner replied.

Upton forced Harry to meet his gaze. "You sure you're alright? Because if you need some time to be with your family and process everything that's happening—"

"No. I need to play, that's what I need." Harry looked him dead in the eye as he said it, hoping to convey the desperation to him. How he took this more seriously than anything. He could already imagine what was being said by the supporters. *He don't get paid millions to not put football first.*

"Okay," Upton relented. "Okay."

Unlike the England manager, Paulo, Upton had a warm demeanour. They both cared about their players tremendously, Harry knew that, but Harry always felt more of a connection to Upton. He'd been Harry's mentor since he was twenty, when he transferred back to Nottingham after a short stint at Chelsea. Upton was there five years ago when Harry's world turned upside down, there to support him through the aftermath of the attack, even showing up to an organised search in the woods. The last thing Harry wanted was to let him down.

With scores level near the end of the first half, Harry's patience wanes. He tries to hold on, but he starts to lose it every time he's near the away section. Usually, he can handle heckling from the crowd – he's been dealing with it for ten years now – but tonight is especially brutal.

He lets out a groan as he catches himself being distracted once again from the play at hand. He lifts his hand to signal he's open but the ball is blocked. He waits for the throw-in as his mind drifts back to Emma and how jealous she's always been. It was one of the things he struggled to deal with the most. How she was always paranoid he was cheating on her. And sure, sometimes she was right, but even when he wasn't, she couldn't get it out of her head. Could never let anything go.

If she had accused him instead, he would've understood. Because he also blamed himself. But to accuse Kaleigh at eight months pregnant? That was downright cruel.

When he first met Kaleigh as Emma's friend, she was this bubbly, happy-go-lucky girl. And while that side of her is still there, she's hardened. And he doesn't want to see her put through the wringer again.

Harry heard the story from Kaleigh. Remembers how she broke down when she told him how the events unfolded that night. She was angry at herself for not fighting the attackers off and hiding instead. He wonders if that's why Emma is angry? But what did she expect?

And why would she believe it gives her the right to ruin Kaleigh's life like this?

Unlike the press claimed, he and Kaleigh genuinely did not get together until a year after it all happened. They'd flirted one or two times, yeah. But it was innocent. He'd been purely focused on football, his saving grace, the only way he coped. And Kaleigh brought out the best in him, made him a good person. He'd never go back to the guy he was.

The thought reminds him of who he is now – who he wants to be – and it helps him refocus on the game. Harry runs in a half-circle, and then signals once again that he's open. Evans obliges and lobs the ball his way, but the defender gets to it first and kicks it behind them. Harry should be annoyed but the ref calls a corner, which is his speciality.

Harry glances at Evans who is now down the touchline from him. He moves his hands up and down in a calming motion. This is it, Harry thinks, imagining the ball curving towards the back corner of the net. Harry pulls his foot up to his hands and stretches his quad before taking a few steps back.

But as he's about to raise his hand and boot the ball, something hits him in the back. His blood boils. *These fucking pricks*. He whips around and grabs the bottle, trying to control the impulse not to chuck it back into the crowd, at the coked-up pisshead who threw it at him in the first place.

He pictures Kaleigh's face, trying to calm him down. How disappointed she'd be if he lost his head. He grunts in frustration and tosses it to the side, before looking to the assistant ref.

"Fucking do something about them idiots," he demands as more shit is thrown onto the pitch.

Then Harry makes the mistake of looking up, staring into the crowd of angry faces in puffer jackets screaming, spit flying as they shake their fists at him.

Harry grabs his crotch with one hand then shakes his fist back at them. *Fucking wankers. Three brain cells between the lot of them.*

Porter runs over, grabs Harry's shoulder and pulls him away. "Don't let them get in your head, mate. Let's just do a short."

Shaken, Harry agrees. As he and Porter set up the play, the crowd starts singing.

"What they sayin, now?" Harry asks, unable to make it out over their thick Scottish accents.

Porter shakes his head. "You don't wanna know."

But then he hears it.

"Turner's missus is a killer. Sold his ex to the highest bidder!"

He turns around and tells the fans to shut up and fuck off. He can't control himself. The smiles on their fat, ugly faces make him want to punch every single one of them. To make matters worse, he then sees the sign they're holding up. It's a picture of Kaleigh behind bars, with dicks from all directions shooting cum at her. It's the most depraved and enraging thing he's ever seen.

Just as he's about to turn around though, he sees a man smirking at him. Hood up. He waves a phone at Harry. "Pick it up next time," the man mouths. "Bloody coward."

Before he's aware, almost like he's watching himself from outside his own body, he's storming towards the crowd.

Thankfully, Porter and Viviano pull him back before he can climb over the wall. He screams obscenities, the ref blows his whistle and gives him a yellow. In response, Upton subs him out.

Harry kicks an empty bottle towards the bench as he exits the pitch.

"Pack it in, Turner! Now!" Upton shouts as Harry passes. He's angrier than Harry has ever seen him, red-faced and stern. He crosses his arms and turns back to the pitch as Harry sits down and puts his head in his hands.

Harry glances at the giant clock on the stadium screen to check the amount of stoppage time left. Four minutes. He wishes he could go out there, score a last-minute goal for his team, wipe the smug smiles off the rival fans' faces. But losing his head also lost him that chance, so he's forced to helplessly watch the opposition take the lead as punishment.

He kicks at the ground with his boot, angry at himself, angry at the lowlifes that riled him up, and angry at the squad for not being able to keep up their winning streak without him.

The only silver lining in it all is knowing that he *is* needed. Hopefully Paulo Santino will see that as well. The thought of England's manager makes his anxiety worse.

All this Emma bullshit needs to end. But with the tabloids and fans taking her accusation seriously, he fears this is just the beginning. He rubs his hands over his face, sweating even though he's been stagnant for the past half hour. The thought of this drama carrying on is something that makes him feel physically ill. He wonders what else Emma has said to the police. Could they be building a case against him now too, while he sits here like a fucking loser? A sitting duck.

He jumps up to his feet and paces to the end of the bench and back, trying to distract himself from the thought of his career crashing down on him, everything he's worked so hard for.

His goal was to make it at least another ten years, to play into his late thirties like Giggs and Ronaldo, play at least three World Cups. But he's certain to peak soon, so it needs to happen for him this time around. It has to. It's non-negotiable.

The ref sounds the final whistle and the Nottingham players sluggishly walk back to the bench while the others celebrate. He doesn't offer false words of comfort or motivation. No "good game, mate, we'll get 'em next time." He doesn't bother with pats on the back. He's too annoyed, too frustrated.

He drags his feet onto the pitch towards the winning team, following the usual post-match routine. He could do without this farce today, but doesn't want to risk Upton's ire again. His eyes meet Theo Abara's as they approach midfield. Abara's jaw clenches when he sees Harry.

Really can't deal with this right now, Harry thinks.

Theo Abara, Leila's boyfriend from five years ago, was once one of Harry's teammates and best friends. They stopped talking after what happened to the girls.

Harry thinks back to Las Vegas in 2019, to their season together before he transferred up north.

"You alright, mate?" Abara says on his approach, unsmiling.

KELLY AND KRISTINA MANCARUSO

"Yeah," is all Harry manages.

The last time he properly spoke to Theo was during the search for Leila and Emma, deep in the woods, careful not to be within earshot of the police. Harry can feel the emotions from all those years ago. The highs and lows. Elation. Disappointment. Optimism. Dread. Until nothing was left but fear. Terror.

"We good?" Abara asks, meeting Harry's gaze. An understanding passes between them.

"We're good," Harry confirms, before walking away.

21

Emma

Friday 24 January 2020

Nottingham city centre was even busier than I anticipated when we first arrived. Groups of uni students stumbled down the streets together, dressed for summer, while packs of men decked out in their AFC Nottingham kits crowded the pubs to watch the match.

We paused outside a Wetherspoons so I could check the score. My heart fluttered when I realised they were level with only a few minutes left. Harry had been so stressed about this game, barely getting any sleep, worried if he didn't start scoring he might not be selected for the England squad.

"Bloody Turner, off his game tonight, isn't he?" a man grumbled next to me.

"Overrated, mate, been tellin' ya," said another. "Get 'im fuckin' gone, I say."

"Let's go," I said to the girls. "Can't watch."

But as we walked away, the crowd started to cheer in excitement.

"'Ere we go, 'ere we go!"

"Go on, Turner, go on!"

I froze, holding my breath in anticipation, praying for them to erupt in cheers. *C'mon, babe, c'mon.*

Instead of joy, the crowd erupted in anger.

"Foul! Foul!"

"That's a fuckin' card, ref, what you playin' at!"

"If that's not a fuckin' penalty—"

"Penalty, Em," Kaleigh exclaimed. "Looks like Harry's taking it!"

"Oh no, I can't." I pulled the girls in the other direction. I could never watch penalties. Couldn't watch anyone on the squad take them. They made me feel faint. A missed penalty meant at least a week of him beating himself up.

I remembered when we were younger and all he would do was practice. His dad was relentless – and often too harsh on him – but Harry was equally as obsessed with the game. It was his life. I could only imagine how Robbie was handling this now, no doubt watching through gritted teeth, rubbing his hands together.

I couldn't escape the game though. As we turned the corner, supporters in green shirts crowded the entrances to every pub, craning their necks from outside in an effort to see the screens. I braced myself for the sighs of disappointed, them all cursing my boyfriend, foaming at the mouth about how they're gonna kill him, but instead, they burst into wild applause. He'd scored.

Kaleigh turned to me and wrapped me in a hug. We jumped together in celebration. I squinted at the TV, just in time for a close-up of Harry to be shown. You would've thought he missed the kick by his expression, which was more pained than joyful. He smiled when Evans and McGugan jumped on him though.

As the rest of the squad piled on to congratulate him, the girls and I found ourselves in a similar situation outside the pub, getting pushed about by overly excited supporters.

"Fuck's sake!" Leila screamed as beer flew through the air. "Where are we, the zoo? Like a pack of fucking animals."

She linked her arm through mine, I instinctively linked mine through Kaleigh's, and we escaped the crowd, nearly getting run over by a black cab in the process.

I smiled as the men broke into a rendition of "Sweet Caroline", happy for Harry and for myself, now a safe distance away.

We walked down the pavement towards one of our favourite cocktail bars – a new Cuban place that opened a few years ago – but Leila, who was still complaining about the beer in her hair, accidentally bumped into a group of men.

"Watch yourself, sweetheart," one said to Leila, who clearly had no interest in apologising.

"Nottingham, full of miserable cunts," he mumbled as we hurried away.

I scowled, wanting to tell them to piss off, but Kaleigh dragged me away before I could open my mouth. "Slimeballs," she said. "Let it go."

"Oi, I know you," the one in the red shirt called out. "Yeah, you're 'Arry Turner's bird!" he said in a thick Yorkshire accent. "Fuckin' wanker should have been carded for that handball not given a penalty." Another yells, fist raging in the air. "And you, yeah, you're with Theo Abara!"

"Shit."

We picked up the pace as they started to make lewd and disgusting comments, quickly turning into a cocktail bar we knew they wouldn't be granted entry to.

The red lights and Latin music of the venue instantly shifted our moods, and we all breathed a collective sigh of relief.

"Starting to think a boring evening at the cabin would've been the better choice," I said.

"Yeah, we didn't think this through, did we?" Kaleigh agreed.

"Tomorrow we're deffo staying in," Leila said. "But right now, I need a fucking drink."

After hours bar-hopping, knocking back double gin and tonics and tequila shots, we reached the pivotal point in the night where you decide to stay or go. Where your body, which seems to be more difficult to control than earlier, hints it's time to leave, but your mind, desperate to keep the buzz going for just a little while longer, convinces you to stay.

I started to think of my bed, merely a few minutes from where we were, and considered crashing there with the girls. But then I realised I didn't have my key, and Harry was staying at a hotel with the rest of the team, so there was no way in. We'd still have to go back to the cabin. I dreaded the 45-minute drive.

"Hey, you wanna head back soon?" I asked Kaleigh, who was ordering more drinks from the bar. I had to scream in her ear to make sure she heard me over the loud music.

She turned around, huge smile on her face. "Sure… After these." She handed me two plastic shot glasses, one filled with yellow liquid, another brown. I crinkled my nose in disgust as I got a whiff of lemon vodka and sambuca. I turned my head, inhaling the air behind me instead, but that wasn't much better. We'd ended up at the kind of place we used to frequent at uni, one that smelled of cigarettes and cheap sprays, mixed with body odour and sweat.

"Where's Leila?" Kaleigh mouthed.

I looked around and shrugged. She'd been with me just a few minutes ago.

"Is it me or is she in an extra bad mood tonight?" I asked Kaleigh.

Kaleigh took one of the shots and held it up to cheers me. "Ugh gross," she said, face contorted in disgust after she drank it. "Um, yeah she's not in the best of spirits, is she?"

"Which is why I'm worried where she's gone." I looked around again, still not seeing Leila, so decided to call her. But when I went to look for my phone in my purse, I couldn't find it.

"Shit, my phone," I said, starting to panic. "Be right back." I pushed my way through the crowd and into the bathroom. I checked the stall for my phone, dread pooling in my stomach when I didn't see it.

Where did I last have it? I asked myself. *When I was in the bathroom with Leila, taking selfies. Maybe she has it?*

Thankfully, she did. When I returned back to Kaleigh, Leila was with her, holding my gold glitter phone case over her head.

"Where'd you go?" I asked.

"Outside for a smoke. You left it on the sink."

I frowned, not remembering that, but then again, I did have a lot to drink.

"Okay, we have to stick together now!" Kaleigh slurred. "My phone is dead." She hiccupped, releasing an odour of sweet liquor into the air.

"Let's get one more drink," Leila suggested. She didn't wait for us to respond before holding her hand up for the bartender. I also knew that one more drink didn't mean just one.

Two more drinks later, and we finally were leaving. But as we walked up the stairs out of the basement club, the same group of men that we bumped into earlier stopped us.

Worried they'd followed us, I tried to ignore them, but one grabbed Leila's arm. "Get the fuck off me, creep," she yelled. But instead of moving away, he moved towards her. "Aw, c'mon love, gizzus a kiss."

It was like everything went in slow motion. He grabbed her head and kissed her on the mouth. His friend was filming, laughing hysterically, as if watching a man assault a woman was the funniest thing he'd ever seen. I shoved him away at the same time Leila did. She threw her hand out and clawed him in the face.

"You're a feisty one, aren't ya?" He laughed, but his eyes were full of fury.

Before he could retaliate, the bouncer jumped in, grabbing him by his collar and dragging him up the stairs. Leila burst into tears, as did Kaleigh, as we tried to get out to street level and away from the men.

SIZZLE

HARRY TURNER'S FURY AS WIFE KALEIGH HUMILIATED AT MATCH

Harry Turner's bride is shunned by fellow WAGs at Europa League match as he takes his anger out on the crowd

C*LEB NEWS UK

WAG WARS: EVERYTHING YOU NEED TO KNOW ABOUT THE KALEIGH CREEDY-TURNER SCANDAL

As Kaleigh Turner's fellow Nottingham WAGs turn on her following Emma Macy's horrifying accusation, speculation as to what really unfolded in the woods that night between the former best friends is at an all-time high

BEHIND THE NET

AFC NOTTINGHAM FANS SUPPORTERS CALL FOR KALEIGH TURNER BAN FOR REST OF SEASON AS HARRY TURNER FAMILY DRAMA LEADS TO DEVASTATING RESULT

"Honestly, if it were up to me, footballers would be banned from dating or getting married. Too much distraction," says a Merry Men supporter after the match, while another called for Kaleigh Turner to be deported back to the States

DAILY NEWS ONLINE

"IT'S DISGUSTING… KALEIGH TURNER SHOULD BE IN JAIL," SAYS VIVIAN ADAMS

The outspoken "Tight Women" presenter made her thoughts known about the latest WAG drama, claiming how "disgusting" it is "people like Kaleigh Turner" sit on mounds of money while "actual hard-working people suffer"

22

Kaleigh

I draw the blinds shut, unwilling to give the paparazzi another photo op. It makes the house darker, but I don't mind. It's more fitting of my mood.

I rub my hands over my face and lay my phone on the island counter. A montage of last night plays on repeat, cutting from a depraved sign of me made by rival fans, to Harry nearly rushing the stands, to me being ushered out by Simon like a coward as fans cheered.

What the hell was I thinking? I ask, even though I know the answer. I was in denial. I had hoped at least Zara or one of my friends from the last five years would come to my defence. That they would at least be willing to hear my side of things, rather than blindly believing Emma.

But as the tabloids pointed out, it was clear the WAGs of Nottingham had taken a side. And it wasn't mine. Which unfortunately meant the public and the media wouldn't take it either. The stories grew more savage by the hour, claiming that I'd grown obsessed with Emma and planned to take over her life.

Photos of me side by side with Emma seemed to be the media's favourite at the moment. They showed comparisons of when we both wore our hair in a bun, or when we both wore a pink dress, or our matching tattoos – which, of course, they failed to mention was Emma's idea in the first place. Not mine.

And then there were the comments which were even worse. Especially after Harry's on-field outburst and AFC Nottingham's loss, which plenty of users blamed me for. Suddenly overwhelmed, I throw my tea in the sink and watch as the ceramic shatters into hundreds of little pieces. Just like my life.

I walk past the mirror and catch my reflection before quickly looking away. I don't look "glowing" or "radiant" like I'm supposed to. I look haggard and dirty, still in an oversized tee and sweats. I turn away, thinking of how this week was supposed to be packed with fancy lunches and business meetings, but instead, my afternoon will consist of more doom scrolling, anxiety attacks, and a visit from Jackie Kilner, the best in crisis PR. A stark reminder of how much can change in less than seventy-two hours. How, since Emma's accusation, I've lost almost everything. All of my brand partnerships are in the gutter. My maternity line sales have plummeted. My publicist and social media manager have "respectfully resigned". I've had to limit comments on my Instagram, killing engagement. My housekeeper has asked for extended leave. And, oh yeah, I have no friends.

I think of the slanderous tabloids, how I used to look at

them and shake my head, pitying the targets of the cruel headlines. And here I am, the new punching bag.

I eye my phone warily, still upset over Zara's post this morning. A photo of her and Emma. Zara's hair is tied back in a low bun. She's squinting as if to show how hard she is hugging Emma who looks like she's finally putting some weight back on her bones. Emma isn't looking at the camera though. She's looking down at the floor at the angle she always liked to be photographed in. The caption reads, *Love this woman. So blessed to have her back.*

A horrible thought comes into my mind then. That life would be so much better if Emma had really died that night.

My mother's name flashes across my phone screen and I don't hesitate to answer, not like usual.

"Hey, Mama," I say.

"How ya doing, lovebug?"

The corner of my lips curve into a smile, the phrase reminding me of coming home from school as a kid. But the positive moment is fleeting.

"I'm... I miss home," I say for the first time in a very long time. Surprising myself as much as her.

"Oh," she says, also caught off guard. "Well, home misses you, honey. You sure you can't just come? Get away from it all?"

I wrap my finger around the edge of the curtain and move it to the side, counting three more media vans.

"I wish," I say. "But I'm too pregnant to fly, remember?"

"Oh gosh, of course." She laughs. "Well, soon enough, alright?"

"Yeah," I say, fighting back tears, wishing I could escape. But then I realise even if I wasn't pregnant, I still wouldn't be allowed to leave the country with the investigation.

"Well, I just wanted to check in on you. It's so dang crazy anyone would believe what she said about you. Hurts my heart, it does."

My mother's instinct to assume the best of me cuts me to my core. I don't deserve her loyalty, not the way I've mistreated her and ignored her over the past few years.

"What are you going to do? Hire a fancy lawyer or something?"

"I have that specialist coming over any minute now," I say, checking the time. "So, we'll see what she says."

"Well, don't let me keep you, handle your business and it'll all work out. Just remember to fight with your wits."

"I know, Mama," I say, feeling another strange sensation.

I hang up seconds before Jackie rings at the gate, thankful I wasn't left alone with my thoughts and the overwhelming temptation to doom scroll again.

I buzz her through before quickly cleaning up the broken mug and turning on a few kitchen lights.

"Thank you for coming on such short notice," I say, extending my hand.

Dressed head to toe in black, she looks like she's here for a funeral rather than a business meeting. She moves her leather bag to her left hand, extending her right to greet me. Her expression is as hardened as her slicked back, raven hair. "Let's see if you still thank me after my assistant sends you my bill."

I hesitate, not sure if she's joking or not until she cracks a smile. I give an awkward laugh and move to the side to let her in.

"Shifting priorities is the nature of my job," she explains, as she looks down at her shoes.

"Don't worry about it," I say, motioning for her to leave her black kitten heels on. "We'll just be going to the kitchen area straight ahead."

She nods, following me down the hall. "When Emma's accusation made headlines…" she whistles louder than the sound of her heels clacking on the marble tile floor, "I knew I wanted this case."

"Mmm." I'm not sure whether to be grateful or offended. I choose to be grateful, thinking of all the successful cases she's worked on before. A cheating scandal of a high-ranking minister, an Olympian caught using drug enhancers, a pop star arrested for murder, CEOs, TV hosts, on and on. All of whom have been able to recover from their scandal.

I sit down beside her, momentarily forgetting my manners. "Sorry," I say, standing. "Can I get you something to drink? Coffee, tea?"

"No thank you," she says, pulling out a black metal water bottle, notebook and pen.

I sit silently, unsure of what to say as she flips to a fresh page and writes the date. "Okay, so let's start with the 'don'ts'. Get those out of the way, yeah?"

I nod, trying to get comfortable in one of my contemporary dining chairs.

"Don't go outside until the frenzy dies down." She writes this in caps and circles it before looking to my belly. "If you think, 'Oh, I'm craving a kebab or a fancy doughnut, I'll just pop out and get it.' Think of your last cover photo and think again."

I shudder, thinking back to the horrendous photo of me at Emma's, mid-meltdown. And of my head buried into Simon's jacket as he escorted me out of the stadium. "For the next few weeks, delivery is your friend. As am I. Which brings me to my next point. Don't go venting to any of your friends." She puts air quotes around the word friends.

Jackie looks at me, eyebrow raised, and I deflate. "Happens with every case unfortunately. But look on the bright side, you'll end up with the people who matter most in the end."

I think of my mother, Harry and his family, knowing that as long as they stick by me, then I'll be okay. I start to wonder if I can convince Harry to transfer to the MLS. Messi is there now, so maybe he'd consider it.

"Your old friends are your enemies right now," Jackie continues. "You need to imagine any one of them could be talking to the press. So be careful of who you talk to and what you say. Got it?"

I think of how Natasha was the only one to reach out since, saying she's there for me. Too bad she's in Barcelona.

"Got it," I confirm to Jackie.

"And finally, don't go on social media."

I bite my lip as my phone continues to buzz in the background.

Jackie holds out her hand, palm up. "Give it to me."

I don't argue, feeling like a child who's too tired to disobey. She turns the phone back to me. "Now punch in your code and go to settings."

I do as she says.

She scrolls down each one of my social media apps and hits delete. "It's for the best right now. Believe me. The internet brings out the worst of the worst, and no person is meant to see or hear the worst about themselves. So not only will this save your sanity, but it will also help the fire burnout faster. Because if you don't give the paparazzi or social media anything to fuel it, then it'll die out once another scandal comes around to take its place."

I raise a brow.

"It'll happen sooner than you think," she says, sliding my phone back.

I turn it over, feeling lighter already. Yet, I'm lost as to what the hell I'm supposed to do in the meantime.

As if she read my mind, she moves on to just that: stay inside, focus on my family, watch and think happy things.

"Is that all?" I ask, wondering if her only advice is to disappear.

"For phase one, yes." She smiles.

I let out an exasperated sigh, my anxiety starting to creep back in. "And what's phase two?"

Jackie exhales. I brace myself, knowing that if she's hesitating then it's probably because I'm not going to like what she has to say. "You need to take back control of the narrative. Make the public doubt what Emma has to say."

I lean forward, intrigued but also confused as to how. Because if there were an obvious solution, I would have already done it by now.

She clasps her hands together and ticks her tongue. "You have to sue for defamation."

I open my mouth to speak but I am speechless. Her suggestion feels wrong on so many levels. "Sue Emma?" I say, the only words I'm able to get out.

"No, no," she says. "You wouldn't be suing her – you can't, I looked into it. If she had made the claim publicly, you could, but it looks like she only said this to the police, which she has every right to. But obviously this leaked somehow. And the tabloids covering it, well, the way this has all snowballed, you could have a case against some of them, as well as anyone who has publicly spread the allegation. Like your 'friend' Zara here who has been commenting publicly about it on social media."

My jaw drops and I flush with embarrassment.

"And don't even think about reaching out to her about this, best to blindside her, along with the rest of them."

"You want me to sue Zara Becker?" I say, eyes wide. "That's like waking a dragon."

"You are a dragon. Well, you need to be one now at least."

"But still, suing anyone would surely make me look like more of a villain, no?" I say, perplexed.

"It will also make you look more innocent, like you're fighting this and are happy to go to court if need be. These stories are causing irreparable damage to your brand. We have to respond from a position of strength. Remind everyone that you're innocent until proven guilty."

I sigh, wanting to continue my argument that I think it's a bad idea. But then I start to think through everything that's happened. The dirty looks, the tabloids, the paparazzi, getting shunned by Zara – which honestly hurts more than the death threats and loss of sponsors.

I wonder if this is what Emma wanted. For my life to fall apart. I think of how close we once were and wonder how she could wish that on me. It's not like I wished any of this on her, regardless of what she thinks.

My eyes sting with tears, angry at how the world works. Knowing how my situation looks. I picture Emma taking my place then, in my garden playing with Alfie and Harry.

Jackie is right, I can't sit back any longer. I have to fight. For myself, for my reputation, my dignity, my freedom. And for my family.

I don't want to open Pandora's box. But what choice do I have?

I give Jackie the okay to work with the solicitor.

Seemingly pleased, she starts packing up her things. "One last question. Is there anything else I should know? As much as I love to do it to other people, I don't like to be blindsided."

I pause, debating whether or not I should tell her everything that happened that night. But that was a can of worms I wouldn't dare open.

"Not that I can think of," I lie.

23

Emma

Saturday 25 January 2020 1:45-2:45 a.m.

The first half of the Uber ride passed in a drunken blur. I stared out of the window, mindlessly watching the raindrops rush across the glass as the car sped down the carriageway. Nothing but headlights illuminated the dark winding road ahead of us, and the only sounds were the squeaking of the windshield wipers and Leila moaning about the lack of phone service. She'd posted a teary video to Instagram while we sat in traffic on our way out of the city centre, and was annoyed she could no longer load new comments.

The car slowed as it turned down the narrow country lane, signalling we'd officially entered the dead zone around the cabin. It was eerie, how unsettling the atmosphere was in the darkness. Like we weren't supposed to be there.

"I can't wait to be in Thailand," I said. "No rain, just sunshine."

"Aren't you going in June?" Kaleigh replied, through drunken, squinted eyes. "That's monsoon season..."

She swayed in motion with the car and I worried she was going to be sick.

"Oh, thanks for raining on my parade."

She hiccupped. "Just saying. But hey, maybe it'll also rain diamonds if you know what I mean." She winked, before hiccupping again.

"He's def gonna propose. Don't you think Harry will propose to Emma in Thailand, Lei?" Kaleigh turned to Leila, who scoffed.

"Honestly, I think he's only taking you there to make up for the cheating. Pretend he's a good guy."

I winced at the unexpected response.

"Leila, why would you say that?" Kaleigh said, eyes wide. She seemed much more alert now, almost like she was shocked out of her drunken stupor.

"What?" Leila said. "You asked me a question, I gave you an answer."

"Oh, fuck off, Leila," I said, done with her attitude. "I should've told you to go home earlier. I knew from the moment we arrived you'd be a miserable cow all night."

"I was just fucking assaulted, Emma, okay?" Leila raised her voice. "You'd be pretty upset too."

I wanted to say it was "just a kiss" and to get over it, but I didn't want to be that person. Regardless of how annoyed I was.

The Uber pulled up to the cabin and Leila jumped out before the driver stopped. Angry, I stormed after her. "You know, just because your relationship with Theo sucks doesn't mean mine does. Can't you be happy for me?"

"Leave it, Emma," she replied, running through the rain to the cabin's porch.

"Leave it? No, you've been such a bitch recently, and on my birthday no less. And then you want to say these horrible things about my relationship for no reason and expect me to 'leave it?' Fuck off, honestly."

Leila stopped and turned, fury in her eyes. "No reason?" She laughed. "I don't want to hear you go on and on about perfect Harry when we know he is a conniving, cheating, disgusting, lying bastard."

"Leila, chill out!" Kaleigh said, finally catching up with us. "We don't know that—"

"No, Kaleigh, I know. *I* know." Leila emphasized the "I". "*I* know Harry is cheating on you, Emma, because *I* fucked him. Okay? Multiple times. Is that what you wanted to hear? He's been fucking ME."

Kaleigh let out a horrified gasp, but I froze, sure I'd heard her wrong.

"What did you say?" I forced myself to breathe, to focus on the droplets of water showering down on us.

"I said, I'm fucking your lying boyfriend," Leila replied.

I recoiled, as if the words had physically slapped me across the face. The past six months started to replay through my mind, all the times Leila had stayed over, how she'd started to visit from London more than ever. Lying to me. Betraying me.

Heat radiated through my body. Within seconds it felt as if my blood was literally boiling.

"I'm going to fucking kill you."

I ran at her, claws out, with the full intention of causing as much harm as possible.

NEW DEVELOPMENT: HARRY WAS HAVING AN AFFAIR WITH LEILA!

7 March 2025 10:01pm

Wow, does this case just keep on giving.

Sources are now claiming that Harry Turner had been cheating on Emma Macy at the time of the attack... but not with who you think. No, Harry Turner wasn't sleeping with Kaleigh Turner (that we know of), he was having an affair with Theo Abara's girlfriend, Leila Adler.

Do we think Harry Turner had more to do with the attack than anyone assumed? Or does this give Theo Abara motive?

Comments:

Sleuthanie: Kaleigh wanted Emma and Leila out of the way so she could have Harry all to herself, all makes sense now

   SandraBollocks: Definitely, I heard she had posters of footballers in her room growing up. Sounds like she calculated this from early on.

Murder4Sport: I always thought Harry Turner got off too easily, same with Abara

   TruthSeeker: They have alibis!

HarlowsNextVictim: Maybe Abara's ex took revenge? Things were nasty between them.

BTSarmy4life: Surely this just proves Harry Turner is a liar?

24

Charlie

Saturday 8 March 2025

My friend's two golden retrievers come bounding towards my car as I creep down the unpaved road – if you can even call it that. The surface is so riddled with potholes, it's more like an obstacle course. Kate claps her hands to call her dogs back while I park.

After a knackering week, we thought it'd do us both good to meet for a morning walk and catch up outside in the crisp country air. We're meeting at Sherwood Pines in Mansfield, near Kate's home. Not far from where the Nightmare in Notts attack happened.

I carefully nestle my vehicle into one of the makeshift off-road spaces carved out by others who, like me, refuse to pay a six-quid car park fee.

"Hello, doggies," I say once I get out of the car, excited to see them.

I'd love to get a dog of my own one day, but I'm not home enough at the moment to make it work; I feel bad enough leaving my cat for hours on end. Plus, I'm not sure Beans would love a canine companion.

After I fuss Mabel and Molly, who is already half-black from the mud, I greet Kate with a kiss on the cheek. A knowing look passes between us, as if to say "what a week".

"How's it been then?" I ask as we start our trek down the forest path.

"Tough," she says.

I swallow hard, thinking of the court case against the football coach who was preying on young boys.

"Honestly, I can't wait for it to be over," Kate says. "And for him to hopefully spend his life behind bars, while people like you pick up the pieces." She knocks me with her elbow.

I give her a wry expression, knowing it's likely I'd cross paths with one of the victims eventually.

"But how are things with you?" Kate asks. "How's everything with Emma Macy going? I saw the news, it's all kicking off between her and Kaleigh Turner."

I shake my head. "And that's not even the latest development."

She raises an eyebrow, clearly waiting for me to expand.

I hesitate, knowing I shouldn't really disclose anything. But it's Kate. I trust her. Plus, I already had to tell Maynard since it's relevant to the investigation, and once the police know, nothing stays secret for long. Especially not something like this.

"Sorry, what?" she says once I tell her about Leila and Harry. "Leila Adler? And Harry Turner?"

I shh Kate, worried someone will hear, even though there doesn't seem to be anyone for miles, just endless trees.

"If you would've said Kaleigh and Harry, I would not have bat an eyelid. But Leila?" She shakes her head in disbelief. "How did the police miss that? Surely there would've been some evidence of this before?"

I throw my hands in the air as we trudge through the mud.

"I suppose he is the star of the beloved AFC Nottingham. Plus, an asset for England…"

"And what?" I laugh incredulously. "You think they purposefully let him off for homicide so Nottingham could stay top of the league?"

She shrugs, holding my gaze, and the more I consider the theory, the more possible it seems. I think of Maynard, who already seemed partial to the Turners, being slightly dismissive of Emma's claims, constantly commenting on how much she's "been through", how "unstable" she is.

"Especially someone with that kind of money," Kate continues. "Bribery and hush money would be easy to find. Plus, it's often the boyfriend, as we know…"

"Well, then there's also Theo Abara, Leila's boyfriend at the time," I add. "Same thing would apply to him. But what would we be looking at then? A crime of passion? Why hurt the other girls? Why would Theo hurt Leila? Why would Harry hurt Leila AND Emma? Surely he'd leave one standing…"

"One was left standing, though…" Kate cocks an eyebrow at me.

A shiver shoots down my spine but I'm not thinking of Harry. I imagine Kaleigh planning this. Kaleigh, who organised the cabin. Kaleigh, who also knew about the affair according to Emma, but never told the police. Kaleigh, concocting a plan to get both Leila and Emma out of the picture so she could have Harry, while also garnering sympathy for herself.

Kaleigh did this to me.

I recall Emma's hoarse words from four days ago, her croaky voice, rough as sandpaper, like she hadn't used it in months. The shadow that crossed her face when I said the person who did this to her was dead. The anger in her eyes, the pain, when she accused her former best friend.

"I hope I can get more out of Emma soon," I say, still unable to make a connection between Kaleigh and Gaz Barker – the only person who was undoubtedly involved.

"You just have to give her time," Kate says. "It's the only way with trauma victims. She'll tell you when she's ready."

"I know." I remind myself that Emma's recovery is the priority, more important than anything else.

"How did you get her to talk in the first place?" Kate asks.

I sigh. "I don't think it had much to do with me to be honest. Harry and Kaleigh Turner definitely triggered it, after they visited that morning. I wasn't there, but Emma's mum told me she had an incredibly visceral reaction to Kaleigh in particular."

"Hmm." I can hear the doubt in Kate's tone. "Do you think her accusation against Kaleigh…"

"Is untrue?" I finish her sentence, knowing she's struggling to verbalise her controversial take.

Kate is a firm "always believe the woman" type, even in cases like Amber Heard and Blake Lively, for example, where the world's already turned on them. It's a side I usually stand with her on, but what do you do when it's two women against each other, both claiming the other is lying?

"I'm not sure," I answer.

"Well, either way, getting her to open up, to tell you this much in such a short space of time, is a huge accomplishment, Charlie," Kate says. "Remember when you called me after the first session? You thought it might take her weeks to talk."

I nod, thinking of the progress I've made, despite Emma turning back in on herself a few times since. A conversation from our last session comes back to me then.

"Leila had been acting weird, was in a bad mood all night," Emma explained. "At first, I thought it had to do with Theo. But then, once we got back to the cabin, she flipped. Couldn't bear hearing about the house Harry wanted to buy, how he might be planning a proposal." Emma stared off in the distance, tears in her eyes.

My heart broke for her then, realising she was probably still in love with Harry. Not that he deserved any of her affection.

"And how did that make you feel?" I asked.

"Angry," she replied without hesitation. "But now, it just makes me sad. You know, the last thing I said to Leila was that I hated her. I thought about that for five years."

My heart pounded as she divulged this, inadvertently revealing that she'd known Leila was dead. We still hadn't ascertained the sequence of events that night, only knowing from Kaleigh's police statements that when she came out of the bathroom, she saw Leila and Emma "dead" on the deck before she ran. But no one knew if Emma was taken first or if she saw what had happened to Leila.

"Emma," I asked, heart thumping. "Were you there when Leila was attacked? Did you see it happen?"

I knew my mistake the second I made it. Once Emma heard my words, when I mentioned the violence, she withdrew. Started trembling, shaking, hyperventilating. "I don't... I can't." And then our session ended.

"I'm just so worried," I tell Kate. "That I'm gonna screw this up for everyone. That I'll say the wrong thing and she'll withdraw or dissociate completely, and I'll be responsible for a mental collapse."

Kate puts her arm around me. "You're only worried because you care. And that is what makes you brilliant at your job. Trust your gut."

I nod, trying to shake my negative mindset.

"I do worry though," Kate says, removing her arm. "That you're getting too involved in this, considering—"

"It's fine," I reply, cutting her off. "I'm fine, honestly. Just trying to help her."

"Okay." Kate holds her hands up. "Mabel! Molly!" she then cries out, picking up her pace as both dogs disappear into the trees at speed. "Can't resist a squirrel, can they?"

She blows her dog whistle and Mabel comes prancing back. Molly, on the other hand, lacks recall. Once she's gone, she's gone until *she* decides to come back.

"Molly!" I call out, squinting through the trees for her.

I catch a flash of blonde darting to the right. I immediately think of Kaleigh's golden locks flowing behind her. I imagine her smirking as she runs, delighted her plan worked.

25

Harry

"What's that guy been in?" Kaleigh points to the telly.

"Huh?" Harry replies, not hearing the question. They started a new series after Alfie went down for his mid-afternoon nap, but his mind is elsewhere.

Ever since the game the other night, he's not been able to relax at all, especially since he's being forced. *"Take the weekend, clear your head,"* Upton said. A task easier said than done.

"That guy looks familiar," Kaleigh says. "The one with the black hat."

"Oh, uh... I dunno," he replies, rubbing her foot. She's sprawled out on the couch, head at the other end with her golden hair tied in a messy bun, feet in his lap. For a moment, things feel normal again.

"If only I had my phone, I could look it up," Kaleigh sighs. But they both agreed they needed to switch off today, put phones away and disable all notifications, save for family.

"I zoned out, what's happening?" Harry asks.

"So, that girl and that guy have been having an affair behind *that* guy and *that* girl's back," she says.

"Right," Harry replies, feeling his cheeks flush. His cock twinges as the man presses the dark-haired girl against the sink, spinning her around and kissing her neck. A memory flashes before him and he's in a bathroom, looking at himself in the mirror as he pounds into a similar-looking brunette. Her back arches as he enters her, his hand caressing her delicate, perfect neck. But he goes limp when the vision changes, her throat now slashed and bloodied.

It's your fault, a voice whispers. It morphs from a female tone to a husky male. And then Theo Abara is yelling at him. But not for fucking Leila. Because he never knew about that. No one did.

Harry clears his throat, desperate to shake the horrific image, and the voice that's haunted him for the past five years.

His chest tightens, heart rate spiking as he looks at his perfect wife, eyes locked on the screen, wondering what she'd think of him if she ever found out. But he was a different person back then. A reckless kid who made bad decisions with money and women. Who couldn't resist the beautiful brunette standing in his kitchen in the middle of the night when his girlfriend was asleep upstairs.

Leila had come up from London to visit Emma, like she did many times before, same with Kaleigh. But that night, he couldn't sleep, and when he went downstairs to play video games, he found Leila there, leaning against the fridge as she ate a yogurt. She was dressed in baby blue shorts and a tank top, nipples erect.

"Sorry," she said, spoon still in her mouth as she slowly licked it. "I couldn't sleep."

"That makes two of us," Harry said.

He still doesn't know how it happened. How it went from them talking in the kitchen about life and football, playing a couple video games together, to them pressed up against each other on the countertop. They were just two horny twenty-somethings, thinking with their bodies and not their minds.

Harry felt bad when he got back into bed with Emma after, but he also felt weirdly exhilarated, knowing Leila was down the hallway. But it was just sex, it didn't matter. No one would have to know. It was a one-time thing.

Until it wasn't.

They started meeting secretly and Harry thought they were on the same page, simply having a bit of fun. He didn't know that Leila felt any different until she asked Harry to leave Emma for her. It was then he'd cut it off: the morning of 24 January 2020.

Harry's watch buzzes, and he realises he forgot to take it off. He's been wearing the watch for so long, it's like a part of his wrist at this point. He's grateful for the distraction though. Until he sees what it says.

A preview of a message from his brother fills the screen.

Mate, please tell me you were not fucking Leila Adler…

Harry blinks, sure he misread it. He must've imagined it because it was on his mind. Because once again, no one knew about him and Leila. Not even Emma.

His heart sinks as he thinks of the possibility though. Of Leila telling Emma. Or Emma realising that Leila took her phone to call him that night.

Leila had been so angry when she realised he was serious about calling things off that she said she was going to ruin everything for him. He was preparing to deal with the fallout already, from the tabloids and from Emma. It's why he'd planned an entire trip to Thailand and started looking at houses. He was done with the playboy life, was ready to settle down. He knew if he finally proposed she'd take him seriously.

But he never had the chance to do any of it.

He bites his lip and then gets up from the couch, needing to look at his phone, despite not wanting to. He opens the text from Simon and sees the link to a tabloid.

Harry's pulse pounds in his ears and he lets out a shaky breath. After he places his phone down, he buries his head in his hands.

"What's wrong?" Kaleigh props herself up on the couch, her swollen belly like a bowling ball under the blanket.

He can't look at her, not yet.

Fuck, he thinks. *What do I do? Do I deny it?*

That's what his mates do. Deny, deny, deny until everyone believes it's the truth. But if he's really a changed man now, he can't lie to her. Not to Kaleigh. That would make him the same coward he was back then.

"Baby, you're freaking me out, what's wrong?" she presses, eyes wide with worry.

He doesn't know what to do. Doesn't know if he can keep it in. All of these complex emotions are going to be the death of him. He can't take it. He needs his wife to tell him what to do. How to handle what is certainly about to be a huge fucking scandal.

"I need to tell you something," he says. He looks up at her but doesn't meet her eyes, hating that he's about to crush her. "Apparently, the press are now running a story, claiming that I... was sleeping with Leila."

He runs his hands across his face as he says the words. He waits for her reaction, for her to ask why they would say that, for her to demand answers. But she doesn't say anything, she's silent.

And then Harry realises, she knows. That if Emma found out that night, Kaleigh would've too.

"You knew?" he asks.

She looks down at her light pink nails, and then starts to cry. He rushes over to the sofa and crouches down next to her. "I was such a fucking dick back then, I'm sorry, Kay. I never told you because... well, I don't know, it never seemed..." He drifts off, unable to find the words.

"It's okay," she says. "It's the same reason I never told you that I knew, I guess. When would be the best time to bring something like that up, right?" She laughs, eyes glistening with tears. Even with snot running from her nose, she's still the most beautiful woman Harry's ever seen.

"How did you find out?" He swallows hard as he asks the question, but he needs to know what Leila said. How much she shared with the girls. And how screwed he really is.

Kaleigh explains how it wasn't until they got back to the cabin that night. How Leila and Emma got into an argument and Leila yelled that she'd been fucking him.

"That's all she said?"

Kaleigh nods.

It's weird to look at her now, knowing that she'd been keeping this secret from him. But it makes sense, for the same reason he kept it from her. What doesn't make sense though, is why she wouldn't have told the police earlier.

"Why didn't you ever say anything to the police?" he asks.

She shrugs, wiping her nose with her sleeve. "It just didn't seem important at the time... I guess I thought they'd waste time looking into you when I knew it wasn't you."

"How?" he asks.

She looks at him like he's asked the dumbest question in the world. "You were irresponsible back then, couldn't keep it in your pants, clearly, but you weren't vengeful or cruel. You're not the killing kind."

He laughs in relief and kisses her on the forehead, wanting to move on, get back to watching their show together. But her tense frame makes him wonder if that's the entire reason why she didn't say anything – if she's keeping more secrets from him. Like he is from her.

26

Harry

Harry speeds down the country road in his Porsche 911 GT3. He knows he should slow down; instead he shifts it into a higher gear, wanting to get to Emma as quickly as possible.

It's obvious she's the one who leaked the news. Had to be. It's clear she's on a mission to destroy Kaleigh and Harry's lives, and he needs to at least try and stop her before things go too far.

After some convincing, he got Kaleigh to agree for them both to deny the Leila affair and let Harry talk to Emma directly. No more tabloid wars, no more hoping for it to pass. Kaleigh already tried to sort things out, but now it's Harry's turn. He'd be Emma's punching bag if need be, let her get it out. And then, hopefully, they could all move on.

It's his word against Leila's. And Leila isn't here. There is no proof.

This ends tonight.

He slams the brakes as a rabbit runs out into the road. The animal's eyes are wide, stunned, scared. He feels an affinity to this creature, caught off guard.

As he pulls into Emma's drive, he's reminded of the time he came to pick her up after their first big fight, after one of Emma's friends claimed she saw Harry kissing another girl at a nightclub. He'd asked his older teammates what to do, and they said if there wasn't proof, to deny.

Always deny it, mate. Deny, deny, deny.

Harry's stomach flips as he tries to channel the old him. The liar. The cheater. He's a different person now and doesn't want to be that person again, but it's a necessary evil.

Emma saw right through him though.

A warm orange glow emanates from the doorway at the end of the corridor. Emma's room. Harry walks toward the light, heart pounding as he moves. He tries to maintain his resolve, but it's more difficult than he imagined, now that he's here.

Despite the space's familiar layout, so much is different to what he remembers. Hardwood instead of carpet. Grey walls instead of patterned wallpaper. But with every step, flashes of the past come back to him, and he can perfectly picture what was once a second home to him. The dizzying sense of a former life knocks him off balance and he stops to gather himself, but the strong scent of floral air freshener prevents his mind from letting go.

Harry stops in front of the door, wishing he never came, as he sees a shadow flit across the light. But he thinks of what he needs to do. How important it is for him to talk to her. To end this once and for all.

He knocks on the painted wood with his knuckle three times. The shadow freezes.

"Emma," he says. "It's Harry, your parents let me in…"

Harry had been so focused on confronting Emma he completely forgot about Jo and Tom Macy until they'd opened the front door two minutes ago, wide-eyed and confused.

"I thought it'd be good for Emma and I to finally talk, if you think she's up for it," Harry had said to them, feeling like a teenager again.

He expected a more hostile greeting, especially with the Leila "rumour" leaking, but aside from Tom's chilly demeanour and Jo's awkward silence, they let him in without issue.

Emma's bedroom door creaks open and Harry stiffens when he sees her. The old jumper drowns her, and her cheekbones are more prominent than five years ago, but she looks more like the Emma he remembers than the wounded creature at the hospital. There's a little more life in her face, more awareness behind her expression.

Harry's eyes flit around the room, which has been redecorated, like the rest of the house.

"Looks so different." He fidgets with his hands.

Emma nods and looks down at the floor.

Harry's stomach twists in knots, imagining what it must feel like for her. Knowing that nobody thought she'd come back, not even her own parents.

After gesturing for Harry to come in, Emma closes the door behind them. He walks toward the bed, still in the same place it always was, next to the window he used to throw rocks at to get Emma to come outside in the middle of the night.

A lifetime ago.

"So, how are you feeling?" He regrets the question the second it comes out.

She doesn't answer.

"Why are you here, Harry?" she says, finally, voice paper-thin. "What do you want?"

He inhales, looking down at his hands, as he tries to recall the sense of urgency he felt less than fifteen minutes ago. Now all he feels is the tense energy in the air between him and the girl he once loved.

"I just came to say..." Harry glances up and away, not wanting to meet her piercing blue eyes. "I... I'm sorry. I'm so sorry." His voice cracks, catching him off guard.

The display of emotion annoys her more than anything and she scoffs. "Stop pretending like you care."

"Of course, I care, Em," he refutes. "Just because things are... different now, doesn't mean I don't care. I always cared. I looked for you for weeks. You have no idea—"

"And he kept me prisoner for years," she says, eyes wet with tears.

"You don't understand," Harry said. "The police, they told me... they said that—"

"I was dead?" she finishes. "I wished I was."

Emma sits down on the bed and starts to cry. Harry awkwardly places a hand on her back. A weird surge of energy pulses through him as he touches her cold, bony body, which was once soft and warm.

"I can't help wondering what I did to deserve this," she says.

"You did nothing," he says. "None of this is your fault." He waits a beat before finishing his sentence. "It's not anyone's fault Emma, aside from... *his*. Not yours. Not Kaleigh's."

"Don't even get me started on Kaleigh." Emma stares at Harry with the same hate-filled glare from the hospital. "She's lying ab—"

"You can't actually believe she had anything to do with it," he cuts in. "I know you're mad at us, but this is too far, Em, please."

She looks at him, this time her gaze pleading and sad. "Don't you even care about my side? Don't you want to hear it?"

He doesn't though. Not really. And he can see it in her eyes, that she knows. Her desperate, longing expression, turning back to stone.

"Of course, you don't," she says. "You don't want to know anything that would fuck up your perfect life, perfect career."

Harry stands, rolling his eyes. The conversation went so well in his head on the way here. He'd say this, then she'd say that. But it's all gone wrong. He's fucked it, but still he tries to bring it back.

"Right, well, my reason for coming here... I thought we could—"

"What?" she says. "Be friends. After you fucked one of my best friends behind my back, then married the other when I went missing?"

"For the record, I never slept with Leila." Part of Harry hates how easily the lie comes out, but the other part is relieved. "And whether you want to believe it or not, Kaleigh and I both care about you and are here for you. You don't have to keep leaking stories to the press."

"Get out!" she shouts. "If you're going to lie to me, just get the hell out."

Harry sighs, shaking his head as he wonders how he fucked this up so royally. He heads towards the door, but stops at her final remark. A threat.

"I'm going to ruin you, Harry Turner," Emma says, her tone biting. "I know everything."

On his way home, Harry calls Kaleigh to explain what happened, that it didn't go well.

Emma's words haunt him. *"I'm going to ruin you. I know everything."*

He doesn't tell Kaleigh why though.

When she hangs up the phone to answer a knock at the door, a new call comes in, from the same unknown caller that's been pestering him since Emma turned up alive. He curses under his breath, ignoring it again and again.

Deny, deny, deny. Until he can't anymore, and finally picks up.

27

Kaleigh

I steady myself as I reach for the flour on the top shelf, trying to focus on my balance rather than my anxious thoughts. Like what Harry and Emma could be talking about at this very moment.

"You knew?" I wobble momentarily, thinking back to the awkward conversation with Harry about his and Leila's affair. *"But why didn't you tell the police or me?"*

Fair questions with no good answer other than I hadn't felt like complicating an already complex situation at the time. But now, it looks bad for the both of us. Like we're hiding something.

It's the only reason I agreed to let Harry talk to Emma alone. As worried as I was about what she'd say to him, or what feelings their conversation could possibly stir up, it was more important that he try and settle things. Get her to see reason and back down. Get her to realise that we're on her side. Not against her.

"It's me and you, okay? I'm not going anywhere." I repeat Harry's words to try and quell my worst fears.

He loves you, I tell myself as I hold the flour and sugar over my belly. *He's not going to do anything to hurt our family.*

Nothing he'll tell you about at least, a cruel voice whispers. *He could be lying to you like he used to lie to Emma.*

My phone pings and I step down instinctively to reach for it, angling myself to the side so as to not accidentally knock over any of the other pantry items.

It's been sorted, the text reads. It's from Jackie, my new publicity manager.

It's a short response to my long-winded explanation of how the Leila story is just another lie. When really *I'm* the one lying. I don't ask how she's sorted it, happy to let her do whatever she needs to change the narrative. I hate that I have to stoop to this, but I'm out of options.

My anxiety spikes, imagining what would happen if any evidence was found to prove this latest revelation. But I believe Harry when he says there isn't any. That it's our word against Emma's. I was hesitant to deny it at first, thinking it'd be better to take the hit, to show that we'll own up to things that are true, no matter how ugly. But it wasn't Leila and Harry having slept together that was the pain point, it was that, if we confirmed it, we'd also be admitting to withholding information from the police. Something which we most certainly couldn't confess to.

"I help?" Alfie asks, eyeing the ingredients lined up next to the stand mixer.

The ends of my lips curl into smile as I look down at his adorable little face, cheeks warm and rosy after waking from his nap.

"Okay, you help Mumma." I turn my phone over and re-focus on making Harry's favourite dessert. A small, hopeful gesture to show him how much I appreciate him standing by me during all of this. Even though it's me standing by him now.

I sigh. The last thing I wanted was for the heat to be taken off me and put on him, but here we are. It's a mess, but we'll get through it. Together.

Somehow, I lose myself in the process of baking as we carefully measure, mix, roll and sample the delicious cinnamon-covered apples. But like all good things lately, it abruptly comes to an end when Harry calls to tell me that his meeting with Emma didn't go as planned.

"I made it worse, Kay. She wants to ruin me."

Shit. My heart sinks. I want to tell him not to worry, that she's just mad. People will see that. But that's what I thought when she accused me, and I was so very wrong. He cusses under his breath as I try to think of something, anything to reassure him. But I'm truly at a loss for words.

Boom, boom, boom. Three bangs on the front door make me jump.

"Someone's here," I say to Harry, after the doorbell rings. "Just drive safe and we'll talk about this soon. Okay?"

"Yeah. Love you."

"Love you, too."

I waddle to the door, worried it could be the police or overzealous paparazzi. I hold my breath, heart racing as I peer through the peep hole.

I frown when I see Zara. Her blue eyes dart from left to right before she rings the doorbell again, impatiently.

I crack open the door and look past her long ponytail, wondering how she got through the gate, but then I remember I'd given her the code a long time ago. Once upon a time when we were friends.

Zara pushes the door open further. "We need to talk."

I cower, tempted to apologise, momentarily ashamed but then I remember Jackie's words. *You need to act from a position of strength.*

I straighten my shoulders. "So, now you want to talk, after you humiliated me…"

"Kaleigh, please, you did this to yourself," she hisses. "Happy to do it out here if you want, but" – she gestures to a van parked on the road – "I'm guessing more of them will be showing up soon. Unless you enjoyed your little meltdown being splashed all over the pages last time."

I flush red and step aside, letting Zara brush past me into the house.

Despite the slight tremble in her hand, she looks well put together, wearing cream-coloured linen pants and a matching trench coat that is draped around her shoulders. I expect her to stop and take her leather loafers off, but she doesn't bother. Just walks straight to the kitchen where Alfie waves hello.

Zara's shoulders relax as she crouches down and says softly, "I need to borrow your mum for a sec, that alright, sweet boy?"

I hand Alfie his tablet as Zara pulls out an envelope from her brown Birkin bag and slaps it on the kitchen island. "Well, you wanted my attention. You have it."

I let tears well on the tips of my eyes. "I told you I had nothing to do with what happened to Emma. How do you think I feel?"

"How do you think Emma feels?" she counters.

"Horrible, traumatised, angry, betrayed... Jealous." I wave my hands in the air, trying to keep my voice low to not alarm Alfie.

Zara shakes her head in disbelief. "So you want me to believe that she's making everything up? After everything she's been through?"

"Yes," I say. "For that exact reason. She's not well, Zara."

"And Leila and Harry?" she says, crossing her arms. She peers at me to study my reaction. I make a point of rolling my eyes.

"As far as I know, nothing happened between those two. So yeah, once again, Emma is just making shit up to punish Harry and me for getting together."

I'm not a liar, but I *can* lie when I need to. I just pray she can't see through it.

"I don't know, Kay. It's still not adding up."

"Things have never added up to me either, okay? I don't know why Gaz – whoever – attacked us that night. Why he killed Leila, took Emma, who, yes, I really thought was dead..." My face flushes as I think of her lying there on the deck.

I'm about to call Emma a liar again, bring up all the petty things she did to others in the past, but decide it's finally time to change tack.

"But," I sigh, hoping I'm not about to make a huge mistake, "I think I might have an idea of why Emma blames me, okay."

Zara's eyes widen. "Why?"

I pause as visions of that night rush to me. A beeping, flashing light in the distance. The glimmer of a knife. Emma's eyes wild with fury.

"Well?" Zara says, throwing her hand out impatiently.

I debate whether or not I should tell her. But I can't risk it. She wouldn't understand. This is a conversation only Emma and I can have. I always knew that deep down. Harry couldn't fix it, nor Zara. I'd need to try one last time. A final Hail Mary before things get really ugly.

"I need to talk to Emma first. *Actually* talk to her."

Zara rolls her eyes. "What are you going to blackmail her or something? Threaten her? I don't trust you, Kaleigh."

"Zara, please," I beg. "It's me. I'm not some calculated killer. I'm only asking you to please convince her to talk to me. If you do that, simply broker a meeting between us, I'll tell my team to back off." I nod toward the papers on the countertop.

She taps her French-manicured nails on the marble and purses her lips. "But what am I supposed to say to her? She doesn't want to see you, you know that."

I bite my lip and think. From what Harry said, Emma is even angrier at the both of us now. So there's no use in trying to play a sympathy card. No, the only way Emma will agree to meet with me is if she thinks I'm willing to admit my wrong, give her the satisfaction of being right.

"Tell her there is something I'm willing to admit, but only if she'll hear me out first. She can then take that information and do what she wants with it. There are things that..." I pause, deciding not to tell Zara there are things that I haven't told the police yet. "There are things I need to ask her about, too."

Zara looks taken aback, but I continue.

"Tell her that I remember everything. The question is: does she?"

28

Emma

I knew that the person I should be the angriest with was Harry. *Blame the guy, not the girl and all that.* But I wasn't. I was heartbroken and angry and wanted to also claw his eyes out, yes. But for some reason, my fury for him didn't come close to the rage I felt towards Leila.

I wondered why the betrayal from him hurt less. Maybe because I'd expected it. In my heart, I knew what he was doing. I thought I could stick it out, let him get his playboy years out of the way, hope nothing too humiliating would happen. He thought with his cock, like most guys.

But Leila? She wasn't some random slag he shagged on holiday. She was *my* friend. She owed *me* loyalty. I think of how she held me while I cried after the *Daily Mail* article came out. Now I knew why she was so livid about it. She wasn't livid on my behalf. She was livid on hers. What had she thought? That he'd break up with me to be with her?

I scoffed. No one understood. How some people mate for life. How she was just a small obstacle in our way. Insignificant.

And it wasn't that I would let it go or let Harry off for this. No, I'd hold it over his head forever and ever. But her? I wanted to strangle her with my bare hands.

Maybe it was the innate jealousy in me, the animalistic, primal urge to stamp out the competition. Or maybe I was just a bitch.

Call me spiteful, fine. Say I don't support women. Well, why would I when they never supported me? What was the fucking point?

I picked up a glass and smashed it on the floor, screaming.

"Emma, stop!" Kaleigh yelled, holding her hands out.

I could tell by the fear in her eyes that my outburst earlier had scared her, when I punched Leila square in the face, causing blood to spurt from her nose. Kaleigh had managed to step in and pull me off her before I could rip out her extensions though.

Relenting to Kaleigh's request, I slunk to the floor with the bottle of Grey Goose. As I took a swig of the vodka, a crying Leila stomped through the hallway, carrying her overnight bag.

"I'm leaving," she said, blood still on her face. "Where are my keys?" Her eyes practically burnt holes into us.

I laughed. "I don't know. And if I did, I'd gladly hand them over. Let you kill yourself on the road." I didn't actually mean it. I didn't think so, at least.

"Ya'll stop it!" Kaleigh screamed. "Leila, you are not driving, you have had way too much to drink. The two of you don't have to talk to each other, but we're stuck here till morning. Deal with it."

I smirked, impressed with Kaleigh standing her ground.

Leila opened her mouth, but Kaleigh talked over her. "And unless either of you magically have service all of a sudden, we can't call cabs or order an Uber. My phone is dead, I forgot my stupid charger, and you both have iPhones, so, yeah, we're stuck, okay?"

Leila let out a scream of frustration, before turning back to the bedroom and slamming the door. I rolled my eyes as Kaleigh followed her.

"She's in the hot tub," Kaleigh said once she rejoined me in the kitchen.

"Well, tell her to get out, I'm going in. It's my fucking birthday!"

Kaleigh sighed, pinching the bridge of her nose as she sunk down next to me, reaching out for the vodka.

"Are you okay?" she asked.

"Oh yeah, I'm brilliant," I laughed, ignoring her sincere tone. "What a dumb fucking question." I started to giggle uncontrollably.

Kaleigh didn't laugh, just chugged. I grimaced as I watched her swallow, worried she might be sick. And I was right.

"Oh no," she said, pushing herself up and running to the bathroom.

I took another sip from the bottle as I sat by myself on the floor, wishing she hadn't left me alone to stew. It was a dangerous thing, to be alone with your thoughts.

I remained in the kitchen, drowning my sorrows in alcohol as I waited for Kaleigh. If she didn't come back soon, I worried I'd start a fight with Leila again. I imagined myself holding her under the water in the hot tub, just to scare her.

I was angry at myself for even thinking about it. I wished I could inflict emotional pain on her, embarrass her, but I wouldn't take it any further than that.

I'm not the bad person, she is, I told myself.

I closed my eyes and leant my head back on the slick white cabinets. The crunch of gravel outside made me sit up. Was Leila trying to leave again? Had she found her keys?

I hated her, but I didn't *really* want her to kill herself or someone else drunk driving. I forced myself up, ready to drag her back inside.

But then I heard her scream.

The first thing I saw when I made it outside was the bloody hunting knife on the decking. And then I saw her, slumped over in a tub of red water.

29

Kaleigh

Sunday 9 March 2025

I turn off my headlights once I reach the top of the Macys' driveway. I put the car in park on the main road, rather than on the gravel, so as not to wake Emma's parents. It's quarter to six in the morning, and the sun has yet to rise.

The darkness at this time unsettles me more than I anticipated. It makes me feel unwelcome, like an intruder. *She invited you here*, I remind myself, looking at the dim light beckoning me from Emma's window.

After agreeing to broker a meeting for us, Zara called me with the plan last night. She said Emma agreed to meet, and that she suggested I go to Emma's first thing in the morning, before the press showed up. They hadn't been camping out, just harassing us during the day when they expected us to be coming and going, so this time should be safe. It'd be the only way for me to arrive without it being plastered all over the papers.

I take a deep breath knowing that, after Harry's disastrous meeting, this is our last hope to end this out of court. Out of jail.

I think of Harry, so on edge and agitated when he got home last night. I walked in on him arguing with someone on the phone, but couldn't make out what he was saying over Alfie's cries. When I asked who it was, Harry told me not to worry about it. I assumed it was Robbie, who'd been on Harry's case ever since he got the yellow.

Hopefully I could settle things with Emma, and everything else would calm down.

You can do this, I tell myself as I wriggle out of the driver's seat.

I'm overcome with a sense of foreboding the minute I step out of the car though. My instincts tell me to go back, to leave. That there is danger here. I think of the thirteen magpies and shiver.

Keep moving, I think. *Get to the house.*

I look around again to make sure I don't spot any cameras, suddenly worried that Zara has set me up. I shudder as I remember the light in the woods all those years ago, barely visible and blinking, like a firefly. A crow caws in the distance, unsettling me even more. But I press forward, following Zara's instructions to go straight to the back of the house, where Emma would be waiting.

Still, something inside me says to run. But instead I creep closer, shrivelled leaves crunching under my feet as I move.

"Emma?" I whisper once I make it around the back of her house. "Are you here?"

But there's no answer.

"Emma?" I ask again, annoyed now. It's ridiculous being out here at this time. I'm sure she's doing this to piss me off.

Alice starts to kick my stomach, telling me she's unsettled too.

"I'm sorry," I whisper to her, thinking of all the reasons I came. The hope for a truce or at least some sort of understanding. A chance for me to explain why I did what I did, to make Emma understand. A chance to finally make amends and put this ridiculous feud to an end. The tabloids' worst nightmare.

"Emma," I say once more, nearly at the other side of the house now. A vision of her pale face lying lifeless in a pool of blood comes to mind. I shake it off but the image doesn't go away.

"Em—" my call is cut short when I trip over something. I instinctively cradle my stomach as I fall to my knees.

"You're okay," I reassure myself, taking stock. It wasn't a bad fall, just a little stumble.

But when I look to my right, I realise I'm not okay. And neither is Emma.

"Emma," I say, panicking. I reach out and jiggle her. "Wake up." But she doesn't respond.

I reach for my phone, shaking as I turn on the flashlight. As my eyes adjust to the darkness, I see the gash across Emma's pale throat. I drop my phone.

A silent scream escapes me, and I vomit next to her corpse.

30

Harry

Harry curses as his phone goes off next to the bed. He has a splitting headache and the loud ringtone isn't helping. But then he sees it's Kaleigh and hurriedly picks it up. She was supposed to be meeting Emma, but this is too early for her to call with an update.

"Everything okay?" he says groggily, wondering if Emma turned her away again. He sits bolt upright when he hears her crying. "Kaleigh, what's wrong?"

"Emma," she sobs. "She's dead."

A high-pitched ringing fills Harry's ears. "What?"

"I got here and she was... dead. Her throat... It was cut."

Boom. Boom. Boom. Harry's heart is like a jackhammer in his chest.

"Harry? What do I do?" Kaleigh cries.

He knows she's asking him a question, but he can't seem to hear or comprehend.

"Harry?" Kaleigh says his name again, but her voice is

muffled, the ringing in his ears now replaced by a white noise that makes her sound like she's calling from a wind tunnel. His mind is stunned, his body frozen, except for the trembling of his hand.

This can't be happening. It's too cruel of a fate. He pictures the fragile girl in front of him yesterday, begging him to listen to her, then threatening him when he wouldn't.

Had she hurt herself? Was this his fault?

"Did you say her throat was cut?" Harry asks Kaleigh. Because you can't cut your own throat.

"Yes," she whispers. "Like Leila. Someone…"

"Where are you right now?" he asks urgently. "Is anyone there with you? Are the police coming?"

"I… I don't know. I'm alone. In her backyard. I didn't know what to do."

Harry pictures his heavily pregnant wife crying on the ground next to Emma's corpse, someone watching her from the treeline.

"Kaleigh, I need you to get out of there right now," he says, realising how much danger she could be in. "Wake up the Macys and get inside. Have them call the police."

Kaleigh begins to sob again, and Harry wishes he could reach through the phone and wrap her in his arms.

"But…" she says, voice quavering. "Won't it look bad?"

"Why would it look bad?" he asks, confused.

"Because I was the one who found her."

Harry freezes, knowing that she's right. But he'd ask questions later. He needed to make sure she'd actually have a later first.

"Sweetheart, listen to me. None of that matters. Just get somewhere safe. I'm on my way."

31

Charlie

I know something has happened the second I see the heavy police presence on the road in front of the Macys' house.

It's 8:30 in the morning, I'm here for my session with Emma, but the pit in my stomach tells me that's not going to happen.

I take stock of the paparazzi and news vans to my left, being held back by police officers. In the distance, crime scene investigators in white hazmat suits walk around the property.

Someone has died, I think, praying it isn't who I think it is. That I haven't failed her.

I make a beeline for Maynard, who is on his phone by the front door.

"DCI Maynard!" I wave to get his attention, stumbling on the gravel in my haste. "What happened?"

He sees me, mumbles something to the person on the phone, and then greets me with a sad smile once he hangs up.

"Let her through," he says to the officers on the street.

"Dr Singh." He huffs out a loud breath as I duck under the blue and white tape.

My heart races as I study him for a hint of what's going on. But deep down, I know. I can feel it in the air, almost tangible. Dread overwhelms me as a wailing cry sounds from inside.

"Emma?" I ask.

He nods sombrely. "She's dead."

I run my hands through my hair, already frizzing from the early morning mist. This can't be happening.

"That poor, poor girl," I whisper. "To think she survived five years of hell for this to be her fate." It's a painful realisation, even worse than the thought that I failed her, that I couldn't help her enough to want to live. It's not the first time one of my patients has killed themselves, but it doesn't make it any easier. Every time is like three punches: one to the gut, one to the heart, and one to the head.

But then I take in the officers collecting evidence and the crime scene tape outside. The blood drains from my face.

"Wait, was it not suicide?"

He shakes his head. "Murdered. Throat slit." He meets my eyes, not needing to say what we're both thinking.

Just like Leila Adler.

"Kaleigh Creedy found her this morning," Maynard says.

"What?" I whip my head up, shocked.

"Said she came to meet her, it was prearranged through a friend, which we've checked," he adds. "Kaleigh said she came around the back to look for her, which had been their plan, and then stumbled across the body."

"She stumbled across her?" I say incredulously.

Maynard raises his eyebrows knowingly. "Yup."

"Well, is she in custody?" I rack my brain, wondering why Kaleigh would come here so early in the morning if not to cause harm to Emma. Regardless of the meeting being prearranged, she'd be angry, especially after the Leila revelation...

"She's been very cooperative," he reassures me. "She's at the station now, waiting for her lawyer before we can question her. And her husband is there too."

"But you haven't arrested her? Surely there's grounds..."

Maynard shakes his head.

"Why not?"

He tightens his lips and looks at me, as if to say he's already answered enough questions. I'm only a psychologist, he doesn't have to tell me anything. But I look pleadingly at him. "Please, I just need to make sense of it all."

His expression softens and I can tell he's considering it.

"We have reason to believe the time of death was between 3:15 and 5:30 a.m. Kaleigh arrived at 5:45. A neighbour's camera picked up her vehicle driving past at that time, corroborating her story."

"But that's not far from the estimate," I argue.

He shakes his head again. "Crime scene investigators said 5:30 a.m. at the absolute latest, they're thinking likely sometime around 4:15."

"And the Macys don't have any security systems?" I ask.

"A burglar alarm they didn't set and no cameras," he replies.

I sigh. "What about the Turners?"

"It's on our list of items to look into."

I nod, momentarily satisfied.

"Do you think it could've been one of them? Obviously the only person Emma pointed any fingers at was Kaleigh Turner. We also know Harry Turner withheld information, failing to mention his affair with Leila Adler…"

Maynard studies me, once again considering if he should divulge any more information. "Maybe there's something else Emma shared with me that could help," I say. "But I won't know unless you tell me what the missing pieces are…"

Maynard hesitates, but then speaks. "Well, Emma's mum did tell us something interesting. Apparently Harry Turner came over last night, to talk to Emma. Said she heard them arguing." He lets the implication hang in the air.

I picture Emma, confronting the love of her life who's since moved on. The pain she must've felt before she died.

"I presume Emma was still alive when he left though?"

Maynard nods.

"But then Kaleigh comes back first thing in the morning and she's dead?"

Maynard nods again, holding his hands out.

I bite my lip. "One of them must be involved. They must be."

But he just shrugs, not giving anything else away.

Inside the house, Tom Macy consoles his sobbing wife. I gesture to them. "Where were they when it happened?"

"Asleep. They only woke up when Kaleigh started banging on the glass door."

A shiver runs through me when I see the streaks of blood on the glass behind them. I think of the last thing Emma told me, yesterday afternoon. How she came outside to find Leila dead, her accusation against Kaleigh finally starting to make sense. I shake my head, tears stinging my eyes. I want to scream in frustration. For Emma. For the fact that we'll never know the rest of her story. And that justice may never be served for everyone involved in this heinous chain of events.

"And you don't have any other leads?" I ask.

Maynard glances at me, and I can tell there is something he hasn't told me yet.

"The neighbour's camera picked up another car, around 4:30 a.m. We asked the petrol station up the street for any CCTV footage of it, too, which they had."

"That's good," I say, hopeful.

Maynard chuckles. It's a tired, frustrated laugh. "It would be great… except it has no plates."

I suddenly feel cold.

"Just like the car caught on CCTV in 2020," I whisper.

Maynard nods, affirming my gut feeling that this is not another coincidence. Whoever killed Emma most likely killed Leila Adler. And that person is out there, thinking they got away with it. Again.

I can't let that happen.

32

Kaleigh

You did this. You wished her dead. Now she is.

Tears flow down my cheeks as my mind struggles to process where I am and what's happened. *You're at the police station. Emma is dead – actually dead.*

I stare ahead at nothing in particular, blinking. My mind is blank, except for when the void is filled by terrifying visions of Leila and Emma's slit throats. I start to wonder if something is wrong with me, if I'm doing something unknowingly. If I'm crazy.

A wave of nausea hits and I feel like I'm going to be sick. I pray that this is a nightmare or a mistaken timeline. That soon I'll wake up in my home and Emma will wake up in hers.

You wanted this, the voice reminds me. But I argue with it. *No, I didn't want this, I really didn't.*

I hold my hands to my throbbing head as I try to piece everything together. But I can't think straight, fear making it impossible to work out what this means. That a killer is still on the loose. They always have been...

I want to grab my knees and curl into a ball, but I can't do that so I push the white metal chair against the table and start sluggishly pacing back and forth, cradling my belly for comfort.

This isn't happening, I tell myself. *This is a vision from the past. I'm in a nightmare.*

"Kaleigh," says Rudy Kirkpatrick-Jones, the lawyer Jackie sent from London. I almost forgot he was here.

"I know this is a lot."

"I don't think you know," I say through my tears, even though I know fighting with him is not going to help.

"I'm sorry." I meet his gaze, which is somehow stern and sympathetic at the same time. His blue eyes are piercing against his pale skin and red hair.

"Don't worry, Kaleigh, we'll get you out of here shortly," he says as I wearily move around the room. "They don't have enough evidence to make an arrest. All you'll have to do is make your official statement and answer a few questions, then we'll get you home. Okay?"

His tone is soft, but it does little to soothe me.

"Let's go through your statement again, same as you told me earlier. That Zara Becker helped you broker a meeting with Emma Macy. It was early in the morning to avoid the press. You have proof of these texts and Zara will confirm this wasn't an impulsive visit. And when you arrived, you found Emma dead."

I freeze as I recall the horrific sight and subsequent events. Banging on the Macys' back door, Emma's dad looking horrified as he ushered me inside. Jo running past

KELLY AND KRISTINA MANCARUSO

me to her daughter's corpse on the ground. Crying, wailing, screaming. I sat on the floor in the corner of their kitchen until the police arrived, refusing to move until Harry got there. That was when Jo Macy began screaming for me to be taken away in handcuffs.

Rudy guides me back to the chair when I start crying again. Overwhelming fatigue hits me as I sit. I'm so, so tired.

He repeats the sequence of events, reminding me of what I'm supposed to say during the interview.

"Can't you just tell them that for me?" I ask, a lump in my throat.

"Unfortunately, no," he frowns. "It must come from you. And after you give your statement, they'll want to ask questions for clarification. But it will be fine, simply follow my lead."

He then holds up his hands and makes a gesture with his fingers.

"One finger down means you can answer. Two fingers down means to skip."

He seems so confident that I start to feel hopeful. "You really think I can get out of this?" I ask.

He looks up and gives me a reassuring nod. "What matters are facts. Like when the coroner will estimate her time of death compared to your arrival. So long as those don't align, they shouldn't have anything to charge you with."

"But what about Emma's accusation?"

"Hearsay. Again, nothing that can be proven."

I nod.

"Anything else you want to talk through together before I let them in?"

214

I shake my head, ready to get this over with.

I hold the plastic cup of water in front of me like a stress ball, trying to focus on my fingers digging into its crinkly sides as I get drilled with question after question by DCI Maynard and an even more cynical Banes.

"Can you identify yourself? Can you state your current or permanent residence? Is that where you were last night before arriving at the Macys?"

I answer with short responses. *Kaleigh Creedy-Turner. Mill House, West Bridgford. Yes.*

Then, at their request, I deliver my statement, explaining my version of events like Rudy coached.

"Mrs Turner, can you confirm that both you and your husband were home between the hours of three and five-thirty in the morning?" Banes asks.

I nod.

"What were you doing at that time?"

"Sleeping," I reply, before clarifying. "I set my alarm for twenty past five and then, like I said, I left the house twenty minutes later around 5:40. It only took about five minutes to drive to Emma's that early."

Banes takes note. "And you and your husband were sleeping in the same bed?"

"Yes." I roll my eyes, showing I think it's a ridiculous question. But my heart races at the lie.

Harry and I were both sleeping in the same house, yes. But I wasn't in our bed at that time, I was with Alfie. Like any three-year-old, he struggles to sleep, so I often sleep with him when he has nightmares. Thankfully, Harry and

I aligned our stories earlier, knowing they'd most likely ask this.

"And do you have proof, any camera footage that can confirm your alibis?"

"We have outdoor cameras that should show when I left the house..." I look to Rudy for approval, but he is studying Banes, who now smirks as if she has something up her sleeve. It unnerves me.

"Ah yes, funny you say that. Because while the two of you were conversing before we came in," she says, "your husband was helpful enough to allow us to check your home camera footage..."

I stop myself from rolling my eyes, cursing Harry for agreeing to something like that. I glance at Rudy and he stiffens, probably thinking the same.

"And interestingly enough, we found that some of the footage is missing." Banes looks from me to Maynard, furrowing her brow in mock confusion.

I swallow hard, feeling unsettled, even though it's not the first time the cameras have played up.

Rudy taps two fingers on the table signalling for me not to answer before speaking. "I've noticed this is quite common with these new phone camera systems. Mine misbehaves all the time. But it's neither here nor there, in this case, is it? Because I've already been informed that the neighbour's security camera has Mrs Turner's car driving past at the time she claims."

The smug look disappears from Banes's face, and she looks to Maynard, annoyed at how Rudy seemed to know this information. I thank the Lord for Jackie's recommendation. This guy is on the ball.

"So, sounds like you have what you need to confirm her movements."

"For now," Banes says to Rudy before turning back to me. "Post-mortem revealed Miss Macy died due to exsanguination from a knife wound to the neck, just like Leila Adler."

She pulls two photos from the envelope and slides them across the desk. A close-up of the knife wound on Emma's neck and a similar close-up of Leila's from five years ago.

My eyes linger on the photo of Leila. I'd never seen it before, and it surprises me how unaffected I feel. While it's grotesque, it seems fake. So different from the image in my head of the fresh wound. My memory of Leila's is more akin to the photo of Emma I stare at now.

My eyes dart between the photos. *Two bodies.*

"Is this really necessary?" Rudy says.

Maynard waves his hand. "We're only trying to see if the photo helps Mrs Turner remember important details from the night when Leila Adler died."

"And how is this relevant to Miss Macy's death last night?" Rudy asks. "Which is the only reason my client is here by the way."

Maynard's face reddens. "Because we believe whoever killed Leila Adler is the same person who killed Emma Macy. And *your* client was the last person to see both of them alive."

"That's not true," Rudy responds before I can. "Mrs Turner was not the last person to see Miss Macy alive, that would be the deceased's parents. And I'd also like to point out that for someone in my client's condition, being heavily pregnant, committing cold-blooded, violent murder would be difficult."

I shift uncomfortably in my seat as the men's gaze flit to my protruding stomach. In any other circumstance I wouldn't tolerate a man referring to my pregnancy as a condition that prevents me from doing anything, but in this moment I'm grateful to have it as an excuse for not being able to murder someone.

"And let's be realistic here," Rudy continues. "Both you and I know it doesn't make sense for Mrs Turner to have murdered Miss Macy, then wake up her parents rather than leave the scene of the crime. All the evidence points to Mrs Turner telling the truth."

"Well," Maynard counters, "we've looked into her phone records actually, and she made a phone call to her husband before the police."

"I was scared," I jump in, hating how that could be used against me. My heart thumps as I say it though, knowing that the main reason I called Harry first was because I knew how bad this would look.

"So why not call 999?" Maynard asks.

"You don't have to answer that, Kaleigh," Rudy chimes in, holding a hand up. He turns back to Maynard and Banes. "She was obviously very traumatised, scared for her life. You both seem to be forgetting that she may also be a target as well."

"She just keeps getting away though, doesn't she?" Banes quips. "And obviously, it's impossible to ignore the fact that Emma accused you, Kaleigh, of coordinating her abduction…"

"An outlandish claim made by a woman who was unwell," Rudy says.

Banes ignores him. "But what about your police statement from five years ago, where you claimed you saw

Emma dead? You didn't see her dead. But you wanted her dead. And you finally got your wish."

I scoff and then look helplessly at Rudy as tears stream down my face.

"Well, seeing as neither of you have any actual evidence against my client, I think this interview is over." Rudy stands and then helps me from my chair.

"Maybe you weren't the one to make the kill, Kaleigh," Banes says as I reach the door. "But that doesn't mean you're innocent. It's better if you own up to your involvement now."

I sob as Rudy ushers me to the door, feeling like my life is over.

33

Harry

"You know how this looks, right?" DS Banes says.

Harry feels like he's twenty-five years old again, sitting in a police station, being questioned about the "death" of Emma Macy. How his hands were clammy and sweaty, his head and heart pounding. He still can't believe he's here again. Except this time, she really is dead.

"I'm not sure why you'd say that," Harry's solicitor says in his posh London accent. Harry finds it weird to have this man he's never met before defending him, but Kaleigh's PR lady promised he was the best. "You've already confirmed that when Mr Turner left Miss Macy, she was alive."

Harry's head spins with a nauseating sense of déjà vu.

"That doesn't mean he didn't go back," Banes says. "Emma's parents confirmed that she was very upset when he left. They could hear them arguing."

Harry's heart hammers in his chest, wondering how much

they heard. He clutches his right hand into a fist, rubbing it with his left.

"Ex-lovers argue all the time," Rudy says matter-of-factly.

"Speaking of ex-lovers," Banes says, not skipping a beat. "Can you tell us about your relationship with Leila Adler."

"There was none," Harry says, sitting back in his chair and crossing his arms. *Deny, deny, deny.*

Maynard sighs. "Listen, Mr Turner, I'd love nothing more – and I'm sure you would too – for you to be out of this police station and out on the pitch tonight."

Harry runs his hands over his face.

"But we need to speak to everyone who saw Emma before she was killed," Maynard continues. "As you can appreciate, we have to interview you because of your connection to the original case, because you saw Miss Macy last night, and of course, because your wife was the one to find her."

"My clients were cleared of having any involvement in the tragic events that happened five years ago," Rudy chimes in.

"Mr Turner, where were you this morning between the hours of three and five thirty?" Banes asks.

"At home, in bed." Harry is growing more frustrated by the minute.

"With your wife?"

Harry nods even though it's not technically the truth. He knows it's a shitty alibi, both for him and Kaleigh, but where else would they be? He winces as a new wave of stabbing pain pulsates through his temples.

"Shame your security cameras can't prove it. What do you think happened there?"

"DCI Maynard, DS Banes, have we not gone over this already?" Rudy complains. "This is quite common…"

"Is it common?" Banes frowns, looking to Harry.

There's been times where the battery died or the connection was bad, so it didn't record. It's not unheard of. But then Harry thinks of the only other person who has access to the cameras: Kaleigh. He dismisses the doubt though as soon as it crosses his mind, worried about the real killer.

"Listen, I know you think my wife and I are these criminal masterminds, but if there's someone still out there, someone who tried to get to Kaleigh once, and has now killed his second victim out of the three, I want to make sure you're doing everything you can to ensure this psycho doesn't finish the job."

Three for three. The thought unsettles him, and Harry once again curses himself for being so foolish, so careless. Is it all about to come back to bite him, after all this time he thought he was in the clear? Is this actually somehow his fault? A pit forms in his stomach.

"Please rest assured we are doing everything we can to find out who did this," Maynard says. "So if neither you nor your wife are responsible, as you claim, who is? Is there anyone you can think of, from five years ago, especially, that would want to hurt Miss Macy now?"

Thump, thump, thump. The pressure building in Harry's chest makes him feel like he's about to take a crucial penalty. Everything on the line.

"No." The lie rockets him back into the past.

Touch. Kick. Score.

Win.

Lose.

Deny, deny, deny.

34

Kaleigh

Monday 10 March 2025

I triple check the locks on all the doors once Harry leaves. He's taken Alfie to nursery on his way to training, so it's just me now. Alone with my fears.

I shiver, thinking of the man from that night. The one that came back for us after killing Leila. Headlights on the drive. Footsteps over my head as I hid below the deck.

I sink into the couch and pull a blanket over my head as I start to spiral, thinking that because of this faceless, nameless man, Leila and Emma are now dead. And I could be next.

The thought forces me up. I waddle over to the kitchen, grab the first chef's knife I find and clutch it tight.

Harry promised he'd get a better security system since ours isn't working properly, but the company can't install it until the end of the week. So I have to be hypervigilant until then.

I stand still, listening for any noise. But it's silent. I ache to hear my son's giggle, but it's best he's not here right now. Not if someone is after me.

The silence consumes me as I realise that I shouldn't have been left alone. That Harry shouldn't have gone back to training. That I should've told him to stay.

I look over at my phone, lying on the couch, and wonder if I should call him. Ask that he come home. But I know I can't. Football takes priority above all else. Tears fill my eyes as I curse the sport that's taken him from me.

Stop being dramatic, I tell myself. *You don't want to be one of those wives.*

If Emma's killer wanted you dead, they would have done it already. The season is almost over anyways.

But it just upsets me more as I think of how this should be one of the most exciting years, with multiple championships and the World Cup on the horizon. How I should be preparing to bundle my son up to cheer on his daddy from the stands, but instead I'm in hiding, the most hated woman in the UK. Jackie practically said so when she emailed me this morning, informing me that she could no longer represent me.

You know you're screwed when you're deemed too much of a liability for a crisis PR firm.

I recall the expression on Banes's face yesterday – who despite the lack of real evidence, clearly thinks I'm guilty on all counts – and then imagine giving birth to Alice in an orange jumpsuit.

My heart flutters and I force myself to breathe, desperate to lower my cortisol. I feel a tiny foot kick the inside of my belly, as if she's telling me to knock off the negativity.

My eyes sting with tears, hating that she'll be brought into the world with so much unresolved tension.

Do something about it then, a voice urges. *Prove you're innocent.*

Not knowing where to begin, I open up a Word document to type out my thoughts.

Goal: Prove I'm innocent.
How: By finding out who that man was.

The question is *how*. I put myself back in 2020, recalling the various theories about who was responsible. It gives me an idea. Somewhere to start.

I minimize the Word document and open Google, typing "Reddit Nightmare in Notts" in the search bar.

Nightmare in Nottinghamshire: Two WAGs Missing After Attack – Jan 2020

Nightmare in Notts: Suspect Round-up – Jan 2020

Leila Adler's body found in River Trent :(– Feb 2020

What Really Happened to Emma Macy? – Feb 2020

Arrest Made in Nightmare in Notts Case – Feb 2020

Why David Allen is Innocent – Feb 2020

Who is Kaleigh Creedy and How Did She Survive? – Mar 2020

Families of Nightmare in Notts victims share new details – Mar 2020

R/SuperSleuth11

Nightmare in Notts: Suspect Round-up – Jan 2020

Below is a list of all possible suspects that the Reddit community has rounded up so far, in order of least to most likely. Click the links to find out more on each suspect. Who do you think did it and why?

- Uber driver who dropped girls back off at cabin
- Mystery car – black vehicle without licence plates caught on CCTV morning of the crime on main road near cabin
- Tom Macy – father of Emma Macy who came into a lot of money following the sale of his business in Feb 2020
- AFC Nottingham supporter or stalker who was potentially obsessed with the girls
- Kaleigh Creedy – Kaleigh was the only one present during the attack and the only one of the three women to escape; police confirmed multiple times that Kaleigh is a victim and

only a victim, not a person of interest

- A drug gang that had been busted and locked away by Leila's stepfather. It's possible an outside gang member retaliated against the bust by attacking Leila.
- Theo Abara - footballer boyfriend of Leila Adler; he had been playing a home game in Nottingham that night but police confirmed he never left his hotel room after the match.
- Kaya Silva - scorned ex of Theo, who left Kaya for Leila (possible Leila was target)
- Harry Turner - striker for AFC Nottingham, boyfriend of Emma Macy; tabloids have alleged Harry was unfaithful to Emma previously; like Theo, he had been playing a home game in Nottingham that night and police confirmed he never left his hotel
- Davey Allen and/or other Sheffield supporters who targeted Emma Macy after Harry Turner handball/penalty drama.

I read through the list of lead suspects from 2020 in order, still shocked how anyone could have thought Tom Macy might have been involved. I move on, not even entertaining the theory.

I skip over the other unlikely suspects and pause on the drug gang theory. That someone could have targeted Leila in retaliation for her stepdad putting their lead members behind bars. But that wouldn't explain why they would come back for Emma a second time. I visually cross them off in my mind as I move on and click the link into Theo.

It's Always the Boyfriend...

7 February 2020 01:13 a.m.
Statistically speaking, a majority of cases are done by someone close to the victim. And more times than you would expect, it's usually the boyfriend/partner.

This case involves two boyfriends: Harry Turner and Theo Abara. This thread is for discussion on Theo:

1. Theo was playing in Nottingham that night but cops confirm he didn't leave his hotel. However, he could have snuck out the back or left in some way that the cameras or the front desk personnel could have missed.
2. Leila was rumoured to have been on the verge of breaking up with Theo. Is it possible she tried to break up with him and he accidentally killed her in a crime of passion? Emma being collateral damage?
3. To add to point #2 – According to phone records, Theo called Leila three times in the hours leading up to her death. Was this normal behaviour or something more?

I frown, feeling unnerved. How did this user know Leila was on the verge of breaking up with Theo when even I didn't know until that night?

Curious, I click into JusticeForDaveyAllen's profile. Bile rises in my throat as I see their latest post: *Why I believe Kaleigh Turner is guilty.*

Don't look, don't look, I plead with myself. But my curiosity has taken me too far now. I can't help it. I click.

Kaleigh Creedy-Turner Discussion: Why I believe Kaleigh Turner is guilty

Posted by u/JusticeForDaveyAllen

First, another moment of silence for Emma Macy. She didn't deserve what happened to her with Gaz and she didn't deserve to die. Just like Davey Allen didn't deserve what happened to him either. This only goes to show how cruel and harsh this world can be. And how cruel humans can be.

Prior to Emma's accusation, I used to maintain Kaleigh's innocence, but after, I couldn't ignore the possibility. And now this? See below a list of reasons I believe Kaleigh Creedy-Turner could be guilty of killing Emma Macy.

1. Kaleigh's story from that night never really made sense. She found Leila and Emma dead and then the car arrived? It's suspicious.
2. Emma literally accused Kaleigh of orchestrating her abduction.

3. Kaleigh had motive to kill Emma, to stop any more damaging stories from coming out.
4. Kaleigh was the one to find Emma dead at a very suspicious early hour in the morning.
5. Kaleigh had a history of sabotaging other women to get her way. I have an insider source who confirmed Kaleigh Creedy tampered with the spray tan of her main competitor right before winning Miss Teen USA.

Comments:

Conspiramacy: I've been saying this for years! I always thought it was sketchy that KCT miraculously escaped this "random attack" and coincidentally fell in love with the boyfriend of her presumed-dead best friend. Everyone used to come at me, saying to leave her alone, but look who was right. Me!

Jesuslovesyou: I stood by this then and I stand by it now: Kaleigh Creedy-Turner is a victim and only a victim. Is it not obvious that Emma was just devastated by the fact her best friend married her boyfriend? I don't understand why people keep making her out to be some evil mastermind.

35

Kaleigh

I stare at the post, unblinking, unmoving. How do they know? How does this random person know what I did to win?

I swallow hard. These were secrets I only ever shared with one person: Emma. I remember lying in bed with her in our second year of uni, spilling our darkest secrets after we'd been drinking all night during Freshers week. Emma told me she'd posted online nudes of another woman after finding them on Harry's phone, and I told her about the time I'd tampered with Gretchan McCarthy's spray tan the day before Miss Teen Alabama – something I'd never admitted before, something that no one knew. It was the worst thing you could do to a pageant contestant because it's not a quick fix or as simple as "go out and buy a new dress" or "redo your hair". No, you can't just buy new skin. The technician was fired, which I felt bad about, but I didn't have regrets about Gretchan suffering, she deserved it after calling me and my mama white trash all those years ago.

I stare back at the screen, infuriated by JusticeForDaveyAllen, knowing that I need to figure out who the hell this is. It has to be someone Emma was close to.

Zara? I wonder. But I immediately dispel the theory. It can't be her, it has to be someone who knew Emma and also wanted to prove Davey Allen's innocence. And Zara hated Davey, thought he was to blame the second he was arrested.

I click into JusticeForDaveyAllen's profile and start scrolling through their posts. They cover everything from Emma's recent death back to Leila's, recapping every event and all the various conspiracy theories as to who the killer could be. None of the posts reveal the identity of the account holder, but it's clear they are vehement defenders, borderline obsessed, with clearing Davey Allen of any wrongdoing.

Deciding it must be someone related to him, I open a new window and type in "Davey Allen" and click into a news article about his death. I skip past the part summarising his alleged crimes, not wanting to read the details again, then stop at the bottom, where it notes that Allen is survived by his mother, Ruth, stepfather Johnathan, and half-sister, Charlotte.

I continue to scroll, hoping to find a family photo. There isn't one, so I start a new search tab for "Charlotte Allen", guessing someone younger is behind the subreddit. Various results pop up, from social media profiles and website links to a collection of images of different women, and I wonder how I'll ever narrow it down. I decide to scan the images, before clicking into the LinkedIn, Instagram and Facebook links.

When nothing stands out, I move onto Davey's parents, but they're just as much of a dead end. I rub my forehead with two fingers and take a deep breath, willing myself to focus a little longer.

"You're so close," I whisper, genuinely feeling like I'm on the right track.

I stare at the ceiling and try to think logically about this again. How the user, who is so obsessed with clearing Davey's name, would also need to be trusted by Emma. They'd have to be someone Emma would feel comfortable confiding in. Most likely a woman around our age. Which brings me back to Davey's half-sister.

"Half-sister," I say aloud, emphasising the first word. "Of course."

This whole time I'd been searching for other Allens, but even Davey's mom probably has a different surname now. I do a bit more digging and find that his stepdad's surname is Singh.

I sit up straight, readying myself to type in a new search. One that pairs the sister's first name with that surname.

Charlotte Singh.

36

Charlie

I stare at my calendar, trying to prepare myself for the heartache that will inevitably hit in one week's time, on the anniversary of my big brother's death. Not that the grief ever leaves. It's something I've learned to live with, following me around like a shadow. But this time of year it digs its sharp claws in.

I should call my mum, see how she's doing. If I had to guess, she's probably already drowning her sorrows at the local pub. Davey was her first child, the little boy she raised completely by herself until she met my father five years later and had me. Davey and Johnathan Singh never really got along though, both of them struggling with the dynamic, vying for my mother's attention.

I watched them fight constantly. Even from a young age I was interested in their behaviours, like how my father treated Davey differently to me and how Davey refused to be disciplined by him – or our mum for that matter. So, when Dad got a new job that required us to relocate to Nottingham, Davey refused to come, deciding to instead stay with a friend in Sheffield. He was seventeen by then, had an apprenticeship with a local joiner, so Mum didn't put up a fight, just let him get on with it. He'd come down on the train to visit me though and, when I was old enough, he started taking me to watch the football.

I think of how he shielded me from trouble, directing me away from any lairy supporters or fights. He taught me what to look out for, taught me how to keep myself safe. I never once saw him do anything untoward, so when he was arrested, I refused to believe he was guilty, that he was capable of that kind of violence.

But then I saw the video of him forcibly kissing Leila, and I started to wonder if maybe he *was* capable.

"Sometimes when I'm drinking I do dumb shit," he'd said to me when I visited him in prison. "I shouldn't have kissed her, Char, I know. Thought I was Billy Big Bollocks in front of my mates, didn't I? But I didn't fucking kill her. I swear."

I remember watching him fall to pieces on the other side of the table in the prison's visitation room, desperate for someone to listen. I'd never seen him like that before, a broken shell of himself. And in that moment, I decided to believe him.

But it didn't matter.

The next week, Davey hanged himself in his cell, unable to cope with spending life in prison for a crime he didn't commit. He knew, just like I did, that the world had already made up their minds about him.

I try to convince myself that working as a psychologist means something. That it's my way of making a difference in society, and maybe I can help someone else's brother before it's too late. But it still tortures me that I never did more for my own brother at the time, that I didn't try harder to change people's minds. Something other than creating a daft Reddit account.

It was awkward when Maynard asked me to speak to Emma, unaware of my connection to the case; my different surname means most people have no idea about my relation to Davey. The only person who knows is Kate, who cautioned me about getting so involved over the weekend. But even she doesn't know how deep I'm in.

I never planned to share anything from my sessions with Emma online, I really didn't. My primary goal truly was to help her. But when Emma pointed the finger at Kaleigh, and I realised the implications – that Davey might've not just been wrongfully accused but framed – I couldn't let it go.

I have my moments when I berate myself for doing it, knowing how unprofessional and unethical it was. But I wasn't leaking anything that wouldn't have eventually come out anyway. That if the stories about Emma's accusation, or Leila's affair with Harry, or the suspicious circumstances of Kaleigh finding Emma's body weren't shared by me, they would've come from someone else, like a leak in the police, ready to talk to the tabloids for a bit of cash on the side (something that happens more often than people think).

Plus, I figured posting on Reddit was better than selling my stories to the press. I still have *some* integrity, unlike the Turners who may have got away with murder while my brother took the fall.

Boom, boom, boom.

The banging on my door knocks me out of my thoughts. I check the time and frown, not expecting anyone until half past ten.

Boom, boom, boom.

I huff, annoyed at the impatient visitor. I brush away any lingering tears before I push up from my chair to see who it is.

37

Kaleigh

The overhead fluorescent lights buzz and hum as I wait outside Dr Charlotte Singh's office at the hospital. A similar energy pulses through me, like a bulb about to burst.

I knew who she was the second the search images loaded, recognising her as the doctor speaking to the Macys outside Emma's room last week.

I deduced that the police must not know about her connection to the case, or else she wouldn't have been allowed to be a part of the investigation due to the conflict of interest. I also suspect that no one knows about her online persona, because that would be the end of her career, sharing confidential information with the internet.

But what's bad for her is good for me. I can use this knowledge as power, force her to take down her negative posts and start convincing others of my innocence, to turn the mob away.

The door opens and Charlotte's expression immediately goes from one of curiosity to concern. The colour drains from her face. She probably thinks I've come to murder her next.

Good, I think for a second. *Be scared of me.*

I smile, but not in a friendly way. I want her to see the fire in my eyes. I want her to know that I know who she is when she's not playing doctor.

"Can I help you?" she asks, trying to pretend she doesn't recognise me. But I can tell it's a front by her flushed face and the fidgeting of her fingers.

She's dressed almost identically to how she was last time, black trousers and oversized jumper. Short brown hair tied back neatly in a bun. Barely any make-up on her comely face. Her eyes are red, and I wonder for a moment if she's been crying.

"I was hoping to speak to the person who runs the profile 'Justice For Davey Allen' please," I say smugly.

Her face goes from red to white, like she's seen a ghost. "Erm, I'm sorry, I'm not sure what—"

"I'm confident you are sure actually."

She scoffs and then tries to close the door on me.

"I know you're his sister," I hiss, one hand on the door, one on my belly. "So unless you want me to report you for your extracurricular, online activities, you're going to let me in right now and we're going to have a chat."

She holds my gaze, and I see a fire behind her eyes as well. She ultimately relents and moves so I can squeeze into her office. She locks the door behind her and gestures for me to sit in the chair opposite her desk, while she sinks into her black swivel seat. She places her phone on her desk, its bright purple floral case taking me by surprise, so at odds with her usual ensemble of all black.

"You put it together then." Charlotte looks resigned.

"Well, you didn't make it that hard." I pause to gauge her reaction, but she remains speechless and puffy eyed. She looks almost as tired as I do.

"I thought it could've been Emma's mom, or maybe one of our mutual friends, but they wouldn't have spared a thought for Davey Allen."

The remark cuts her, and I flush, feeling bad despite my ire toward her. Because despite everything she's done, it's looking like her brother really was innocent. I clear my throat.

"I knew it must've been someone related to him, and even though it took a little while to work out your last name, I eventually figured it out."

She shrugs and lets out a long sigh. I wonder how someone like her, someone so intelligent, could be so foolish. But I suppose her brother is her blind spot.

"It's about to be the anniversary of his death, you know." Her eyes well up with tears. "Not that you'd care."

My immediate reaction is to roll my eyes. But again, I'm reminded that Davey Allen most likely had nothing to do with it, and feel a weird sense of shame about it all.

"How'd you get on the case anyway?" I ask. "I'm guessing the police don't know he's your brother?"

"I was there," she says. "That night at the pub. When Emma burst through the door, like some scene out of a horror film. I was the first one to see her, to speak to her. My fingers were covered in blood as I checked her for a pulse..." She drifts off, caught in the memory.

I look down at my hands, imagining the event as she continues to explain.

"Of course I was interested in knowing what she had to say, though I had no interest in being on the case, really. But they couldn't get her to talk, so the DCI asked me – begged me – to see if I could get her to open up. I've worked with women like her before, plenty of victims of abuse. And I thought if I could get her to talk, it would help her, it would help the police, and yeah, maybe it would finally exonerate my brother."

For a moment, I forget why I'm angry. It makes sense, her reasoning. But then I think of the PR nightmare, the loss of friends, the stress her actions have caused me. The accusations from the police...

No, I think. *What Charlotte has done to me is no different than what others did to her brother. She of all people should've refrained.*

"Why put me through what he went through then?" I ask, on the verge of tears. "It's ruined my—"

"Ruined your life?" She finishes my sentence. "No offence, but your castle crumbling wasn't something that concerned me. I'd just been told by a woman who'd been through hell that you were the reason she was there. I know it was rash of me, idiotic, foolish, whatever, to post the new findings online due to my station, but... my brother took his own life because of these accusations, I..." Her voice cracks and she looks away.

"Exactly. So why do that to someone else?" I press. "Did you ever think that maybe I'm being wrongfully accused too?"

She studies me. "Are you?"

"Yes!" I cry.

"Why would she accuse you then? I don't believe it was a case of jealousy. She meant it when she said it. I also know that she found Leila outside in the hot tub, dead, and you were nowhere to be seen."

"That's what she said?" I scoff, outraged.

"Is that not true?" Charlotte asks.

I pause. It is true. But Emma omitted a key detail. That when I came outside, she was the one holding the knife. I want to tell Charlotte, prove to her that Emma only told her fragments of what happened. But if I share my version of events, I have to reveal what I've been keeping a secret all these years, too.

"Why don't you tell me what happened then?" Charlotte asks when I don't respond.

"Oh yeah, so you can plaster it all over the internet," I retort.

"Well," she says, scrutinising me, "if you're innocent, then won't hearing your side clear your name?"

My heart pounds through my chest as I'm overcome with emotion, everything bubbling to the surface. Anger, grief, guilt. And I wonder if it finally is time to tell the whole truth.

But to her? To this unprofessional online gossipmonger?

I shift my belly forward and ready myself to leave before I overshare. But then I think of Emma, and the conversation we never got to have. All hope of a reconciliation ruined.

I exhale loudly, weighing the decision. How if Charlotte took this to the police without the full context, things would look even worse for me. If she truly cares about justice though, and sees that I *am* innocent, then she can help clear my name.

All I'd have to do is come clean about that one thing. Blood rushes to my face as I think about it.

"Okay," I say. "I'll tell you what really happened.

38

Kaleigh

I recap everything from that night, up to arriving back at the cabin. The thought of it gives me chills. The wooden structure, only illuminated by the Uber's headlights, hovering over us in the darkness.

The memory makes me want to clam up and find some way to push it away as usual. But I know I have to stay in it this time.

"I don't know what Emma told you," I tell Charlotte, recalling Emma and Leila shrieking at each other outside. "But she and Leila got in a huge fight when we got back to the cabin."

Charlotte nods.

"Did Emma tell you how she threatened to kill Leila and then punched her in the face, nearly broke her nose?"

Charlotte shifts in her seat and I can tell Emma didn't go into that much detail.

"Well, that's what happened."

"Okay." Charlotte says, gesturing for me to keep going.

"Leila wanted to leave, wanted to take Emma's keys and drive home, but I stopped her obviously, because she was so drunk." My voice cracks, wishing I'd let her go. I blink rapidly, not wanting to cry. It feels like it's all I've done lately.

"So I separated them," I say. "I genuinely thought they were going to kill each other. That's important to remember, okay?" I emphasise this, needing Charlotte to understand.

She nods and I continue.

"I'm in the kitchen with Emma, sitting on the floor, slugging vodka straight from the bottle. The room starts spinning around me, so I run to the bathroom to be sick, leaving Emma alone."

"Where was Leila at this point?" Charlotte asks.

"She's outside... in the hot tub." Sweat prickles at my forehead and I force myself to breathe again. "I hear her scream, so I run outside to see what happened and... there she is." My throat burns as I say it, as tears slip from my eyes.

I clench my fists, squeezing my thumbs as I envision Leila slumped over in a pool of red. I exhale, trying to steady myself, as I picture the scene again. And this time, it's as if I'm having an out-of-body experience, like I'm watching a movie.

"I rush over to Leila and pull her out of the water, foolishly thinking I could save her, give her CPR. But before I see it, I feel it. In the weight of her head, the way it lifts too easily from the front."

My stomach churns at the thought and for a moment I think I might be sick. I pause and focus on my breath. *In. Out. In. Out.* I clear my throat.

"And then I see Emma. Holding a large hunting knife." I picture Emma, eyes wild as they meet mine, before my gaze drifts to the knife in her hand, blood oozing from its razor-sharp edge onto her arm.

I look into Charlotte's dark brown eyes before I tell her what I did next. "You have to understand. Emma said she was going to kill Leila. And when I saw Emma holding the knife, I truly, in my heart of hearts, thought she'd hurt her. And I was scared of what she would do to me next, and I panicked, and..." I look away to the wall, unable to face Charlotte any longer as the guilt washes over me.

I close my eyes as I recall shuffling backward, feeling behind me for something, anything I could use against her, in case she came for me next. My hand knocked into something cold, a decorative stone, heavy and rough. I lodged my hand around the stone and pushed myself up.

I sob, as I finally own up to what I did.

"I grabbed a rock and just... hit her."

I recoil, remembering the feeling of it making contact with Emma's skull. How she fell to the ground and the blood that began to pool around her head. And then, how after someone showed up, I panicked and ran, not realising she was still alive. That I could have helped her.

39

Charlie

I stare at Kaleigh Turner as she describes the horror that unfolded that night. Naturally, I wonder if she's lying. If she has some sort of personality disorder, whether she's a compulsive or pathological liar and has convinced herself this is the truth. But, her body language, her demeanour, her confession... all point to honesty.

It makes sense now, why Emma would've blamed her. Emma potentially thought Kaleigh killed Leila and then hurt her, while Kaleigh thought Emma killed Leila and was going to kill her next. It was a devastating, tragic misunderstanding between two friends, one they'll never get to reconcile.

I believe Kaleigh – to my own chagrin. Because accepting her innocence means accepting that I was wrong. Not only about her involvement, but wrong to do what I did: falsely and publicly accuse her like others did to Davey.

I bite the inside of my cheek as I look at Kaleigh in a new

light. Not as a suspect or someone who framed my brother. But as a victim, like him. Like Emma.

Hypocrite, I think to myself.

Feeling ashamed, I stand up and make my way across the desk. "Kaleigh," I say, placing a hand on her back. "It's okay."

"It's not though, is it?" She dabs her nose with a tissue. "If I hadn't freaked out and just assumed she'd hurt Leila, we could've escaped together and they would've never taken her."

They. The word sends a chill down my spine as I think of Gaz Barker and a mystery accomplice.

"What happened after you hit her, before you ran? What exactly did you see?"

She inhales deeply and then exhales a shaky breath, before continuing. I listen intently as she explains in more detail what unfolded.

"I was sitting on the deck, between what I assume are my two dead best friends. And I didn't know what to do. Would the police think *I* killed them both? Or could I just tell them the truth – or what I thought to be true in that moment – that Emma hurt Leila so I tried to stop her from hurting me in self-defence? Either way, I wanted to call for help, I really did, but I genuinely couldn't. My phone was dead, theirs had no service. And that's when a horrible thought crept in. What if it wasn't Emma? What if… it was someone else? What if the real killer was there, lying in wait?"

The colour drains from Kaleigh's face. She rubs her arms, now covered in goosebumps, like mine. I imagine a faceless man, hiding in the night, watching Kaleigh, waiting to take Emma.

"And then, I saw something in the woods. A light."

"Like a torch?"

"No, no," she says. "A small light. Like from a phone maybe? It blinked a few times and I thought I could hear it beeping."

I nod, remembering this from her original police statement.

"So I sat there, frozen, for about twenty minutes, paralysed in fear. Thought maybe if I didn't make any noise, they'd leave me alone."

I think of the rest of Kaleigh's original police statement, how she said a car pulled up next, and she saw someone wearing black.

"But then someone arrived, didn't they?" I ask, picturing Gaz Barker.

Her eyes well with tears again, and I can see the fear on her face, feel it radiating off of her as she confirms.

"A car pulled up," Kaleigh says. "It broke the trance I was in. I didn't know what to do so I hid. I climbed over the wooden rail and wedged myself under the deck. In the wet mud."

Kaleigh scratches at her skin instinctively, her body remembering the event as if it's happening in real time, a tell she's recalling a memory, not lying.

"I could hear him, getting closer. First the gravel crunching from the drive, then his distant voice, talking to someone on the phone, or so I assumed. And then his footsteps." Kaleigh swallows hard. "I held my breath, forced myself not to cry. Even though Leila's blood was dripping through the creaking wood above me." She twitches.

I picture the scene, the horror she must've felt.

"There's two bodies," Kaleigh whispers, looking down. "Need to get them out of here. Clean this mess up."

I go cold as she lifts her gaze, her brown eyes meeting.

"That's what he said."

40

Harry

Harry takes his boots off before entering the house. Once inside, he offloads his items into their designated place. Keys on the left hook, jacket on the right hook and boots in the silver-wire pull-out bin underneath. His chest is tight with anxiety, as it's been ever since Emma came back and even more so since her death.

Her death. The fact still knocks the wind out of him.

He glances at the storage unit, perfectly neat and tidy, everything organised into their assigned unit. He wishes he could compartmentalise the rest of his life that easily. Home life here, emotional trauma there. Football, separated from all the rest. But unfortunately, he can't. A fact that's becoming clear on and off the pitch. He's too drained to worry about it now though, just wants to eat something and go to bed.

He pushes open the utility door, noting how the house seems quieter than normal. No TV playing from the kitchen,

KELLY AND KRISTINA MANCARUSO

no giggling or screaming Alfie. Harry doesn't like it, makes him think of what his future could be like if they stay on this path.

"Kay?" he calls out, before registering that her car wasn't in the drive when he returned home.

He wonders where she could be, used to her always being home these days. The paparazzi camped outside made it difficult for her to leave, trapping her inside the house.

But while home is Kaleigh's cage, it's become Harry's refuge. The stadium used to be his source of comfort and energy, where he always wanted to be, but now he feels like an outsider, like he doesn't belong. His teammates avoid him, his coach is frustrated with him. The thought of having to travel to Scotland on Thursday to face-off against the same team as last week makes him want to disappear. He doesn't know if he'll be able to cope with the raucous fans again, trying to see how far they can push him before he snaps. As if he's a wild animal being poked.

"*Useless piece of shit, you are, Turner!*"

Poke.

"*Your missus in prison yet, Turner?*"

Poke.

"*Want me to sort her out for you so you can focus, Turner?*"

Poke.

"*I got money on this game, Turner, don't fuck it up or I'll fuck—*"

Snap.

Harry grunts, slapping himself in the face to stop the onslaught of comments. Stop the images of them screaming at him, spit flying from their mouths as their mates howl with laughter.

Keep your head straight, he imagines his dad saying. *World Cup is next year, you need to stay focused.*

But then he thinks of Banes's face at the police station, taunting him in a different kind of way. A scarier way. He imagines himself in a different cage: a prison cell.

Harry starts to spiral, thinking of Theo Abara, of that night five years ago. His foot on the ball, his heart racing. The phone call. The text. And then he thinks of worse things. Of Leila and Emma's bodies. Of someone coming for Kaleigh next.

He whips his head around, grateful for the sound of the garage door opening, meaning she's home and safe. He wants to hold her, to feel her in his arms.

She walks in and looks up at him. His heart sinks. Her eyes are red, cheeks wet.

"What happened?" Harry says, rushing over to her. He places his hands on her belly. "Are you... is Alf—"

"He's fine," Kaleigh whispers. "I asked your mom to pick him up from nursery."

Harry relaxes a little, relieved everyone is physically well. He wraps his wife in his arms and presses his lips into her soft hair. "Come on, let's sit down."

Harry guides Kaleigh from the utility through the kitchen to their sitting room. He helps her onto the sofa and sits next to her, placing one hand on her shoulder and the other on her hands, which fidget in her lap.

She leans into him, wanting to be held. So he holds her and doesn't say anything, just lets her tears soak into his shirt. He wonders why she's so upset. Is it about Emma? Has it only just hit her? Is it something with the police?

"I've been lying to you." Her voice is barely audible.

"What?" Harry stops breathing, caught off guard, his brain on high alert as Emma's warning about Kaleigh rings in his head.

She pulls back and wipes her hand under her eyes, smearing brown eye shadow and mascara further up her cheek.

"I don't want there to be any more secrets between us," Kaleigh says. "I know why Emma blamed me. I… I left out something from that night." Harry wonders if she can feel his heart beating out of his chest.

"That night," she continues, "Emma and Leila got into a huge argument. Over you. Emma was so angry, she said she'd kill Leila. Not long after, Leila was actually murdered. I thought it was Emma. When I saw her standing with the knife I… I hit her." Kaleigh cries out, burying her face inside her hands.

"Hit who?" Harry shakes his head. "Kay, I don't un—"

"Emma." Kaleigh snaps. "I thought she killed Leila and was going to hurt me, so I… I… hit her on the head, knocked her out. I thought I'd killed her, but not on purpose! Then when *they* showed up, I realised it hadn't been Emma that hurt Leila – I was wrong. And it's all my fault Emma was even taken in the first place. But I swear I didn't mean…" She looks up at me, pleading eyes filled with tears.

"Shh, shh, it's okay," Harry says, comforting her as he tries to process everything. He gulps, feeling guilty for how he treated Emma this past week. Still, it doesn't change anything. Doesn't change how he feels about Kaleigh or his loyalty to her. He knows her heart, trusts what she's saying. He's on her side, always would be.

Till death do us part.

"Kaleigh," he says. "It's not your fault. You can't blame yourself for what Gaz chose to do."

An uncomfortable feeling settles in his stomach when he remembers that it wasn't just Gaz. That someone must've been working with him, and they're the one who killed Emma. The skin on the back of Harry's neck prickles as an unwanted notion crosses his mind, something he'd been worrying about all week. Something he thought he didn't have to worry about ever since Davey Allen was arrested all those years ago.

"Oh, and to top it all off," Kaleigh sniffles, "I told somebody all of this to try and make things better. And I think I accidentally confirmed that you were having an affair with Leila in the process."

His heart hammers now, more worried than before. "Who did you tell?"

"The psychologist. You know, the one that we saw at the hospital with Emma."

Harry stares at her in disbelief, so many questions running through his mind.

"It's a long story," she says, voice nasal from crying. "I think I might've just made everything worse. It's all my fault, all of it. And…" She looks down at her belly and bursts into tears again.

Harry grasps Kaleigh's hand and squeezes it before letting it go, realising just how sweaty his palms have become. *Should he tell her?*

Kaleigh finally looks at Harry, her honey brown eyes boring into his. But they don't hold hope like they usually do. They look dim and hollow.

Harry stands up and shakes out his arms, but it doesn't stop the nerves from coursing through his veins. He never wanted to tell her, knows she'll never look at him the same way if he does. But what else can he do? He can't stay silent, stand by like a coward and let her think she's to blame. Especially when he knows the truth.

41

Harry

Harry always wondered what it would be like to make it to the top. To have everything he needed and everything he ever wanted. He imagined he would be happy. Satisfied. But he wasn't. He wanted more. More cars, more clothes, more women, more money.

And it was all there, available to him, with the swipe of a card or the mere mention of his name. Until it wasn't.

He explains to Kaleigh how this dose of reality hit in 2019 after a trip to Vegas with Theo and a few other teammates. They'd just finished their best season and went to celebrate. From the finest dining to the hottest clubs, nothing could interrupt Harry's high. Drinking, eating, fucking. More and more. Over and over again until he found a new kind of high: gambling.

Harry played and played, rolling the dice, calling out numbers, pushing out chips, pulling levers. He'd win. He'd lose. Then win some more, his bets getting bigger and bigger every time – just like his losses.

But Harry didn't care about the losses. Not yet at least. He was Harry-fucking-Turner. He'd be fine. He had the money. And if he lost, he'd win it back.

Only he didn't. He kept losing, which only spurred him on, a devil on his shoulder telling him to keep going, that it was worth chasing the high of winning big again. He knew he needed to stop. But he couldn't help himself, getting into other forms of gambling, placing a new bet whenever he'd get a chance, whether on horse races or other sport. He'd then try to pay it back by doing every cheesy ad campaign and endorsement he could think of. Until even that couldn't make him enough.

"You have to understand," he says to Kaleigh, recalling the feeling of his addiction, "I owed so much money. I was in deep. With no way out. Until Theo showed me one."

Kaleigh remains silent, as if she's holding her breath. Worried where her mind is wandering, Harry continues, explaining that the solution was harmless, something that wouldn't hurt anyone. A win-win.

"So unbeknownst to me," Harry says, "Theo was making money on football… through betting."

"Like match-fixing?" Kaleigh says, shocked. She's stopped crying now, distracted by Harry's confession.

"Nothing that major," Harry says quickly. "It was stupid shit, like he'd plan to tackle someone in the first half and get a card. And these bookies would give him 30k, just for doing that."

Kaleigh frowns, looking suspicious, but Harry continues, explaining how Theo liaised between him and the bookies, and they'd agree over coded texts what Harry could do for similar sums. Smaller amounts of money for things that really wouldn't affect the game like minor tackles, and larger amounts for things like booting the ball wide that could have a bigger impact. It's called spot-fixing.

"But I was stupid and naïve," Harry says. "Didn't realise that once you're involved with these people, the asks only get bigger, and then they have stuff to use against you, so you better listen to them, yeah?"

Harry can see Kaleigh trying to piece together what happened, her full lips pursed, eyes wary. "What did they ask you to do that day?"

Harry exhales, readying himself to share his own secret. *If she can do it, so can I*, he tells himself.

"It was a massive game, we needed to win…"

Kaleigh nods. "I remember watching you take the penalty… with Emma." She says Emma's name in a whisper and her eyes well with tears again. Harry talks faster, wanting to distract her from her own demons by sharing his.

"I got a text only a couple of hours before the match."

Harry remembers it like it was yesterday. How his heart sank.

"They wanted me to miss a penalty if I got one. Said I should get a chance at one, but I needed to miss it."

"You mean they set that tackle up?"

Harry nods, swallowing the lump in his throat. Before the game, he foolishly agreed to the plan, justifying that if the tackle was a set-up, then him missing the kick was fair. He hadn't realised how different he'd feel in the moment though.

He vividly remembers charging towards the net, following the ball that'd just been served to him. The ball hit the grass, he tapped it under control, then sped past Theo Abara – who was playing for the opposition following a transfer.

Then he was in the box, his only obstacle the keeper. Harry zoned in on the left corner, pulled his foot back, and *BAM!* He's taken out from behind, a clean swipe right under his left foot from Abara. Harry hit the ground, rolling, tasting dirt and grass and blood in his mouth. He rolled over, groaning as the ref blew the whistle and signalled a penalty kick.

You'll be given a penalty. Miss it. 70k.

It was as if he was at war with himself from the second he registered what had happened. He looked from his excited teammates to a steely-eyed Theo, who nodded at him knowingly.

As Harry walked up to the spot to take the kick, he thought of his team, down one goal. He thought of the ardent supporters. He thought of his dad. He thought of himself and how this opportunity could make or break him.

"I couldn't do it, Kay," Harry says, voice shaking. "I couldn't do it. Couldn't purposefully miss. I thought they just wouldn't pay me. Never thought they'd—"

He struggles to finish the words. To admit to what he'd feared for so long.

42

Kaleigh

I can feel the blood drain from my face as Harry finishes his confession, explaining how he received a text later that night, telling him he'd face consequences.

"And then the next day, the police told me what happened," Harry says.

I want to comfort him, tell him that it's okay, that I appreciate him telling me this dark secret like I appreciated him for understanding mine, but I can't ignore the anger bubbling inside.

"You knew who did it all this time? And you never said anything?" I think about Emma, taken and held prisoner. How she could've been found earlier. How she might still be alive today.

"No!" Harry says, horrified. "That's the thing, I don't know who they are."

I open my mouth to argue, tell him he still could've given the information to the police, but then I realise that if he did, if he admitted to match-fixing, he would incriminate himself. A small voice also reminds me of my own lies.

"I tried…" Harry continues. "I tried to tell the police that I thought it could be someone wanting revenge on me, tried to point them in the right direction. But then they connected Davey Allen, found his DNA on Leila. And I started to think maybe it was him, that maybe the people who threatened me were just bluffing."

"You thought they just left you alone?" I ask, wondering how he could be so naive.

I look at him, feeling uneasy being near him for the first time in my life. But then, as he breaks down in front of me, I remember our vows. *For better, for worse.* And I also remember the part I played in all this, how he opened up to me now so there would be no secrets between us, so I wouldn't blame myself. But somehow, things feel more dire.

I hold his face in my hands and press my head to his. We sit there together in our guilt for a moment before I pull away.

"Did you tell anyone else about this?" I ask, expecting him to say no.

"Dad knows," he says.

I think of the disappointment Robbie must've felt finding out his son was involved in match-fixing. "What did he say?"

"What do you think? He said I was a fucking brainless git."

My anger redirects from Harry to Robbie. I knew Robbie had been tough on him and Simon growing up, but especially Harry, pushing him to extremes. Not that you'd ever know by their relationship now. With how inseparable they are.

"Dad tried to help. Tried to take care of it. But he could only do so much, ya know? Get so far. If these people don't wanna be found, they won't be. When they didn't get back in touch, we figured that it was over. That Dad's message got through to them. Or that I really had paid my price…"

"But why Leila?" I ask. "How is that *you* paying a price?" The memory of my friend's sliced throat sends my blood ice cold. I swallow down my sick. "Why not kill Emma and be done with it, why kill Leila? Did they know about you two? Maybe they did and that's why they hurt them both?"

Harry shrugs and doesn't say anything. He won't meet my gaze, but he squeezes my hands and kisses them. My stomach churns when I realise what he's leaving unsaid. That they would've killed me or taken me too if I hadn't got away.

Three bodies. Not just two.

I imagine the same person who sent the text then going to the cabin for his revenge against Harry. Me and my friends, collateral damage. All for a stupid game of football.

"We have to find out who did this," I say. "They can't get away with it. I won't be able to sleep knowing they're still out there…"

"Kaleigh, we can't," Harry says. "Were you not listening? I don't know who they are. My dad couldn't even track them down. And even if we knew who they were, don't you see how dangerous that would be?" He exhales and lowers his tone. "What makes you think they wouldn't go after you… or Alfie."

My jaw clenches when he mentions Alfie.

"Why would you say that?" I push Harry away.

He places his hands on my shoulders and stares at me. "I'm not trying to scare you for the sake of it, Kay. I'm telling you this because these people are dangerous."

I start to cry again, fear and frustration taking over.

"How can I just let this go? Surely you have a phone number or something we can pass along to someone. They don't have to know it's us, but they need to be caught."

Harry holds his head in his hands and sighs. He knows something, I can tell.

"Tell me!" I shout.

"They always used different phone numbers and it would come in as unidentified anyway. But I have the name of the company they wanted me to transfer the money to, and where it came from when they paid me. But I've already tried to track them, it's a shell company. It's impossible—"

"Just tell me," I demand.

And he does.

43

Charlie

Tuesday 11 March 2025

I'm on my way into work, walking through the car park, when a white Range Rover pulls up beside me. I pay it no mind at first, until the driver rolls down the window and calls out to me. It's strange to hear my formal name, Charlotte. My friends and family call me Charlie, and everyone else Dr Singh. But Kaleigh Turner and I became acquainted under unusual circumstances.

"Kaleigh, is everything okay?" I ask, approaching the vehicle.

She looks dishevelled. So much different to our first encounter at the hospital one week ago, and even worse than yesterday, like she hasn't slept at all.

"Sorry to turn up like this. I was hoping to…" She looks around, not finishing her sentence. "Do you have a minute?"

Already late for an appointment, I don't. But I'm too curious to know why she's here.

"What is it?" I ask.

Kaleigh is distracted by a cry from the backseat.

"Sorry, one sec." She grabs the iPad on the passenger seat, turns it on and passes it back to Alfie. "Look at the pretty cars, Alfie."

"Like Unc Simon's vwoom vwooms," he says, appeased.

"Yes, just like Uncle Simon's vroom vrooms."

She turns back to me, cheeks flushed. "I don't always give him an iPad." She blushes like all parents trying to defend their screen time choices.

"It's actually not as bad as you think," I say, putting her at ease. "Some screen time is completely fine."

She smiles, grateful, as I wait impatiently for her to get on with it.

Kaleigh looks back at Alfie once more before lowering her voice to speak. "I need to tell you something, but... you have to promise you won't tell the police."

I frown, not wanting to make any more promises. When we parted ways yesterday, we agreed that we'd keep each other's secrets. She wouldn't say anything about my Reddit side gig, and I wouldn't divulge what she told me about that night.

"I'm not sure I can make any promises, Kaleigh."

"Do you want justice for your brother or not?" she says. "Because believe me you'll want to hear this."

I sigh, unable to resist. "Fine."

"Okay." She takes a breath and looks around. "I think, well... I'm almost positive, I know who did it."

My heart jumps. "What? Who?" I lean in closer.

"I mean, I know who theoretically did it. Not a person per se," she corrects.

My shoulders deflate and I want to roll my eyes.

Kaleigh looks from left to right and then back at me, her large black sunglasses making her look like a paranoid conspiracy theorist. She lowers her voice even more and leans so close I can smell the vanilla latte on her breath. "It was the match-fixers, bookies, whatever you call them."

I raise an eyebrow, not expecting this answer. It reminds me of something a schizophrenic patient would say, and I wonder if I was right about Kaleigh not being mentally sound. But then she explains, and I'm not so sure what to think.

Kaleigh divulges how after our meeting yesterday, she opened up to Harry. And Harry, who must've felt guilty that Kaleigh felt at fault for everything, finally told her the secrets that *he'd* been keeping all these years. Told her that if anyone, he was to blame.

I want to say something sarcastic, like "how very noble of him", but stop myself.

"They set him up for a penalty that night and he was supposed to miss. But he didn't," Kaleigh continues, almost breathless.

I cock my head, intrigued for a myriad of reasons. I'd heard about this kind of thing in sport before and knew it happened, but it was so rare for anything to ever be proven. If this got out...

"They told him he'd regret it. But he didn't think they'd mean..." Kaleigh trails off, looking around again, clearly paranoid someone's listening in. "I've never seen Harry so scared. He didn't want me to say anything. Thinks if I do, they'll come after me or..." She stops, unable to say her son's name.

And suddenly the pieces start to fall into place. It'd been established that Gaz was into shady business and it's very possible that his accomplice was into something like match-fixing. Maybe they were more than an accomplice and were the mastermind. Like any organised crime syndicate, these kinds of people aren't afraid to go to the cruellest lengths to punish those who hinder their profits. The 2020 attack could've very well been retaliation against Harry, to teach him a lesson.

"But why kill Leila?" I ask.

Kaleigh shrugs. "Collateral damage. Or maybe they knew about the affair, thought they'd hurt him twice? Or maybe..." She pauses before explaining Theo Abara's involvement in it all.

My mind spins with all the revelations, all the essential information police needed to know all those years ago, but obviously Harry and Theo would never confess to that voluntarily.

My blood runs hot as I think of Davey and how he got dragged into it all. The DNA on Leila's fingernails could be explained away by the confrontation in the bar. But had he actually been framed to take the fall?

"Kaleigh, this is important information the police need to do their job though," I say. "I think we should tell them."

"No!" she snaps, horrified at the suggestion. "Can you imagine the field day the press would have? Harry's career would be over! And it wouldn't surprise me if police jump the gun and try to pin everything on him, too. Then that would be *another* unjust arrest, something neither of us want. Don't you dare tell Maynard. And don't you even think about posting anything on your little Reddit because I will turn you in so fast." She pokes a finger at me.

"Okay." I hold my hands up, trusting she'd make good on her threat. "I won't say or post anything. But what are you expecting *me* to do with this information?"

Kaleigh fishes in her purse for something and then hands me a small piece of paper, torn out of a notebook. "This is the name of the company Harry received payments from. I thought maybe you know someone – that isn't Maynard or Banes – that could help you find out more. I tried and couldn't get anywhere. But if we find out who owns it…"

Then we find the killer.

44

Charlie

After my appointment, I sit at my desk, fixating on the tiny piece of paper from Kaleigh with the name of a company on one side and her phone number on the other. I flip it from front to back, back to front, as I wonder how something so small could carry so much weight. How it could represent so many different things. Like Kaleigh's trust.

I should go to Maynard straight away with the information. But I won't. I'll keep my promise to Kaleigh, still feeling guilty about everything I posted about her on Reddit. We're unlikely allies now, both wanting the same thing: justice.

Harry's lucky to have her, I think, not feeling any kind of loyalty towards him.

I recall a patient from a few years ago, who was involved in something similar. He didn't have a Kaleigh looking out for him, and ended up in prison. He was a boxer who'd taken so many blows to the head that his brain developed early onset dementia. But before that, he had explained to me how he got involved in match-fixing, how boxing was the only other sport that rivalled football in corruption. And how the boxer eventually turned to a life of crime when he could no longer pay off his debts.

I know Harry's situation is a bit different though, that he only did it a few times when he was younger, even though it looks like those harmless occasions turned into something catastrophic if Kaleigh's theory is correct. But still, I don't hold much sympathy for him. He got himself into the situation by being irresponsible in the first place. And then omitted essential information which resulted in multiple people being killed. All to protect his career.

But then I think of myself in my twenties. And all the young offenders I also see who make bad decisions. I find athletes, actors and musicians are particularly fascinating in terms of the way their psyche works. I try to imagine what it would be like to be given all this fame and money practically overnight at such a young age. Without proper guidance and maturity, it's no wonder Harry got in over his head.

I sigh, doubling down on my decision not to tell Maynard. I'd do what I promised Kaleigh and try to figure this out with her.

I read over the name of the company again, EC Holdings Mgmt, trying out the name on my tongue to see if it rings any bells. But it doesn't. A name as anonymous as its owner or owners. Whoever "they" are.

I find myself starting to rip the paper as my anger grows once again at the injustice of it all. That this person had continued to roam free while Leila, Emma and my brother were buried in the dirt.

I'm going to bury them, I think, feeling like I'm on the right path. Albeit a dark one. But then I remember that no, even if I could bring myself to kill, it wouldn't be good enough. I need the real killer to be convicted publicly so I can fully clear Davey's name.

"Focus," I say aloud this time as I type the company name into my search bar. But no website or anything of note shows up, except an ad to a corporate registry database. I click the ad, which is unlike me, input my information, pay the fee, and finally find something. The location of where the company is registered: the British Virgin Islands.

I know I should stop and prepare for my next appointment, but instead I open a new tab and type in: *How to form an anonymous business in BVI.*

The results load quickly, showing a combination of sponsored companies who can help create anonymous offshore accounts to websites defining what an offshore account is and how to make one. I click into an article that seems more professional than the others.

I skim through the parts that explain what a shell company is and how it's used to operate business away from the watchful eye of the law. Basically, a perfect way to clean and wire dirty money. Match-fixing money.

I continue to scroll, skipping over the requirements needed to open and manage one, and pause on the words "owner identity". According to the article, the name of the owner may be shown on British Virgin Island Bank paperwork but will more than likely be the information of the registered agent, which isn't always the same as the owner.

I tap my pen on my desk, unsure what to do next. So I turn to Reddit for help, searching for: *How to find out the owner of an anonymous shell company registered in BVI.*

As usual with the platform, there's already plenty of threads on the niche topic. I click into one and read through the responses, overwhelmed by the sheer amount of information and acronyms. SEC. CPA. LLC. EDGAR. I keep scrolling, scanning the page for any clear instructions, pausing on a response that gives me an idea.

CorporateWarped: *There is no easy way for a member of the public to find out the owner of a shell registered to BVI. Would need help from a forensic accountant or a hacker tbh.*

I think of my uni friend Callum Moss, now a forensic accountant.

Callum and I met during a group project for our Forensic Psychology course at uni. While I was most interested in the criminal mind and the "why", Callum was interested in the way they operated – the "how", like money laundering.

I open up my Instagram and click into his page, scrolling through his grid. I blush, thinking of the few times we'd been more than friendly. As far as I can tell, Callum is single now, only posting pictures of him and his dog from time to time.

Nothing to lose, I sigh as I slide into his DMs. I ask if he's free after work, telling him drinks are on me because I have a forensic accounting question.

I start to gather my things, already a few minutes late for my session in the psychiatric wing, when his reply comes through.

So good to hear from you, Charlie! Would love to
help. Why don't you tell me what it is now in case
I need to research and then we'll catch up for
drinks later? Just tell me where and when!

My face reddens as I realise I accidentally set myself up
on a date. I'm surprised by the butterflies swirling in my
stomach, a feeling I hadn't experienced in months, if not
years. I reply, letting him know when and where, and also
tell him I'm looking for information on the owner of EC
Holdings Mgmt, a shell company registered to the British
Virgin Islands.

To my delight, Callum is as reliable as I remember.

I think I found something, he texts, only a couple
of hours later.

45

Kaleigh

A pit forms in my stomach as I gather all of the dirty laundry from around the house, wondering if I'd aired too much of mine.

Did I tell Charlotte too much? Can I really trust her? The worries pile up in my mind. *What if she accidentally tips off the bookies, sends them on an unintended final revenge plot against my family?*

Maybe I made a mistake, looking into this when Harry had begged me not to. And especially after we'd decided not to keep any more secrets...

I'm still surprised at how much we'd been hiding from each other and even more surprised at how sharing our deepest secrets ended up bringing us closer. It's a relief and a burden at the same time. Because, now more than ever, it makes me want to do anything to protect Harry and our family. And I won't feel safe until the monster is caught.

My phone's ringtone interrupts my thoughts, and I fumble for it as it slides to the bottom of the laundry basket. I grab the dirty clothes in stacks, holding my breath as I get to an armful of Harry's training shirts.

Once half empty, I turn the basket upside down until my phone falls on top of the load.

"Hello?" I answer.

"Kaleigh, it's Charlie. Dr Singh."

My chest tightens, praying that she's calling to tell me she's found something and not because she's decided to tell the police. I take her using her nickname as a good sign though.

"Hi Charlie," I say, trying it out. "Have you found anything?"

"Yes," she whispers.

She doesn't stop to wait for my acknowledgement though, launching into details as I walk to the living room to check on Alfie. "The company disclosed an affiliation with a special purchase vehicle out of the British Virgin Islands."

"Okay?" I say, as more of a question than a statement because I have no idea what this means.

She senses my confusion and simplifies it for me. "It means the owner messed up. Basically, they disclosed a connection to a separate shell company that is made for the sole purpose of buying expensive luxury goods like a yacht or an exotic sports car."

"Okay," I say again, feeling like a complete idiot for not understanding.

"By law, the beneficial owner of a luxury asset or SPV has to register with the BVI authorities, which means if we can find the record we can find the real owner's name."

Finally, I get where she is going and let out an excited exhale. "That's amazing. How do we find it?"

"Well, that's the tricky part," Charlie sighs. "You can only request access to the database if you can prove illicit activity. But since we're not going through the proper channels here, we're kind of stuck."

"Hmm," I try to think of anyone who may be able to help. I think of my friend Natasha then, who once bragged about her "amazing financial advisor" in the British Virgin Islands who helped her save a ton on taxes, and tell Charlie I may have another way.

"I have an idea, I know someone who may be able to help," I say. "I'll call you back."

I close out of my phone app and click into WhatsApp before finding Natasha's last message to me. I just want you to know I'm here for you, love. I believe you xx.

I think of Jackie then, of how she told me to trust no one. How anyone, even my friends, could be talking to the press. But I mouth a big "screw you" to Jackie and reply to the only friend I seem to have left.

Thanks, doll. Sorry it took me so long to respond. It's been a lot. I actually have a favour to ask… something that could help me find the person responsible. Give me a call when you can xoxo

I finish loading the laundry when another idea pops into my head. A better way to kill time while I wait for Natasha's response. I throw on some leggings and bring Alfie a pair of shoes.

"Put these on so we can go see Uncle Simon's vroom vrooms."

"We're here, baby," I say to Alfie as we pull into Turner Classic Motors, Simon's car dealership and repair shop, passed down from Robbie.

I leave a space between Simon's vintage convertible and my Range Rover. I can't get out of my car these days without having the door wide open.

Before we head in, I check my phone to see if Natasha has responded, even though we just spoke. She called me almost immediately and I explained the information I was looking for. She said she was confident "her guy" could track something down, to leave it with her. So I did.

While I wait for him to come through, I continue with my plan to learn whatever I can about how luxury cars are bought and sold to see if it sparks any other leads.

Alfie's still sleeping, as he usually is after any car ride that lasts longer than fifteen minutes. He wakes slowly, opening his big, beautiful eyes, the same warm shade as Harry's. "That's it, baby. Let's see the vroom vrooms and then get ice cream. Okay?"

He instantly perks up. "Ice cweam!"

I smile as I unbuckle him from his car seat. We hold hands as we walk to the showroom around the front.

"Simon?" I call out, admiring the pristine, gleaming cars parked inside. I hold Alfie close, knowing Simon wouldn't love his nephew's oily fingerprints smudged across the paintwork.

Simon doesn't answer, so I head through to the back of

the shop where his office is. I frown, still no sign of him. That's when I hear some noise in the distance, coming from the warehouse. I sigh, feeling winded at the thought of walking across the lot to the metal-clad building, but I waddle forth nonetheless. A cramp hits me once I reach the door and I pause to catch my breath.

Once inside, my senses are overwhelmed. Clinks and clanks echo through the large metal interior, which smells strongly of petrol and paint. I spot Simon near the back, polishing a bright blue car. I cramp again on my way to greet him, passing rows of vehicles, ranging from vintage to modern, all at different stages of the restoration process.

Simon startles when we reach him. "Shit, you scared me. You shouldn't be here."

My heart sinks. "Sorry, I should've called ahead."

"No, no," he corrects. "Here I mean." He gestures around him. "Fumes and tools everywhere. Bad for both of ya."

I instinctively pull my coat over my mouth as Alfie hugs Simon's leg. "Hey, little man, let's get you and your mum out of this dingy place."

"Ohh, I wanted to see the vwoom vwooms," Alfie says, disappointed.

"We can see the real nice ones in the showroom, how 'bout that?"

Alfie doesn't answer though, just starts sprinting ahead of us. I let out a laboured exhale as I try to keep up with him. Simon notices though and runs ahead to make sure Alfie doesn't touch anything he isn't meant to.

I smile as I follow the two of them, a perfect uncle and nephew pair, wondering how Harry could have ever fallen out with Simon so badly that they hadn't talked for over a year.

But then I think of Harry's confession earlier and how different he was back then, and wonder if the fault actually lay with my husband.

Alfie weaves in and out of the cars once we make it back to the showroom. "Careful, Alf," I warn as he picks up speed, getting dangerously close to bashing into the vintage Mustang.

Simon grabs Alfie's hand and guides him into the front seat of an old red car where he begins to play with the steering wheel.

"So tell me about the world of luxury cars," I say, not really knowing where to start. I figure learning something is better than nothing.

Simon frowns. "Well, what do you wanna know?"

I want to tell him the real reason I'm interested. That Harry was threatened by match-fixers the night me and Leila and Emma were attacked. That I believe that's the person who killed Emma. That if I can just find out the owner who purchased a luxury sports car in the British Virgin Islands for EC Holdings Mgmt, then I could find the real killer.

But that'd be a bit much for now. So I stick with a simpler explanation. "Don't know, just curious."

I try to think of what I could ask to learn more about the financing side of things. Like why someone would need to create a special company to purchase one. "What do the most expensive or rare ones usually go for?"

Simon lets out a whistle. "It varies a lot. If you're talking a new Rolls-Royce, you're looking at a few hundred thousand. Or if you're talking about a rare, historic one, could be looking upwards of that, into the millions. A couple years back, the Mercedes Uhlenhaut Coupé sold at auction for a hundred-fifteen mil."

"One hundred and fifteen million pounds?" I ask, taken aback. "And how would the financing work on something like that? Would you have to put it in a specialty purpose vehicle fund or something?"

"Well, that's oddly specific." Simon furrows his brow. "That kind of money though? Who knows. Most of the people I deal with have the cash to buy outright. Or they'll pay in instalments, we set up a finance plan for them. I don't really know much about where they funnel that money from, so long as I get it."

I nod. I continue to let Alfie climb in and out of cars for a little longer, wondering what else, if anything, I should ask until I finally get a ping from Natasha.

46

Charlie

I fish a protein bar out of my bag as I type up my notes from my final session of the day. It was a difficult one, an assessment with a young male offender being treated at the hospital after a bar fight.

As with many offenders of his sex and age, he was curt and distant when we started our one-to-one. This is usually because these individuals have been coldly communicated with by police and other law enforcement up to this point. But as we progressed through our session and he started to believe that I was there to help him, to understand what had happened without the motive of using what he says against him, he opened up.

He broke down, turned into a puddle of tears and snot. And I couldn't stop thinking about my brother. How broken he was after his arrest.

"I swear to ya," Alex said, catching me off guard. Same accent, same phrasing my brother once used, "I didn't mean to kill him, I just... I don't know, he kept winding me up then shoved me so I whacked him."

I could tell straight away that Alex was not a narcissist, on the contrary, his admission of the crime and apologetic display of regret also pointed to him having compassion, empathy, and also that the problem seemed to be controlling his impulses.

Impulsive violence. Suspected ADHD.

I finish typing my suggestion to the court, that Alex should be further evaluated for a behavioural disorder, before closing my laptop. Cases like this are the ones that often stay with me, keep me up at night, cycling through a million what-if scenarios about my brother. My heart thumps, thinking of the possibility again of Davey being framed, and I'm angry all over again, imagining these bookies out there choosing him as their scapegoat.

I check the time, twenty minutes until I'm supposed to leave to meet Callum. The thought of a cold beer touching my lips sets me slightly at ease, though I hope this pub visit doesn't end like the last one did. With a girl covered in blood.

I think of how much my life has changed since that night, how it's rocketed everything back from the past. How it's brought me here, now, to withholding information from the police and looking into alleged sport corruption at the highest level. I laugh at how ridiculous it seems, me trying to figure out how to identify the owner of a specialty vehicle purchased by a shell company.

I lean back in my chair, running through the new variables. Match-fixing. BVI. Luxury purchases. Mysterious vehicles...

"Hmm," I pause, cocking my head to the side.

This isn't the first mysterious car flagged in connection to the Nightmare in Notts case. My heart begins to race as the pieces slot into place. The car caught on CCTV the morning of Leila's murder. The car caught on the neighbour's camera the morning of Emma's murder. Both without plates. And then of course, the latest development, an uber-expensive car purchased by a shell company that Harry Turner was paid through for match-fixing.

That's three links to cars.

Four, a voice whispers. Chills shoot down my arms when I recall something Kaleigh said this morning to her son. Something about "Uncle Simon's pretty vroom vrooms".

I whip out my phone, fumbling as I type in "Simon Turner cars Nottinghamshire". And there it is: *Turner Classic Motors, Nottinghamshire's classic car sales and repairs, owned by Simon Turner.*

My hands are shaking as I pick up my phone to call Maynard, needing to verify he's looked into Simon Turner before.

"Dr Singh?" Maynard says upon answering.

"Hello, DCI, you alright?"

"Sun's shining for once, so can't be doing too bad," he jokes.

I force a laugh before quickly moving on. "Look, I'm sorry to bother you about this, but I just found out that Simon Turner owns a car dealership in the area, which I'm sure you're aware of. I was wondering if he's been questioned at all, or if you've had a chance to search his place, you know because of the stolen car connection in both 2020 and now…"

"Uhhh," Maynard drags out. "I mean, he's not actively on the radar, no. There's tons of car dealerships in the area, but obviously we'd need a warrant to search any. So we'd need a solid connection."

"Is it not enough that he's related to a suspect?" I ask.

"Eh," he says dismissively before pausing. "Still not enough. Nothing concrete that would convince a judge to grant a search warrant. Unless there's something I'm missing, something Emma said to you?"

Not Emma. I sigh, realising I can't share my reasoning with him without breaking my promise to Kaleigh.

"No," I say, deflating. "Got ahead of myself, sorry for wasting your time."

But what I really want to tell him is that we may have been looking at the wrong Turner all along.

47

Kaleigh

Desperate to distract myself while I wait for Natasha to get back to me, I decide to make an artisanal cheddar loaf.

I uncover the bowl and inhale the delicious, rustic smell as I sprinkle in a little salt. A voice whispers that I should be doing more to find the killer. That if an onlooker were to report on our family status at the moment, no one would think anything was wrong. They'd see a happy family living their perfect little life. Not a pregnant murder suspect and her match-fixing husband. But what else can I do? I just have to wait.

I gently knead and stretch the dough, ignoring the cramp tightening across my abdomen.

My phone pings and a bubble with Natasha's name appears. I try to take my hands out of the dough but it sticks. I don't care though. I tap into my phone, getting the sticky paste all over it as I open Natasha's text, reading the miracle I'd been hoping for.

I found a name!

I wait impatiently as three dots pulse on the screen.

My guy knew a guy, who was willing to look into
it for a fee ;)

Aka bribed him, I think, moving my hand in circles as if that'd get her to tell me the name faster.

Name is Eddie Cranston. Hope this helps xx

I thank her profusely before wiping my phone with a tea towel, repeating the name to see if it rings a bell. But it means nothing to me.

"How's it going?" Harry leans on the kitchen island, gesturing to the bread.

I look at the mess around me. "It's... going."

I tilt my head up and stand on my tippy toes to give him a kiss. "Love you," I say, wanting to savour this small moment of peace among the chaos.

But I can't help myself. I need to know if he recognises the name.

"Hey, babe, do you know an Eddie Cranston by any chance?"

I decide it's best to keep it vague for now. To see if he knows without telling him what I'd done.

He drops his phone and looks at me with a raised brow. "Why do you know that name?"

I stop kneading, fingers sinking into the dough, unsettled. "You know them?"

He laughs, suspiciously. "Simon had a fake ID by that name when we were younger."

Thump. Thump. Thump. Harry continues talking but I don't hear what else he says over my heart beating so loudly, the blood rushing in my ears.

"Simon?" I said, hoping he can't sense my concern.

No. It's not possible. It can't be him. But then I think of Simon's cars, the fight him and Harry had about money long ago, and things start to add together.

"Yeah…" Harry studies me intently. "Why? Where'd you hear that?"

I feel the colour drain from my face. Harry stands from the island high top and walks over to me. "Kay, what's going on?"

I debate whether to tell him or not but know that it's useless. I can't keep a secret this explosive.

"Um, so don't get mad, okay." I hold my hands up as tears well in my eyes. "But I did some digging, into the name of the company you gave me… and Eddie Cranston is the owner."

I watch Harry's face shift from confusion to rage. He doesn't bother to ask any questions before storming away. Fuming.

"Where are you going?" I call after him, even though I already know.

I quickly grab Alfie and buckle him into his car seat, trying not to panic him in the process, then head in the direction of Simon's house, desperate to make sure Harry doesn't do something he'll regret.

48

Harry

Harry trembles against the steering wheel as rage courses through his veins. His brain short-circuits as he tries to process what he's learned. That his own brother is the one behind all this. The bookie. The murderer. The accomplice. The betrayer.

He remembers a younger version of his lean and lanky older brother, getting them into trouble, gaining them entry into clubs and casinos. He always found a way around the rules with a sleight of hand. "Steady Eddie" they used to call him, a name earned from his cool demeanour, ability to lie. When it became clear Simon didn't have the skill or drive to make it as a footballer like Harry, he started working with their dad at the car dealership, quickly taking over the front of house and turning it into a lucrative business.

Harry scoffs, feeling like a proper fool for not seeing through him all these years. He tries to reconcile images of his big brother with the villains he imagined in his mind.

The men who haunted his dreams. Masked and wearing all black, sitting in a dark room with ties to the worst of humanity. Quite literally calling the shots, manipulating the game. Ordering to hurt those Harry cared about.

His own brother.

He thinks of their falling out, and the large sum of money Simon begged for years ago. He wanted to lend it to him but he didn't have it, had lost it gambling himself. Did he do this in retaliation? It doesn't make any sense.

Harry's rage grows as he pulls onto Simon's drive and sees his precious Jaguar E-Type convertible. *Is that what their lives bought you?*

He's tempted to sideswipe it, but resists, wanting to take his anger out on Simon aka Eddie. Harry slams his car door behind him after he parks, and approaches the house, ready to demand answers.

"What the fuck, Har?" Simon opens the door after Harry's furious bangs. "You trying to break—"

But Harry shoves him before he can finish the sentence. He can see in Simon's eyes that he knows why he's there.

"Har, chill." Simon backs away, holding his hands out.

Harry has so much to say to him, but doesn't know how to communicate it. So instead, he just swings, punching his brother square in the jaw. Simon stumbles backward, groaning in pain. Harry swings again, but Simon ducks, and then tackles Harry to the ground. They wrestle, trying to get a grip on the other while delivering blows, until Harry flips Simon over, pinning him down.

His hands are wrapped around Simon's neck, ready to squeeze, but a scream cuts through his rage.

"Stop!" Kaleigh yells.

"Daddy, no!" Alfie cries.

His son's desperate plea snaps him out of it. He looks at them, standing in Simon's doorway, terrified. Harry follows Kaleigh's horrified gaze to Simon, sprawled out below Harry, face cut and bloodied.

Kaleigh glares at Simon and Harry as she tries to soothe Alfie, who is now crying into her shoulder.

"Guess I had it comin', didn't I?" Simon spits blood from his mouth.

"Piece of shit," Harry grumbles.

"That's no way to talk to your brother," Simon replies, trying to stand. "After all the mess I've cleaned up for you."

Harry laughs at the sheer cheek of him. "Cleaned up? You mean got me into. How could you fucking do that to me, your own brother?"

Simon sighs, wiping blood from his nose as he sits on the stairs. "Jesus. I just needed the money. It's not that big of a deal."

"Not that big of a deal?" Harry storms back towards Simon. "You…" He bites his lip so hard he breaks skin as he points a finger in his face.

Simon wipes the blood spilling from his nose with the white cuff of his shirt, but Harry doesn't feel an ounce of sympathy, only shame that his son had to witness the violence. "I made money off you, yeah. I wouldn't have had to if you'd helped me when I needed it."

Harry and Kaleigh exchange looks of disgust and shock.

"So you what? Killed Leila and Emma for money?" Kaleigh says from behind Harry, cupping one hand over Alfie's ear.

"What?" Simon asks. "I just wanted a fucking piece of the pie. I didn't bloody hurt anyone."

"You texted me that night." Harry pulls at his hair while shaking his head, remembering the text. **You done it now. You'll regret this.** Emma and Leila's deaths were a retaliation. "Don't fuck with me, Simon."

Alfie lets out a loud wail and Harry flinches, knowing they really shouldn't be having this conversation in front of him.

Simon continues, yelling over Alfie's cries and Kaleigh's shushing. "So I blackmailed you. Made some money when you were being a shit of a brother. It doesn't mean I hurt Emma. You know I would never." He says it vehemently. "She was like a sister to me."

Harry and Kaleigh both glare at Simon, not believing him.

Simon's face pales when he realises they actually think he's responsible. His eyes fill with tears, surprising Harry. "I had *nothing* to do with Leila or Emma. I just… You're my brother. You were supposed to help me. Couldn't even sell one of your fancy cars?" Simon spits out more blood. "I did what I had to do but I didn't fuckin' hurt anyone. Especially them girls."

Harry lets out a long exhale, considering that maybe the two events weren't connected. That maybe his defiance of the match-fixer was separate from whatever happened to Leila and Emma that night. But then who was working with Gaz? Why?

"If it wasn't you, then who was it?" Kaleigh asks, wondering the same.

Simon groans, seemingly over the conversation. Ready to move on. "How am I meant to know? All I know is it wasn't me. I stopped after they died. Felt too bad for you."

Harry searches his brother's eyes, looking for any hint of a lie. But Simon looks as sincere as he's ever been.

49

Charlie

Turner Classic Cars is closed by the time I arrive. Sign pulled across the front door, lights off. From my recon spot across the street, all I can see are shiny classic cars behind the glass, sitting in darkness save for the reflective glow of the nearest streetlight.

My engine idles as I bring up the recent news article – the one that features an image of the car caught on camera the night of Emma's murder. The grainy screenshot shows a black saloon-style vehicle. I note the all-black wheels and distinctive stretched bonnet.

I run through my plan one last time: casually walk around the back, try to enter, then see if I spot the car anywhere and take photos. If I get caught, just feign ignorance, pretend I didn't know it was closed and say I was hoping to speak to the owner about buying a car for my brother.

My face reddens as I think of Davey. "I'm doing this for

291

you, big brother," I whisper, hoping his spirit is with me. "And you too, Emma."

I know deep down I shouldn't be here, that it's dangerous and careless. But I also know that there's a possibility the evidence that could clear my brother's name – and lock away Emma's killer – is sitting inside that very building.

I have to try.

I text Callum, telling him I'm going to be a little late. I decide against texting Kaleigh though, not knowing how far she'd go to protect her family, like the lengths I'd go to exonerate mine.

Justice For Davey Allen. I think of the subreddit I created years ago, all the time I spent looking into the case, to be here now, possibly on the cusp of uncovering the truth and finally getting the justice I set out for.

I exhale and exit my car, before striding across the street. I keep my head down, face hidden below a cap to avoid being caught on camera, while wondering why Simon Turner would do this. Was he just in it for the money? Had he committed any violence himself? Or was he involved in an even more sinister, perverse capacity, like Gaz Barker?

I think of the only established connection between Gaz Barker and Simon Turner – pub owner and pub patron, the same relationship Gaz had with most of the community. Hopefully my call to Maynard would prompt a deeper search though.

I pause when I reach the car park, wondering whether to check out the showroom or warehouse first. If I was hiding a vehicle, I'd tuck it away in the warehouse, so I head straight there, stopping when I reach the large roller shutter door. Knowing I won't be able to simply sneak through that, I walk around the side of the building, hoping to find a pedestrian entrance. I spot a dim light near the back and jog towards it, fishing the hairpin out of my pocket on my way. I've never picked a lock before, but I'm praying I can make it work with the help of YouTube.

Turns out I don't even need to try. While the door appears shut, the latch is not fully seated, and it opens with a simple pull. Adrenaline courses through me as I step inside, feeling both invigorated and on edge.

I inhale the fumes and exhale nervously as I survey the space.

To my left are two rows of cars that eventually blend into a shadowy expanse of darkness, and directly in front of me seems to be the workshop floor. A green vintage Porsche is propped on one hydraulic lift, while a more modern-looking white BMW sits on another, sans front wheels. To its right is a doorway, illuminated by a single overhead light.

An unnerving thought occurs to me as I register the light and the open door. Like someone either left in a rush without locking up properly, or they're still here. I stand completely still, listening for any signs of life. But there's nothing, just eerie quiet in a place usually filled with noise.

Two minutes, I promise myself. *Then get the hell out.*

I walk straight, then turn left down the path between the long rows of cars. I use my phone's torch light to inspect the cars as I go. They're all in various states of repair, some with missing bonnets and exposed engines, others missing wheels or windscreens. There are a few black cars, but none close to the shape of the one I'm looking for.

As I make my way back to the workshop floor, I notice a separate structure, next to the exit. When I walked in, I thought it was a wall, but now I see it's a sort of booth, big enough to fit a single car. I peek inside, noticing lines of bright blue sprayed on the ground. This must be where they paint the cars.

I instinctively glance at the gleaming blue BMW I passed. My heart slows as I recognise its long, sleek shape. I walk over to examine it, deflating when I spot the chrome wheels. Not black.

Sighing, I decide it's time to go. As I survey the workshop one last time, my eyes land on a couple of tyres between the two hydraulic lifts. I shine my light in their direction, gut clenching when I see the black alloys fitted inside the tyres. I look at the white BMW propped above, noting its back wheels, fitted with the same matte black alloys as the ones on the ground.

My heart beats stronger and faster, like a war drum, as I look from the white BMW to the newly painted blue one, imagining Simon Turner disguising it. Sanding off the black paintwork, then spraying it blue and swapping its black alloys for chrome ones. And then hiding the car in plain sight.

My gut tells me that this is it. This is the car caught on camera that night. I fumble with my phone to record my finding, shocked that my hunch was right, that the evidence is here.

"Can I help you?" a gruff voice says from behind.

I freeze.

Slowly, I turn and face Robbie Turner, who is now standing in the doorway.

"You," I gasp. Every detail of the case runs through my head, and I see it all differently.

My gaze lands on a long piece of metal in his hand and I begin to tremble, my body warning me I'm in serious danger.

"Sorry," I say, attempting to keep my voice light. "I was looking for Simon."

Robbie doesn't say anything, just stares at me. My eyes dart around the space, searching for an escape route. But he's blocking the only exit. I gulp, wondering if there's any way I can get past him. My phone feels heavy in my hand, and I clutch it tightly. I know there's some way to call 999 by pressing the side buttons, but can't remember if I hold them together or press rapidly.

"Slide your phone across to me," he says, noticing the movement of my fingers.

"Please, I—"

"Now," he commands.

I look at my phone through tear-filled eyes, not wanting to say goodbye to my last hope. But I don't see any other option, so I obey. I move slowly, trying to buy myself time.

I glance from my left to my right as I bend down, wondering if I have a better chance of surviving by barricading myself in the office, or attempting to break through the shutter at the end of the warehouse. I choose the latter, and the second I slide my phone across the floor, I turn on my heel and make a run for it between the rows of cars.

I glance behind me as I sprint, panic rising as Robbie closes the space between us. Before I even make it halfway, he catches me, swiping at my feet with the metal rod. My head slams onto the cold concrete and I groan as the searing pain sets in.

As my vision starts to waver, I try to make sense of it all, wanting to at least die with the satisfaction of knowing *why*. I taste warm blood in my mouth as I roll over.

"Why?" I ask as he hovers over me.

"Had to protect him, didn't I?" he says, voice cracking.

It takes me off guard, how matter-of-factly he delivers the statement, tone tinged with helplessness rather than anger. Like he truly had no choice. *But why?* I want to ask again, still not understanding.

The notion is scarier than dying: that no one will ever know the truth. That my brother's name will never be cleared, that Leila and Emma's killer will never see justice.

Their only hope is Kaleigh Turner now.

I think of her then, completely oblivious to the danger she's in, before Robbie strikes my head with the rod, and everything goes black.

50

Kaleigh

I check my phone, wondering if I'll hear from Charlie soon. She said she was meeting someone at the pub tonight who might be able to give her more information, and I'm on edge that she's somehow found out it's Simon and has gone straight to Maynard.

I think about the shocking turn of events the night has taken, Simon admitting that he was the bookie blackmailing Harry. Yet I believe him when he swears he had nothing to do with Leila or Emma's deaths.

But if it wasn't Simon, then who?

I pinch the bridge of my nose, feeling utterly defeated, as fear creeps in once again. The killer is still out there, and we have no leads at all.

Lorraine hands me a cup of tea and I wince as another cramp hits me.

"You okay?" she asks, eyeing my belly.

"Braxton Hicks," I say, smiling gratefully, trying to disguise my mental state. The fact I'm hanging on by a thread.

"He got you good," Lorraine says, handing Harry a bag of frozen peas. She looks at me and rolls her eyes. I give her a knowing head shake.

"What's going on?" Robbie says when he gets in. "What's so important I had to rush back?"

Haggard and sweaty, he seems more high-strung than usual, like he's had an extra-long day. Too bad it's only about to get worse when he hears about the fight, and what Simon's been up to.

"What the fuck, mate?" Robbie says when he finally sees Harry's face.

"Language, Rob!" Lorraine nods to Alfie, playing with his toys on the floor.

Robbie fusses Alfie's hair. "Hey, little man."

"Hi, Granddad," he replies, making my heart melt.

"What's this all about then?" Robbie asks Harry as he takes his coat off and hangs it on the back of the chair.

Harry gestures for Robbie to follow him into the other room.

"You boys are gonna put me in an early grave, I swear," I hear Robbie say as they walk off.

Fifteen minutes later, they both come back into the kitchen. Robbie turns the TV on and sighs. "I need a stiff drink."

"Me too," I mutter, wishing I could join in.

"Oh shit," Robbie says, staring at the breaking news headline.

"Shit," Alfie repeats.

"Alfie, we don't say that," I correct him. He sulks and then goes back to playing.

"What is it?" Lorraine asks, looking over her shoulder from the sink.

"Helicopter crash at East Mids," Robbie says.

"Mumma, look what I found." Alfie hands me something.

"Thank you, baby," I respond, not paying attention as I take it, eyes glued to the news.

"Just pulled two bodies from the wreckage," Robbie says.

I freeze and then clear my throat. "What did you say?"

"Helicopter crash at East Midlands Airport." He points to the TV.

"No, after that…"

Robbie looks at me, confused, but repeats himself anyways. "They pulled two bodies out," he says, then mutters, "what a bloody mess."

I feel the blood drain from my face, but not because of the news. Everything else becomes muffled, drowned out by a high-pitched ringing in my ears.

Two bodies. Out. Mess.

I hold onto the counter for balance as I'm transported back to the cabin, under the deck, my friends' blood dripping through the cracks as I stifle my sobs. I picture a man creeping across the decking above me, on the phone to Gaz Barker, telling him to clean the crime scene.

"There's two bodies, need to get them out of here. Clean this mess up."

I replay the phrase over and over again in my head, refusing to believe what my gut is telling me.

No, I chide myself. *This is Robbie. Harry's dad. My father-in-law. Alfie's doting granddad. He wouldn't. He couldn't. It doesn't make any sense.*

I force myself to take a breath, to calm down. Exhaling,

I look at my hand, at the item Alfie handed me. A chill washes over me when I see what I'm holding. A phone with a purple floral case. Just like Charlie's.

"Hey, baby," I whisper to Alfie, unnerved. "Where did you get this?"

He points to Robbie's coat and alarm bells immediately sound in my mind. Why would Robbie have Charlie's phone?

No. No. No. I push the unimaginable explanation away as the room begins to spin around me. I hurriedly shove the phone in my handbag before I run to the sink to be sick.

"Oh my god, Kay, you alright?" Harry rushes over to help me.

"Don't... feel well," I say, feeling like the walls are closing in on me. Like I'm about to faint.

"Let's get you to lie down, love," Lorraine says.

"No," I say, looking at my husband. "Harry, I need to go to the hospital. The baby..."

Thankfully that's all I have to say to kick him into gear. Although, I fear I may not be lying as another tight cramp comes on.

"We'll watch Alfie," Lorraine says. "You go."

"No!" I protest, not wanting to leave my son with Robbie. "Please, Harry, I want him with us."

"Kay, but—" Harry tries to argue.

"He's coming with us," I demand.

Harry relents and helps both me and Alfie into the Range Rover.

As we're about to pull away, Robbie runs outside. He's looking for something, checking his pockets and around his car.

Then, he stands still as a ghost as he watches us drive away.

51

Kaleigh

I scream from the passenger seat as a bone-tearing sensation radiates through my lower half. I breathe deeply through the pain, wondering how I missed the warning signs. But I've been so distracted, assuming the cramps were either Braxton Hicks or a symptom of the heavy stress I've been under, I missed what they really were. Contractions. Early labour.

Shit, I think, knowing that based on the length and intensity, I'm probably at least six centimetres along.

"Are you... I thought you still have three weeks to go," Harry asks from the driver's seat, eyes flitting from me to the road.

I breathe deeply through the pain as a call comes in. Robbie's name lights up the display on the dash.

"Don't answer it," I snap.

Harry hesitates, hovering his finger over the green button.

"I just need quiet," I lie, staring at the name.

I writhe in pain as another contraction hits and I think of all the times I left my son in Robbie's care. Unable to accept the thought that he's a murderer, I go through another round of denial. Maybe I'm misremembering, jumping to conclusions. But then I think of the purple phone stuffed in my bag. And Charlie. I let out a sob, not wanting any of this to be true.

"It's okay, Kay, we'll be there soon," Harry says, kissing my hand, having no idea what's really going through my mind.

"There's two bodies." I think about what I heard that night. The words that haunted me for so long. Distant and muffled, spoken by a faceless monster from the shadows of the past. But when Robbie uttered them today, it was as if all the white noise disappeared and I heard the voice clearly.

"Take me to the police station," I say, now knowing what I have to do.

Harry looks at me, stunned. "No, you need to get to hospital."

"It's too far." I pause, wondering if I should tell Harry. But I can't just yet. "Take me to the station. Please. Unless you want to deliver this baby on the side of the road."

He doesn't question me again, just presses harder on the accelerator.

When we arrive at the police station, Harry helps me out of the car and guides me toward the entrance, shaking his head. Confused officers greet us on the way in.

"She's in labour," Harry says, prompting them to jump into action.

"We'll call her an ambulance," an officer to my right says as he helps me inside.

"Thanks," Harry says, sounding lost. "I'm just going to get my son."

Once he's gone, I look to the officer again and say, "I need DCI Maynard... or Banes."

"Banes? She's right there," he says, calling her over.

Banes's eyes widen when she sees me. "Mrs Turner, are you—"

"My bag, the purple phone..." I say through laboured breaths. "Take it. It's Char... Dr Singh's. She's... he... he hurt her." A sob escapes me at the thought.

She follows my instructions, not missing a beat.

"It's him," I say, starting to cry. "He killed them. All of them..."

She pales, eyes flitting toward the car park. "Who? Your husband?"

"No." I scream as another contraction rips through my body. "Robbie Turner."

DAILY NEWS

HARRY TURNER'S FATHER ARRESTED FOR BRUTAL MURDERS AS FOOTBALLER'S WIFE GIVES BIRTH

The shocking arrest comes a week before World Cup qualifiers are set to kick off, leaving fans worried "family drama" will see AFC Nottingham star absent from England squad

Thursday 13 March 2025   *Bethan Jones, editor*

Nottingham – Robert Turner, the 60-year-old father of AFC Nottingham striker Harry Turner, has been arrested for the murders of Emma Macy and Leila Adler, as well as the attempted murder of an unidentified woman.

The arrest is the latest jaw-dropping development in the "Nightmare in Notts" case, which captivated the nation in 2020 when three women were attacked in Sherwood Forest.

Police allege Robert Turner was an accomplice to Gary "Gaz" Barker, the now-deceased pub landlord accused of the 2020 murder of Leila Adler and abduction of Emma Macy. Barker had been holding Harry Turner's former girlfriend captive for the past five years, prior to her harrowing escape on 28 February and subsequent murder at the hands of Robert Turner on 9 March.

Police also alleged that Robert Turner tried to kill another woman on 11 March in an effort to hide his involvement in Macy's death.

"Robert Turner savagely attacked a colleague of mine when she discovered a link between him and the murder of Emma Macy," said DCI Maynard of Nottingham City Police, the lead investigator on the case. "Since then, more evidence has come to light that has led to his arrest for the murder of both Miss Macy and Miss Adler, including a newly discovered connection to Gary Barker. While Mr Turner's motive remains unclear, we are confident that justice will finally be served for these heinous crimes."

The shocking arrest coincides with the birth of Harry Turner's second child by wife Kaleigh. The sole survivor of the "Nightmare in Notts" attack, Mrs Turner (née Creedy) was also questioned in the death of Emma Macy earlier this week, but police have since cleared her of any involvement.

The police have also cleared David Allen of any involvement in the 2020 attack. The Sheffield supporter was arrested in February 2020 before sadly taking his own life.

Meanwhile, football fans have taken to social media to express their concern over Harry Turner's potential absence from England's World Cup qualifiers next week, sending the player well wishes amid the news.

Comments:

AFCNottsFan: Harry Turner can't catch a bloody break, can he? Poor bloke.

ItsComingHome: I wonder if his wife didn't go into early labour if he still would've played in the qualifiers, shame she couldn't keep it in for another two weeks

   StrayKidLaur: Pack it in, mate.

MerryMenOfficial: All of us at AFC Nottingham sending thoughts and prayers to Harry and Kaleigh at this difficult time

NicoleAlexander: #Justice4DaveyAllen

52

Charlie

One Week Later

I sit up in my hospital bed, nursing a migraine like I have for the past forty-eight hours since waking from my coma. The sequence of events leading up to my near-death experience runs through my mind as I try to make sense of it all.

Harry Turner's match-fixing revelation. The link between the cars and Simon Turner. My foolish idea to uncover evidence at Simon's warehouse. The shock when I found the car. The panic when Robbie found me. And the terror when he tried to kill me.

My heart rate spikes as I flash back to that moment, watching him swing the metal rod towards my head, sure I was going to die.

I close my eyes and try to focus on my breathing in an attempt to calm myself. I imagine what I would say to a patient experiencing PTSD symptoms as my hands begin to tremble.

Deep breaths. You're safe now. It's just a memory, it can't hurt you.

But the physical pain in my head and tightness in my chest argue otherwise, realising I never truly understood what my trauma patients were experiencing. I take a few more deep breaths, reminding myself that at least my efforts were not futile. I actually did it, achieved the justice I'd been searching for all these years. With the help of Kaleigh Turner of all people.

According to DCI Maynard, my first visitor after I woke up from the five-day coma, Kaleigh showed up to the police station – while in labour no less – and told Banes it was Robbie.

Recalling our conversation earlier that day about Simon Turner's possible involvement, Maynard ordered a team to his place of business, where they found Robbie Turner behind the wheel of the blue BMW, with me bloody and unconscious in the boot.

Maynard didn't go into detail about what they thought Robbie was going to do next.

"You must've had a guardian angel watching over you that night," he said to me.

And I'm sure I did. At least one.

Before he left, Maynard explained how Robbie confessed to everything, even disclosing his previously unknown relationship to Gaz Barker.

"So Robbie and Gaz were in on it together?" I asked.

Maynard nodded. "Apparently, they've known each other since their early twenties, when they were both mechanics, probably got up to a lot of shit we don't know about. Robbie claims he had no idea that Gaz had Emma alive all this time though."

I frowned, having more questions than before. "So, Robbie thought they killed Emma that night?"

"Guess so. Said he still takes responsibility for Leila and Emma's deaths. And apologised for hurting you for what it's worth."

I grimaced, apology not accepted.

"It still seems weird, though."

Maynard shrugged, but then raised a reprimanding eyebrow. "There are still a lot of gaps we're trying to fill. But let's get into that when you're back to full health."

I still don't know how much I'll tell him, feeling more loyalty to Kaleigh now than before. If I was going to keep my internet alter ego a secret, the least I could do for her was let her keep her husband's secret.

I look around the room, at all the flowers and balloons that have piled up over the past week. Roses from Callum, shop-bought carnations from Maynard, an M&S bouquet from Kate. I was so grateful when she told me that she'd been looking after Beans.

And then there was the card from my mum and dad. *When you're better you'll need to pop by the pub back home. They're planning a party for you already. Some of Davey's old mates coming down from Sheffield, too. You've done him proud, Charlie. Done us all proud.*

A knock at the door comes and I sit up, wincing in pain.

"Hey," Kaleigh says softly as she walks in the room.

She'd texted earlier asking if she could pop by. I'd responded with an enthusiastic yes, wanting to hear how she pieced it all together in time to save me.

"I got you these." She holds up the most beautiful bouquet of flowers I've ever seen, already in a vase with a large white bow wrapped around it. "I didn't know what colours you liked or if you hated lilies like some people do, and I didn't know, with your head injury if you'd be sensitive to strong smells, so I got ones that don't smell too strong, jus—"

"They're lovely, Kaleigh, thank you."

She nods, smiling as she places them down alongside the other bouquets. "These are all so beautiful," she says. "You must be very loved."

I want to laugh. She has a very different bedside manner to the piss-taking I'm used to in dire situations like this. The first thing Kate said was, "Bloody hell! If you wanted a bit of attention you could've just asked." Although she did follow it up with a teary and reprimanding, "I told you that you shouldn't have become so involved." Kate didn't know the half of it though, only that Davey was my brother.

"Can I get you some water or something," Kaleigh says, looking around the room awkwardly.

"No, I have some here, thanks," I say, also trying my best to navigate my way through this strange conversation with my unlikely ally.

She rubs her hands across her brown cable-knit dress, and without the flowers blocking her, I see she is no longer pregnant. I remember Maynard telling me she went into labour that night.

"You've had the baby?" I ask, praying that everything went well.

Her smile tells me everything is okay. She pulls out her phone and shows me a photo of a baby girl with a little pink hat on.

"This is my sweet Alabama Rose," she says proudly.

"Of course it is," I smile, imagining the shit I'd get if I named my baby after my birthplace of Sheffield.

"I was going to name her Alice, actually," Kaleigh says. "But I don't know, after everything that's happened, and I'd been so homesick, Alabama just felt right. We call her Allie for short though. And then Rose because she's also... a little English rose."

Her face flushes a little when she says this, probably worried I'm judging her. Which I am. But not as harshly as I may have before. If it wasn't for her, I'd be dead.

"Thank you." I reach out for her hand. "For figuring it out, going to the police. How did you know?"

She holds my hands tightly, eyes welling with tears as she explains what happened. How Harry got in a big fight with Simon and called Robbie home to help him deal with it.

I gulp, realising that if Harry and Simon never fought, Robbie may have finished me off in one go rather than having to come back.

"We were watching the news and Robbie said something," Kaleigh continues. "Something about two bodies."

I get chills, remembering what she told me that day in my office. What she heard the attacker say that night. She explains how Alfie went digging in his coat pocket and handed her my phone. How she pieced it together from there.

I shudder, feeling incredibly lucky to be alive.

"How's Harry holding up?" I ask, knowing how difficult it must be for him.

She sighs. "He's smitten by little Allie, so that's helped soften the blow. But, yeah, he's... not in a great place as you can imagine. I keep telling him he should go to counselling, to therapy, but you know men with things like that." She rolls her eyes.

I nod, understanding how difficult it is to get men to voluntarily seek professional help.

"But hopefully I can convince him to speak to someone," Kaleigh says. "Think it would be really good for him. Simon, too."

Simon.

Of course. Everything's been such a blur because of my injury, but the rest comes back to me now. The last thing Robbie said to me, about covering for him.

"Has Simon been arrested too?" I ask.

"No, thank god he wasn't involved," Kaleigh says, shaking her head. "In what happened to Leila and Emma, at least."

An unsettling feeling washes over me as I recall the words Robbie uttered before he tried to kill me. *Had to protect him, didn't I?*

I stiffen, realising what this must mean. But I daren't tell Kaleigh yet. Not until I'm sure.

53

Kaleigh

One-week-old Alabama Rose stirs in the car seat next to me as the prison comes into view, as if she can feel the same change in the air that I do. A tense, menacing shift.

"We'll go somewhere nice after this, I promise," I whisper, wishing her first trip out wasn't so depressing.

I probably should've left her and Alfie at home, especially since all they'd done so far was sit in the car with Harry, but I couldn't bear to be apart from my children for longer than absolutely necessary.

"Thanks for driving us and keeping the kids entertained while I do… what I need to do," I say to Harry, stroking his neck from the backseat as he pulls into the visitor parking lot.

Needless to say, he isn't in the best of spirits. He should be getting ready to face-off against Albania in the first round of World Cup qualifiers at Wembley; instead, he's driving me to the prison that's holding his father, only to wait in the car while I go inside.

We've been arguing about this for the past twenty-four hours, with Harry changing his mind from staying at home with the kids, to eventually driving me to visit Charlie and then Robbie. The only thing he hasn't wavered on was his refusal to see his dad.

But regardless of what he wants, *I* need to face Robbie. I need closure. I need to look him in the eye and understand how he was able to play happy families with me for so long after murdering my friends. I need to know why. Because accepting the media's theory that he was a "psychopath stage dad", who killed Leila and Emma to eliminate "negative influences" in Harry's life, wasn't working for me.

Nor was Lorraine and Simon's reasoning that he did it to protect Harry's secrets, both the affair with Leila and match-fixing, which apparently everyone in the family knew about except me until recently.

I place my hand on Allie's belly to soothe her, our little ray of light in this dark time. I'm overcome with emotion as I look from her perfect little face to my son's, asleep on the other side of me, feeling an explosion of love and protectiveness.

My former friends and business associates had all reached out after the article about Robbie made headlines, but I didn't want anything to do with them. I only wanted to focus on family, to be with my babies and husband, and my mother, who was due to fly out to the UK next week. I even booked tickets to fly home at the end of June when baby Allie would be three months old, promising never to take my family for granted again, their quirks and all. This ordeal had somehow healed us – me especially. Made me see everything in a new light and realise there are things far more important than appearances.

Sadly, Harry's family was shattered.

They'd taken Robbie's arrest completely differently, with Harry refusing to speak to his dad, heartbroken by the betrayal, and Simon and Lorraine visiting him nearly every day. As much as I hated Robbie, a small part of me respected Lorraine standing by him. It made me wonder where I would draw the line if Harry ever did something like that.

I stare at baby Allie again and move my fingers over her perfect bow lips. I think about how she came into this world, under so much stress, the opposite of what I wanted. The only silver lining is that Harry is here with us now instead of playing football – not that England fans see it that way.

I was so thankful that Harry made the decision to take time off on his own, that I didn't need to put any pressure on him to call Paulo Santino and tell him he wouldn't be able to participate in international week. He realised he couldn't leave me alone with a newborn and a three-year-old, after I just found out that his father was responsible for the most traumatic event of my life. And of his.

I imagine how differently things could have unfolded, where we'd be right now if I hadn't managed to put it all together that night. If Harry hadn't called Robbie home and Alfie hadn't handed me Charlie's phone. Would Robbie have had time to clean up, like he had twice before?

Maynard and Banes came by yesterday for one final line of questioning and basically said as much. That if I hadn't gone straight to them with the phone, Charlie wouldn't have survived and Robbie would've most likely gotten away with a third murder. This of course prompted a separate line of questioning as to how I became acquainted with Dr Singh in the first place, which I carefully navigated without giving away either of our secrets. I simply explained that I reached out to her after realising she was the doctor helping Emma, that I wanted to prove to her I was innocent, since I already felt like the police had made their minds up about me. This prompted a denial from Maynard, but the guilt-tripping worked because he stopped asking questions, although Banes made it clear that they really should've been informed about my and Charlie's side investigation. But considering the two of us were responsible for putting the real killer behind bars, they were happy to let it go.

I think about my visit to Charlie, relieved she's doing okay. Although she seemed a bit pale when I left, told me a migraine kicked in and she needed to rest.

"You sure you want to do this?" Harry asks as he puts the car in park.

"Yes," I respond without hesitation.

The furniture in the visitation room is screwed to the floor, including the empty lime green chair across the small plastic table from me.

I tense as Robbie comes in, escorted by an officer. His wrists are shackled as are his feet. My blood goes cold as he sits, eyes downcast, not meeting mine.

"How are you?" I don't know why I ask. Out of habit, I guess. My mind is still trying to accept that he's not the kind man I thought he was.

"Doesn't matter," he says. "How are you? And baby Allie? Lorraine told me." His eyes light up when he says his granddaughter's name, but then something clouds his expression. Probably realising he'll never meet her. Never know her.

"She's doing well, thank you," I say. An inner voice screams at me to not make this easy for him by making small talk.

"I imagine you didn't come here just to tell me that though," he says.

I clear my throat, trying to ignore the tightness, like I'm suffocating. "Why... How..."

But I can't get the words out. It's difficult dealing with this postpartum when my emotions and hormones are already all over the place. I wipe a tear from my hot face and force myself to look at him.

"Why us? Why that night? Why did you kill Leila? Why Emma? I need to know. You owe me that much."

The questions pour out in quick succession, rapid fire.

He sighs, before going quiet and staring at the ceiling.

My mind races. "Was it because Leila was sleeping with Harry? You didn't want her tarnishing his reputation or jeopardising his career? Or did she and Emma know what Harry was doing, with the match—"

He clears his throat loudly, cutting me off.

"Why then?" I want to pound my fist on the table in frustration, but I contain myself, not wanting to get thrown out before I get answers. Instead, I clutch my hands together and dig my nails into my trembling palms.

"Did you really not know Emma was down there the whole time? Did you—"

"No," he says sharply. He looks me dead in the eye when he says it and then looks away.

"If I'd known—" His voice cracks.

I look at him in disgust. "What? You would've put her out of her misery sooner?"

"Gaz was supposed to..." Robbie clenches his jaw as he blinks away tears. "He told me he took care of the bodies. I thought she was dead. Just like you did."

I flinch at his words, my guilt and shame hitting me again like a ton of bricks. That if I hadn't hit her that night, she could've run away with me.

But his words are a knife to the heart for another reason, too. Maynard said that Robbie confessed, but to hear it in person – to hear him admit that he was actually in on it with Gaz – makes me feel physically ill. I imagine my father-in-law killing Leila and dumping her body while Gaz stowed Emma away as his own prisoner.

"Why though? Why did they have to die? Why did you choose us? It doesn't make any sense." I let the tears fall, but keep my hands on my lap, worried if I let them go, I'll attack him.

"Darlin', I never chose..." he says, unable to keep quiet. "I would've never..."

I want to scream, to spit in his face. How could he say that? When what he did is clear as day.

I remind myself he's a good liar, has been keeping these secrets for years now. He's a bad, bad man. A monster.

Robbie exhales a sharp breath before speaking. "Sometimes good people do bad things... for reasons they don't want to. That they can't control."

"What does that mean? Of course it was in your control."

He sighs, but doesn't say anything, just runs his hands over his face. And then, without warning, he starts to sob. Anger courses through me as I watch him break down. He never shed a tear for Emma and Leila. He's only crying now for himself because he's been caught.

"I'm sorry, sweetheart. I'm sorry."

Visions of Leila and Emma's bloodied corpses cross my mind as I try to harden myself toward him again. Not knowing what else to say and knowing I'm not going to get the answers I came for, I push my chair back, ready to leave.

"Kaleigh," he says. "Look after Harry, will ya? Keep making him feel safe, support him like you always have. He's lucky to have you, I always told him that."

I swallow hard, meeting Robbie's sad eyes.

"And make sure he wears that watch of his," he says seriously. "If he tells you he's starting to get strange calls, you let Simon know."

I frown. "Why?"

"Just promise me, okay?" Robbie pounds his fist on the table, making me wince.

I scoff at the nerve of him, telling me how to look after my own husband after everything he's done.

"I won't be there anymore, Kaleigh," Robbie calls out as I walk away. "Do you understand what I'm saying?"

No, Robbie, I don't, I think. But something in my gut warns me otherwise.

54

Charlie

I gaze across the dark hospital room, looking at the overflowing bouquet of flowers Kaleigh brought. I've been staring at them ever since she left, my mind racing with questions.

If Robbie didn't mean he was protecting Simon, he must've meant Harry. But why? Why murder two innocent women within five years of each other? What could he have been protecting Harry from? His secrets getting out? The notion seems so trivial. Although plenty have killed for less...

No, something feels off. I'm missing something crucial, I know it.

I ponder an alternative answer: Harry was also involved. He was Gaz's accomplice. But that doesn't ring true either.

From what I know about Harry from Kaleigh, he was as devastated by Leila and Emma's deaths as she was. He thought he was to blame because of the match-fixing, something he'd been riddled with guilt about. And sure, he could be lying to Kaleigh, to everyone. But that level of deception would be psychopathic. And him telling Kaleigh in the first place proved he was empathetic by nature, a trait that doesn't exist in psychopaths.

An uneasiness prickles at the back of my neck as I think of another possibility.

Heart pounding with a slow, steady kind of dread, I pick up my phone. I almost call Maynard, to ask him to explain everything again, but I know I need to call someone else first.

After I convince Kate that I'm doing fine, I ask the question. "Can you think of any notable cases where an offender didn't *remember* committing a violent crime?"

She laughs. "Well, many claim they have no memory of committing a crime..."

"Sure, but any cases you can think of or worked on, where you were convinced they genuinely didn't remember?"

"Like *actual* homicidal amnesia?" she asks.

"Yeah, I guess so."

"Charlie, why are you asking this?" she says accusingly. "You need to be resting. They caught him."

"Just humour me," I beg. "*Pleeease.*"

I picture her rolling her eyes on the other side of the phone as I drag out the word.

"Well," she sighs. "There's homicidal sleepwalking, I suppose..."

I think about a few previous patients of mine who were sleepwalkers. They weren't violent offenders, but were found behaving bizarrely by family members in the middle of the night. One man was mowing the lawn, another was eating cotton balls while asleep. One woman would wake up covered in wrappers. Her husband was convinced she was just binge eating or having a midnight snack, but one night he followed her out of bed and realised she really was sleep-eating, and had absolutely no memory of it.

"That .defence *has* been attempted before," Kate continues. "One man, for example, had murdered his wife, but her colleagues told police he'd already threatened her multiple times, so the attempted defence of 'sleepwalking' was thrown out. But there was one case where a man was acquitted due to this defence. Apparently, in a sleepwalking state, he'd driven to his in-laws, killed his mother-in-law, injured his father-in-law, and then covered in blood, drove to the police station to turn himself in. But the jury found him innocent, believed he truly wasn't conscious when committing the crime. It's a fascinating case."

I imagine the unlikely scenario of Harry slitting Leila and Emma's throats while he was sleepwalking, and shake my head.

"What about something more... serious. So not sleepwalking, but cases that were put down to a serious mental illness or disorder."

"Various illnesses and disorders can cause psychotic states, that have, on occasion, been used to explain violent behaviour," Kate says. "There's schizophrenia, bipolar disorder in extreme cases. Obviously the majority of these people aren't violent though and are much more likely to be victims than offenders. I mean, you know this..."

I hear her take a swig of her drink.

"There's also dissociative identity disorder, of course. Once again, another heavily stigmatised disorder; these patients are much more likely to harm themselves rather than others."

I recall a patient I worked with who had DID. How the battle was to prevent one of her identities from self-harming. It was devastating.

"But," Kate says, "I do remember an extreme, outlying case where a lawyer argued that a man's 'alter' personality bought plane tickets, got on the flight, bought a gun and shot his wife's lover before flying all the way back home. He'd been caught on camera, yet still claimed he had absolutely no recollection of any of it."

"Convenient," I mutter.

"Yes, but various psychological assessments found he actually had DID."

"Jesus," I say. "What could trigger that level of dissociation?" I know the answer before she says it though.

"Severe trauma of some sort, an event that caused the brain to rewire itself."

After I end my call with Kate, I have an idea. I force myself out of bed and make my way down to the nurse's station.

I have to stop and lean against the wall as I go, to get the dizziness under control, but my curiosity propels me forward.

"Dr Singh, what are you doing?" Siobhan says, jumping up from her desk. Siobhan and I know each other fairly well, having worked together in the past. "You shouldn't be walking around like that."

"I'm okay, don't worry," I say, hoping it sounds half believable. "But I *am* stressed."

"I don't blame you," she says, guiding me to her chair in the nurse's station. "I'd be too if I only just woke from a coma. What are you like," she tsks.

"I'm not stressed because of that," I explain, feeling a slight twinge of guilt for my planned ruse. "I'm stressed because I was working with a high-risk patient before this happened, and I can't stop thinking about them, wondering if they're okay."

Tears sting my eyes as I think of Emma, how she isn't okay.

"I'm sure they're being well looked after," Siobhan tries to reassure me.

I raise a knowing eyebrow, trying to ignore my moral compass. "How would you feel if you got knocked out and didn't know what was going on with one of your patients?"

She smirks, understanding. "So, what can I do for you? Can I give someone a call?"

"Before we try that, I was wondering if I could quickly log in on one of these computers? I could walk down to my office, but—"

She sighs. "No, no, don't be silly. No need for that. Just be quick, okay?"

She logs out of her account and gestures for me to log in.

"This is very awkward, but would you mind... Patient confidentiality and all."

I feel like a horrible person as I say it, and she looks a bit miffed at first, rightfully so, but then rolls her eyes and leaves me to it. I reckon I don't have long until her supervisor comes back and tells her off, as she should definitely not have let me do this. My heart pounds as I log in and then search the system for Harry Turner's medical records.

I scroll back as far as I can, searching for his childhood years, and if there's anything on file. I see a file called "Psychotherapist assessment" dated 2007, when Harry was around twelve years old. I click into it and my stomach drops. It all fits together.

"Everything alright, Dr Singh?" Siobhan asks, concerned.

I clear my throat. "Yes, not ideal, but I found what I needed."

I log off and let Siobhan escort me back to my room. Once she's gone, I pick up the phone and call Kate again. As it rings, all I can think about is the significance of what I found in Harry Turner's file.

When Harry was twelve years old, he was brought to a psychotherapist to do an assessment following an incident at the football academy. One of the staff was found dead onsite. It was then discovered that this coach had been sexually abusing some of the boys, based on evidence found in the room. Harry Turner's mother brought both of her sons in to speak to someone and make sure they were unaffected.

"Well, hello again," Kate says.

I don't waste time with pleasantries. "The case you worked on, William Norton. Did he have any connection to AFC Nottingham's Academy? Or are you aware of another coach or scout who was also involved in a grooming scandal around a similar time?"

"What?" Kate says, confused.

"I'll explain later, I promise."

She sighs. "Umm, I don't think Norton was ever around… Hang on, let me check."

I tap my foot impatiently as adrenaline pumps through my veins.

"Oh," she says, excitedly, followed by a much more ominous, "Oh."

"Yes. Some of the victims also claimed that they were abused in Nottingham. By George Thomas, who hanged himself in 2007."

My stomach swirls with unease, heart racing now.

You need to rest. You just suffered a brain injury. I imagine Maynard's likely response to me sharing my new theory, that Harry could be the killer but be totally unaware of his crimes.

And maybe it is crazy. Maybe that knock on the head has impacted my judgement. But then why am I so sure this is the missing link?

I scroll through images of Harry Turner from when he was a child at AFC Nottingham's youth academy. A sad-looking boy, standing right in front of George Thomas, his hand on Harry's shoulder.

What happened to you, Harry? What's going on in your head?

55

Charlie

Two days later, Kaleigh Turner greets me outside her house.

"Thanks so much for coming," she says, as if I'm the one doing her a favour.

I still can't believe how easy it was, how quickly she was able to get Harry to agree to meet with me for a counselling session. I'd suggested a home visit to "make him more comfortable", but really, it's because I'm still on sick leave and can't take meetings at the office. In any case, I most definitely *shouldn't* be assessing potential murderers.

You're reaching, a voice warns again. *You have no evidence.*

But if Robbie Turner cleaned it up...

I quiet the thoughts as Kaleigh ushers me inside their lavish home, knowing I need to be fully focused for this session.

"Harry's just in here," Kaleigh says, guiding me to a room to the right.

Harry puts his phone down as I enter, standing to greet me.

"Thanks for doing this, babe. It'll be so good for you." Kaleigh kisses him on the cheek before she leaves.

He smiles and then gestures for me to sit on the sofa across from him.

"I'm really sorry," he says, surprising me. "About what my... What happened to you. I'd like to pay for any private treatment you need, just let Kaleigh know, alright?"

"Oh," I say, caught off guard. "No, no it's not your fault." *Or is it?* I think.

"Well, the offer is there." He gives me a sad smile.

"Thank you," I reply.

I'm warmed by the kind gesture, and suddenly feel bad about my ulterior motives. But if it's what I think, then Kaleigh and her children aren't safe. This is necessary. Although, the irony that I'm having to lie in order to uncover the truth isn't lost on me. Regardless, I press forward.

"But we're not here to talk about me... I know you've had a rough couple of weeks, too."

He looks down at his hands, nodding.

"I know there will be elements of this that are difficult to talk about. So I just want to let you know this is a safe space." The words feel wrong. I'm not sure this is a safe space. For either of us.

"Well, Kaleigh told me a lot of athletes do this kind of thing. That it can help them focus. Do you specialise in that?"

"I'm a trauma specialist actually."

"Trauma?"

I nod. "Yes, I help people struggling with PTSD, like Kaleigh and Emma."

His Adam's apple bobs at the mention of Emma's name. And then I note his trembling right hand.

"But, you've been through a lot, Harry. I often find high performers like yourself try and push grief away, push distractions away, focus even harder on their work, or sport. But this way of coping is unsustainable. Eventually, they crash. So, I told Kaleigh that I think it'd be quite good for you to have the opportunity, at a minimum, to express how you're feeling. And in turn I may be able to help you navigate everything that's happened. You may not think you're a victim in all this, but you are."

"Nah, I'm not having that," he says. "Not after what's happened, what my d—" He shakes his head, refusing to finish the sentence.

"Harry, I'd love to talk to you about your childhood if that's alright?"

"Why?"

"That's what psychologists do," I reply, smiling. "Your childhood can affect your entire life, the way your brain develops, how you process things, especially stress."

He nods. "My childhood was fine," he shrugs. "Just a lot of football really."

"I suspected as much," I say. "And is this the first time you've spoken to a psychologist, had you ever seen one as a child?"

"No... well, actually, yeah once."

"When was that?"

"Dunno, when I was about twelve, I think." His face reddens at the memory.

KELLY AND KRISTINA MANCARUSO

I carefully watch his hands and feet, seeing if his body language gives anything away. My eyes land on his watch as it flashes. I think about what Kaleigh said, about the small light flickering in the woods that night. *A tracker, perhaps? For Robbie to find him?* It sounds ludicrous, but also clever. It'd be what I'd do if I had a child with dissociative identity disorder, to keep track of them.

"Can you remember why you went to the psychologist?" I ask, trying to keep focused.

He sighs and crosses his arms. Closing off. But I remain quiet, hoping he'll fill the silence.

"Some sick fuck, pardon my language," he says. "But some sick bastard was working there. He forced some of the boys to do things, apparently"

"What kind of things?" My stomach roils at this, knowing the answer, but I need Harry to think back.

"Just sick shit," Harry says, followed by a subtle twitch. "What does this have to do with anything?"

I hold my breath as I observe him, not wanting to let him dodge the question. "It may mean nothing. Or may mean something. Did any of the other boys talk about it?"

"I don't know..." He runs his hands through his hair as he shifts in his seat. "One of my mates told me the guy made him... you know." He gestures towards his crotch. "And if he didn't do what he said, they'd never play again. That all the top footballers did it..."

"Your friend told you that?" I ask.

Harry twitches again, before contorting his face in confusion, like he thinks he's misremembering.

"I can't really remember. It was so long ago." He scratches his head.

"And this never happened to you?" I question. "You were never..."

He looks down at the floor, and I notice his fist clench before making a small, sharp movement. Like slicing a knife.

The body keeps the score, I think, noting that while Harry may not remember things he's done, the body hasn't forgotten.

I recall the one time I'd dealt with a patient with DID in the past, watching them briefly dissociate as their repressed memories came back to them, their body reacting when they're confronted with trauma.

"Harry?" I prompt, before repeating the question. "Did these things ever happen to you?"

He looks back up, shaking his head. "No... Fuck no, thank god."

"So this coach never said anything like that to you?" I carefully repeat his words now, studying him closely. "That all the top footballers did it..."

His eyes flit sharply from the floor to me, sending a shiver up my spine. My heart hammers in my chest as I continue.

"Don't tell anyone or you'll never play again..."

His eyes then move rapidly to the side, then around, like he's disoriented.

"I bet hearing that would've been quite terrifying for a young boy," I press.

If my theory is correct, the abuse at the hands of the coach caused Harry to dissociate in order to endure the trauma and cope in the aftermath. That dissociation resulted in the creation of an alter, another personality. A hostile one created to protect the host, in this case, young Harry.

An icy chill prickles the back of my neck as Harry's eyes gloss over.

He stares straight ahead, then his head whips to the couch, where his phone is.

"Sorry," he says, pointing. "Always ringing."

"That's okay," I say, eyeing his phone that doesn't seem to be vibrating or ringing. I take a deep breath, feeling unnerved. "So your parents, Harry, how did they feel about what happened at the academy? Did they want to pull you out?"

"Mum did, yeah," he replied. "Dad didn't. He said if anything I needed a focus, that football was my medicine."

I nod as he confirms my suspicions.

"And so your mum never brought you back to the psychologist."

"Nah," he says. "She fought with dad about it, said they'd leave it up to me. Obviously I didn't wanna go back, just wanted to play football."

"Would you say your dad pushed you into that?"

He shrugs. "Sometimes. But I'm here now, so his method worked, I guess."

"It sounds like you were close to your dad. I can't imagine the betrayal you must feel now. The confusion."

He shakes his head, face now flushed, eyes glossy. "I just don't get it," he says.

"Why do you think he did it? Anything you can think of?"

"Well, obviously he was protective of me, my career."

Had to protect him. Robbie's words ring in my ears.

"Guess Leila and Emma at one point both wanted to ruin it. So he thought he could stop them. I don't know."

"They wanted to ruin your career?" I cock my head to the side. "Why would you think that?"

"Because they told me," he laughs.

"Both of them?"

He nods, and I can tell he wishes he hadn't said it.

"But surely other people have wanted to ruin your career, like journalists, managers, opponents..."

"Yeah, but that's not... personal. I don't know, I guess Dad took this personally. So fucked up, I can't..."

I wonder if that's it then, if when his alter feels threatened, it wakes up.

Fear creeps along my spine as I imagine a clever, lucid alter. One that is manipulative and angry, but also fully aware. Smart and calculating. Throwing rocks to lure Emma outside before slashing her throat. Doing something similar to Leila... Then, Robbie right behind him, ready to clean up the mess.

"Sorry, I have to take this." Harry waves his phone at me, confirming my suspicions when I see the black lock screen. It isn't actually ringing.

"Hello," he says, as he walks out of the room.

I sit on the sofa, trying to take everything in. Is it enough to substantiate my theory? It's not like I saw him switching alters. The twitching was there yes, but subtle, potentially just down to speaking about a stressful situation.

It certainly isn't enough to bring to Maynard. What am I supposed to say, that I suspect England's star striker to be a real-life Norman Bates? Even Kate would reprimand me for making such an allegation. There are way too many loose ends, way too many holes.

I sigh, touching my fingers to my temples, which are now pulsating with pain. I reach in my purse and take two Naproxen.

"How was it?" Kaleigh asks, entering the room.

I jump, startled by her sudden appearance. "It was good," I lie. "We made good progress."

She nods, a slightly concerned expression on her face. "Did he say who he's on the phone with by any chance?"

I shake my head, biting my lip. "No, just that it was important."

She nods again, gazing in the direction of Harry.

"How are you doing though?" I ask.

"Good," she says. "I—" But she's cut off by a wailing baby.

I fight the urge to tell her to be careful but stop myself, not knowing how to explain. "I'll get out of your hair, okay? That's probably enough for today anyway. My Uber will be here any minute."

"Thanks again," she says, opening her arms.

As she wraps me in a hug, I start to second-guess myself, panicking about leaving her and the children in danger.

"Actually," I say, breaking away from her. "Maybe it would be a good idea for you to let Harry be alone for a bit until I can help him finish working through it all." My heart races as I say it.

"What do you mean?" She frowns, searching my eyes for any hint of a joke.

"I just mean it might be best – safer – to give him some time to work things through, give him some space. You could stay with me if you need to." I know how unprofessional it sounds when the words leave my lips, but I didn't know what else to say.

Kaleigh scrunches her face in bewilderment.

You have to say something, I think. *You have to explain.*

I place my hands on her shoulders and look her in the eyes. "Kaleigh, I think you need to leave," I whisper, knowing full well how crazy it sounds. "He's dangerous."

She shrugs me off, visibly upset. At that moment, Harry appears in the hall.

"Everything okay?" he asks, walking up behind Kaleigh and putting an arm around her shoulder.

I swallow hard as I meet his gaze, wondering who I'm *really* talking to. Unable to say it's fine, I abruptly turn on my heels and leave, not sure what else I can do.

56

Kaleigh

I sit under the starry nursery ceiling in my rocking chair, trying to soothe baby Allie, as well as myself.

I can't shake the image of Charlie looking at me earlier, the fear in her eyes as she warned me that my husband was dangerous.

She's suffered a traumatic brain injury, I tell myself. *She's clearly lost it.*

I think of what one of my professors once said. That many psychologists go into the profession because they have problems of their own. They think if they study the human mind, they can learn how to not only fix others, but also themselves. Sad, how this seems to be the case with Charlie. Whatever she thinks she knows, she's mistaken.

I look around Allie's nursery, dimly lit with tiny fairy lights. It reminds me of summer nights under the Alabama moon, chasing lightning bugs with my siblings behind our grandmother's house. The memory of home momentarily comforts me. But then, unbidden, I hear Granny's voice.

Darkness lives in these woods.

It's what she'd repeat at the beginning of every summer to make sure we didn't wander too far, insistent there was nothing enchanted about the forest. Not the good kind of enchanted at least.

A cold chill runs down my spine as I remember the final part of her warning.

And if you're not careful, it'll follow you home.

After Allie falls asleep, I get myself ready for bed, staring at the monitor as I brush my teeth. I click into it and see Harry hovering over the crib, checking her breathing.

I sigh, disappointed that his session with Charlie only put him more on edge. I think of his behaviour earlier, how agitated he seemed afterward, arguing with someone on the phone.

I used to think he was speaking to his dad, but it couldn't have been him today.

The thought of Robbie calls back *his* strange comments. About supporting Harry, keeping an eye on him, his watch, his phone calls… I spit in the sink and drop my toothbrush before I walk over to Harry's phone to settle this once and for all. I enter in the same passcode he uses for everything and click into the call log. But there are no recent incoming or outgoing calls.

I look back at the baby monitor's video feed and am reminded of the missing camera footage from the night Emma was killed.

I think of Robbie breaking down and replying with answers that only created more questions. I think of Simon and Lorraine, strangely empathetic to Robbie, visiting him every day and trying to talk Harry into forgiving him. *"He did what he did out of love."*

I think of Harry attacking Simon. Simon saying how he's always had to clean up Harry's mess.

"There's two bodies, need to get them out of here. Clean this mess up."

Boom, boom, boom. My heart hammers in my chest as I think of Robbie's words that night.

Could he have said "his mess" instead of "this mess"?

Stop, I demand. *You're being ridiculous. It's over.*

I look at my lock screen, a photo of Alfie holding Allie, and try to focus on my beautiful, perfect children. How I'd do anything to protect them from this world.

But can you protect them from their own father?

A horrible, sinking feeling grows inside of me as I watch Harry on the monitor, still hovering over Allie's crib. I drop Harry's phone back on the bed where I found it and rush toward the nursery. When I arrive, Harry looks at me and smiles, his warm eyes glistening with tenderness.

No, everything's fine, I think, as I melt into my husband's arms. *There's nothing to worry about.*

57

Harry

Harry tosses and turns in bed, trying not to disturb Kaleigh, who has finally managed to fall asleep. The past few weeks have taken their toll, and she hasn't been herself, even more on edge since her prison visit the other day. Harry tries not to think about his dad and everything he's done. It hurts too much to know that Robbie is responsible for Leila and Emma's deaths.

Harry can't help but feel that it's his fault too, in a way. After all, if he never got involved with them they'd still be alive. He doesn't think the guilt will ever leave him, and he's okay with that. Feels like it's the least he deserves after everything. Not that Kaleigh agreed. When he told her he felt responsible, she fired back, told him if anything, he was a victim. It was embarrassing, how she was comforting him when she just pushed their daughter out of her own body.

A pang of sadness hits Harry, followed by a surge of protectiveness over his children. It hurts knowing his father won't be around to watch them grow up, but the thought of Robbie ever being alone with them, like he'd been with Alfie so many times, scares Harry even more.

He thinks back to their conversations, trying to make sense of it all. He replays what he said to his dad, searching for a reason why Robbie would think he needed to kill Emma and Leila.

He told his dad about the fight with Emma, the night before she died, but he never told him about Leila. Why would he? He thinks about the call he had with Leila that night, the one thing he doesn't think anyone else knows about.

After Harry tried to break things off with her earlier that day, Leila phoned him drunk from Emma's phone, knowing it was the only way Harry would pick up. She'd threatened him, said she knew what he was doing with Theo – the match fixing – and that she was going to tell the tabloids. But Harry just hung up on her, too tired to deal with it, calling her bluff.

Was his dad listening in maybe? Had he tapped his phone? Harry had only told Robbie about the match-fixing after the girls went missing, confessing to him in tears, sure that the attack was a cruel retaliation against him. His dad was angry at first, told him he hoped he learned his lesson, but that he'd take care of it.

Harry hadn't realised it was just an act. That Robbie had already taken care of who he saw as the real problem, and let Harry believe it was a consequence of his actions, to scare him into not doing it again.

A pain stabs Harry in the side of his head, and he turns over again. His brain cycles through images of his dad, his son, his daughter, his wife, football... everything that's worrying him at the moment. He should be celebrating with his England teammates right now. Instead, he's left wondering if he'll be off the World Cup squad for good. Will he have to wait another four years? *Could* he wait another four years? The thought of being dropped again sends him into a spiral.

The last time he felt this out of control was when Paulo told him he'd be off the squad if the drama surrounding him got any worse. The night before Emma died. It was a similar amount of stress he felt all those years ago in 2020 after *that* match. The bookies demanding payment. Leila demanding he break up with Emma. Harry spirals all the way back to his childhood. To his coach George Thomas.

He thinks of the questions the psychologist asked today, how strange it was for her to bring it up.

"You can't let her get away with that," the voice on the phone said afterward. *"She knows."*

"Knows what?" Harry asked, genuinely confused and frustrated.

He wishes the man would leave him alone. But he always found a way to Harry. Peppering him with phone calls or showing up whenever Harry was the most stressed. After meeting with Emma the other night. After fighting with Leila five years ago. At the academy when he was a kid, the night Coach Thomas killed himself.

The sharp pain in Harry's head grows stronger. He prays it doesn't turn into a full-blown migraine. Breathing in and out, he tries to focus on something else. Tries to ignore his problems.

Eventually, Harry, the coward, falls asleep.
And I wake up, ready to take care of his mess again.

Acknowledgements

The first people we have to thank are our husbands, Mark and Chris. Sorry if the dedication at the beginning of the novel seems a bit sinister now (lol), but we wouldn't have finished this book on time without you both and your constant support. You held the fort while we wrote around day jobs, our debut book launch, family obligations, and more, making sure we were eating real food and forcing us to take breaks when we needed to. You also kept us in a positive headspace after writing such a dark story for a year and a half. We love you both more than we can put into words, but one day we'll try to write you into the romcoms you deserve! Also, special thanks to Mark for making sure our Nottinghamshire slang and car knowledge was satisfactory, and for letting us post you on social media for extra likes. Chris, you're next!

The next two people we need to thank are the two incredible women who made our publishing dreams come true. Thank you to our extraordinary editor Bethan Jones and amazing agent Millie Hoskins, the first two people who read *Scandal* in its earliest iterations (well before it was even called *Scandal*), and whose essential feedback helped shape it into what it is today. We're so lucky to have you both in our court, not just from editorial and agenting perspectives, but for all the support and pep talks over these past few years. Grateful is an understatement!

To social media GOAT Zoe Giles, editorial icon Peyton Stableford, marketing mastermind Jo Liddiard, sales baddie/ Harlow Hayes stan Lauren Molyneux (#WWFBD), publishing queen Vicki Mellor, PR stars Polly Grice, Lydia Gittins, and Robin Wane, our stateside heroine Tyler Aoki, copyediting ace Jill Sawyer, and the rest of the amazing Head of Zeus and Bloomsbury teams: Thank you so much for all your hard work behind the scenes and for championing *Rumoured* and *Scandal*. We hit the publishing team jackpot with you all!

To our insanely talented cover designer Simon Michele and the HoZ art department: *Rumoured*'s cover is a huge reason so many people bought it off the shelves, and you've knocked it out of the park *again* with this one! Thank you times a million.

To our crime-writing confidants Sian Gilbert and Victoria Vazquez: You're the best. We're so happy Pitch Wars brought us together. It was like the bus ticket to the publishing theme park, and after somehow sneaking in, we're all on the author rollercoaster together. I hope you love that really cool metaphor (analogy? who knows; brain fried) as much as we love you.

Thank you to Mom, Dad, Nancy, Aunt Cindy, Jayne and Barry for being pillars of support in one way or another. Whether it's helping with child/dog care, feeding us, whisking us away on vacation, or just being there for emotional support and cheering us on: Thank you, we love you, and we appreciate you so much. Special shoutout to: Mom and Dad, our biggest cheerleaders since birth, for driving to all the bookstores to check for *Rumoured*; Dad for reading it twice and giving a copy to all your friends; Mom for being the best grandma and watching Elena almost every day so Kristina could write; Aunt Cindy for your eagle-eyed proofreading help; and Jayne for watching Dany all those times and sending countless meals and cakes to keep Kelly going.

Thanks to all our colleagues who bought a copy of *Rumoured* and made us feel extra special by asking us to sign it. Special kudos to Kelly's colleagues who had to deal with her swivelling around in her chair to ask the most random questions about football and British-isms for the past year and a half. Double kudos to Andrew Whitehead for helping with the fictional team name!

Thanks to: Jonny Upton, Si Ratcliffe, Richard Ducker and Scott Loach for all your football knowledge; Sam Ratcliffe for insight into the life of a detective and answering lots of weird crime questions; Inny Loach for answering our WAG-life questions; Megan McGugan for forensic psychology knowledge (and for being my biggest cheerleader since our roommate days); Shivvy Davis for prison insight (lol!); and Mariah Cummings for moral support and special Wednesday dinners!

Lastly, thank you to readers of *Rumoured* who took the time to review it and reach out to us on social. Your kind messages really helped propel us through this book and mean more than you'll ever know <3.

About the Authors

KELLY AND KRISTINA MANCARUSO have been crafting stories together since they were children in upstate New York. Now, they collaborate on opposite sides of the Atlantic.

An HR program manager for a Manhattan-based firm, Kristina has a bachelor's degree from Stony Brook University, where she was named valedictorian by the College of Business. She still resides on the East Coast with her husband, daughter, and two German Shepherds.

A senior creative copywriter for a software company, former PR manager Kelly now lives in Nottingham, England, with her firefighter husband and beloved dog. She has a bachelor's degree from The University of North Carolina at Wilmington and a master's degree from the University of Nottingham.

Their debut thriller, *Rumoured*, published in 2025. *Scandal* is their second thriller.

Did you love **SCANDAL** ?

Then don't miss

The twisted thriller from the Mancaruso Sisters.
Is Harlow Hayes an innocent popstar –
or a heartless murderer?

It's time to find out...

Available to enjoy in paperback, eBook and audio